wish i may

wish i may

by LEXI RYAN

Cover © 2013 Sarah Hansen, Okay Creations
The Road to You excerpt © 2013 Marilyn Brant
Out of Line excerpt © 2013 Jen McLaughlin
Interior Formatting by E.M. Tippetts Book Designs

dedication

For my big sisters, Kim and Deb.

about this book

I grew up wishing on stars.

My father taught me to believe…in destiny, in magic, in happily ever after. Dreams were my scripture and the starry night sky was my temple. Then Mom stopped believing, left him, and took us with her. At the age of sixteen, I cashed in my dreams to pay the rent, pawned my destiny to keep my sisters together.

Now, seven years later, I'm returning home, grieving the death of my mother, and settling my sisters back into the life Mom threw away. I never intended to stay. I don't want to deal with my father, who is so invested in the spiritual world he forgets the physical. I don't want to face William Bailey, whose eyes remind me of the girl I was, the things I've done, and the future I lost.

This would all be easier if Will hated me. As it is, I have to hold my secrets close so they won't hurt him more than they've already hurt me. But he wants to be in my life. He wants what I can't bring myself to confess I sold. He wants me.

I find myself looking to my stars again…wondering if I dare one more wish.

prologue

William
Seven Years Ago

CALLY TILTS her face to the starless night sky as if waiting for its kiss. "I can't see the stars." She squints, trying to make them out through the thick storm clouds hanging over us.

I turn her face to mine and trail whisper-soft kisses beneath her ear and along her jaw until she relaxes in my arms. "We don't need them tonight," I promise, though I know it's only true for me. Cally always needed the reassurance of wishes and destiny—a byproduct of a combination of shitty home life and odd-duck father. Tonight, she needs all that more than ever.

"She's being so selfish, taking us away from our life here. Taking me away from you."

We've had this conversation a hundred times since her mom announced their move last month. I know where she's headed with it, and I won't let her go there. Not tonight. "Don't give up on us." My voice is hard and I have to concentrate on not holding her too tightly, but I already feel her slipping away. "She can make you move, but she can't take you away from me. You're mine. In New Hope, in Nevada, in Timbuktu, you'll always be mine."

1

Rolling over her, I support myself on my elbows and cup her face in my hands. I rub my thumb over the pale skin of her jaw, the flush of her cheek, the rosy pink of her kiss-swollen lips. She threads her fingers through my hair and pulls me down so she can run kisses along my jaw.

"Can we really survive a long-distance relationship?" she whispers.

"It'll only be long-distance when we're apart. You'll be back for prom. We'll see each other this summer."

"Prom."

I run my hand up her side and brush the underside of her breast with my thumb. "Prom. Just like we planned. Then when school starts, you can visit me at the dorms."

"You deserve better," she says.

Under me, she parts her legs until my knee slides between them. She moans into my neck. "There's nothing better than you." I flick my tongue against her ear.

When I pull back, tears glisten in her eyes. "I don't want to wait for prom night. I'm ready now."

For a year, we've been together and held off on sex because Cally wasn't ready. She feared having sex too young would make her like her mother. Even if the fear wasn't entirely rational, I understood. "Are you sure?"

She shifts under me and wraps her legs around my waist so only our clothes are between us. Adrenaline and arousal pump through me at the thought of making love to her. Then a tear rolls down her cheek, and I know I can't.

"Not tonight," I whisper. "Not while you're so sad."

She lifts her eyes to the clouds again. "So this is what goodbye feels like."

"No," I growl. The apology in her eyes breaks my heart.

"We have to say goodbye," she whispers. "I leave in a few hours."

I wipe away the tears on her cheeks. "We aren't going to say goodbye because this isn't the end of us. It's only the beginning."

She squeezes her eyes shut and more tears roll down into her hair, and I can't do anything but press kisses to the path they left behind. I hate how helpless I feel.

"If we don't say goodbye, then what do we say?"

"Look at me." I don't speak again until her big brown eyes are locked on mine. "This isn't goodbye."

"We can't pretend that everything is going to be the same."

"*Hello*, Cally."

"William—"

"It doesn't need to be the same. I love you, and I'm telling you *hello*." My chest burns with this tightness, but I reign in my emotions, knowing I have to hold us both together. "Hello, Cally."

She wraps her arms around me and pulls me close again. A tear that isn't hers splashes onto her cheek. I bury my face in her neck to hide my own fear, and she whispers, "Hello."

chapter one

Cally

"IN ONE hundred feet, turn left onto Dreyer Avenue," my GPS instructs.

I inch forward, peering out my windshield and scanning the manicured lawn to the left for any sign of a road where there is nothing but grass.

"Recalculating," the computerized voice tells me. Her tone suggests frustration with my inability to follow simple instructions. "In one hundred feet, take a U-turn, then turn right on Dreyer Avenue."

"There is no Dreyer effing Avenue." I pound on my steering wheel. This is the fifth time since I returned to Middle-of-Lots-of-Cornfields Indiana that the fucker has tried to turn me into someone's yard. Thirty minutes ago, she repeatedly directed me to drive right into the damn river. Good thing I decided to drop the girls off at the hotel when we got to town, lest they see their big sister go homicidal on an electronic gadget.

Yanking at the wheel with unnecessary force, I pull the car over and throw it into park. My chest is tight and my eyes burn with tears I swore I wouldn't shed today. I made it through the last month without crying. I won't cry now.

It's bad enough that I've been reduced to this. Bad enough that I have to rely on my estranged father at all. Bad enough that I have to track his hippie ass down since he's too goddamned paranoid to carry a cell phone. But here I am.

"You shouldn't hate him so much," my mom told me six months ago. *"He hasn't had an easy life."*

"I don't hate him. I'm ambivalent."

But that was before Mom's "heart attack" (code for *drug overdose* that may or may not fool my sisters). That was before the funeral and the grief and the bills. That was before my life disintegrated around me, as if it were built of nothing but dust.

I'm exhausted, one sister hates me and the other isn't speaking, and my ass is sore from being stuck in this car.

Fresh air. That's all I need. Then I'll follow the road back toward the highway and ask a gas station attendant for help.

I unbuckle and step out onto the paved street. God, it feels good to stretch.

I can't get over how *green* everything is. It's as if I've forgotten the color can exist in nature. The scent of cut grass is almost as rejuvenating as a solid night's sleep for my state of mind. The air is warm and sticky, and children are playing in the sprinkler on a front lawn down the street.

I remember doing that as a kid. Before the move. Before the end of our world as we knew it. Is it too late to give my sisters a chance at that childhood?

Doubt lodges like a soggy lump in my throat.

"Can I help you?"

I snap my head up, startled. "No, I'm good. I—" My eyes connect with the owner of the voice, and I lose my capacity for speech.

"Holy shit." The Adonis from my past narrows his eyes. "Cally?"

The sound of my name on his tongue catapults me back in time and suddenly I'm sixteen again, his cool cotton sheets sliding against my skin as his fingertips trace the line of my jaw, the hollow of my neck, the curve of my hip. I'm sixteen again and licking sweet strawberry wine from his lips.

Time has been kind to William Bailey. Bare-chested and glistening with sweat, he has an iPod strapped around his thick biceps and a T-shirt tucked into the side of his running shorts. He's bigger than he was at eighteen, more built, which is saying something since he was New Hope High School's star football player back then. My gaze drifts south but gets snagged at the ripple of his abs and the trail of blond hair disappearing into the band of his shorts.

Sweet Jesus.

The sound of him clearing his throat has me yanking my eyes back up to meet his.

"Look at you. You're all grown up." He grins, and my knees go a little weak. How could I have forgotten the effect this man's smile has on my knees?

"I could say the same for you." I bite my lip. Hopefully no drool has escaped.

That knee-killing grin grows wider. I'm toast.

This isn't what I expected. Not that I expected anything from William. I *hoped* to make it through my few days in town without seeing him, but of course not. Here he is. Looking for all the world like he's actually glad to see me when he should hate me.

"You live here? I mean around—" *Shit.* How am I supposed to construct a coherent sentence while looking at his bare chest? And that's not even taking into account the memories flooding my mind at the sight of him. I may have never had sex with him, but I have enough memories of doing *everything else* to rival even the most creative fantasies.

Shifting my gaze to those deep blue eyes is no better. A girl doesn't forget those eyes watching her as their owner slides his hand between her legs for the first time.

I study the ground and wave a hand to indicate the spot where Dreyer Avenue definitely is *not*. "I'm looking for my dad."

"You're in the wrong neighborhood." His voice has that low, delicious treble that makes my insides shimmy.

When I sneak a peek up at him through my lashes, I catch him studying me with his own assessing gaze.

I can imagine what he sees. We've been on the road for two days, pulling off only for gas and restroom breaks. We stopped in Kansas last night so I could get a few hours of sleep, and then it was back in the car at four a.m. for another full day today.

I would categorize my ensemble as "road trip chic." My snug-fitting black yoga pants end just below my knees, and I'm wearing a T-shirt that says *Peanut butter jelly time!* The outfit is topped off with bright orange flip-flops and the ponytail I threw my hair into this morning.

So, you know, the exact outfit I *wouldn't* have chosen to be wearing for a reunion with my first love.

I lean into my car for the scrap of paper with Dad's address and shove it into William's hand. "Can you help me find this?"

He doesn't look at the paper but frowns at me. "Seriously? You're lost?" He pauses a beat. "In New Hope?" His tone suggests that I've gotten myself lost in a paper bag. And, okay, New Hope *is* pretty damn small, but I haven't lived here in seven years, and it's changed a lot. The good areas are all run down now, the factories are closed, and the vast expanses of open land by the river have been developed into fancy neighborhoods with yuppy McMansions so ostentatious I can practically smell their oversized mortgages.

"My GPS keeps trying to get me to drive into the river."

At least that wipes the scowl off his face. "Yeah, GPS systems haven't kept up with the developments around here real well." He rubs the back of his neck, and the movement sends the muscles in his arm and shoulder flexing. Between his sweaty muscles and my memories, I'm pretty sure my panties have all but disintegrated.

I clear my throat and resort to asphalt-gazing again. How hard is it to put on a shirt? "If you can point me in the right direction, I'll get out of your hair. I'm sure I'm the last person you wanted to see today."

His grunt has me looking up at him again. Those blue eyes, those crazy blond curls. That mouth. "Cally..."

I sink my teeth into my bottom lip as our gazes tangle. He takes a step toward me, and he's so close, I have to lift my chin to keep my eyes on his, have to curl my fingers into my fists to keep from touching him. He's sweaty and solid and so damn gorgeous.

I wait—for him to tell me how horrible I am for what I did to him, for him to ask me why I did what I did. I don't know what I'd say. It's hard to imagine that, once, leaving New Hope—leaving William—seemed like the worst thing that could happen to me. I was so wrong.

But he doesn't ask and he doesn't move away from me. His gaze dips to my lips for the briefest moment, and the way my body responds to his nearness, even all these years later, even after...everything...it only confirms what I suspected.

After seven years. After the lamest breakup in the history of breakups. After breaking his heart and dismissing my own, I'm still very much *his*.

William

Cally.

I can hardly breathe. My brain doesn't have time for something as trivial as oxygen when it's so busy cataloguing her features, memorizing the exact shade of her mocha eyes, warring with the anger and regret that have sprung to life as if they never left me to begin with.

I never thought I'd see her again. I didn't think I wanted to.

The moment I step closer, I realize my mistake. Being near her is like a sip of water to desert-parched lips. It whips something through me—memories, lust, first love. *Heartbreak.* She tilts her lips up to mine, and I actually think for one goddamned ridiculous minute that I might kiss her, that I want to. That I would swallow all my pride and forgive her for just one taste.

I step back before I can give in to the impulse, and her cheeks blaze to life, her blush as cute as the rest of her. That's the word for her: cute. Sweet smile and peppy ponytail, she exudes cuteness.

Except her ass. Her ass doesn't even land in the same stratosphere as cute, and those tight little pants do nothing to hide its soft, round curves. And her breasts. There's definitely nothing *cute* about the way her T-shirt stretches across their fullness. Or her go-for-miles legs. Not to mention the narrow strip of skin exposed between the hem of her shirt and waistband of her pants. Just looking at the single inch of flesh below her navel, and I practically taste strawberry wine.

Moonlight. Her warm skin under my tongue. The sound of her moan as my mouth dips lower.

The memory grabs hold of my senses and won't let go.

Fuck. I can't even lie to myself. Nothing about her says *cute.* Everything about her says *sex.* And *mine.*

"Directions?" she asks. "To my father's house?"

"Do you want me to walk you there? It's close."

I immediately regret the impulsive suggestion. I should be giving her directions, putting her in the car, and sending her back out of my life. But I want to be close to her for a minute, to prove to myself that I'm bigger than a seven-year-old shit breakup.

Or I want to prove to myself she's more than just a dream.

She worries that plump bottom lip between her teeth because, obviously, she's trying to torture me. How can I want her so much when I thought I hated her?

"I don't bite, Cally."

She mutters something I can't quite make out. It kind of sounds like "Damn shame," but I can't be sure because she's grabbing her purse and avoiding my eyes.

"Are you staying long?" I ask as we start walking. My voice sounds too damn hopeful and I hate that, but what are the chances she'd show up here again, let alone find herself lost right in front of my house?

She's here to see her dad, I remind myself. That shouldn't come as a surprise, but as far as I know this is the only time she's been back since she moved away.

"No. Not too long. Maybe a couple of days. I…my mom died, and I need to get my sisters settled in with my dad."

I stop walking and turn to face her, all my bitterness and aggravation falling away.

She's looking at the ground, those worry lines making an appearance again. I grab her hand and squeeze. "I'm sorry." I don't ask what happened. Having lost both of my parents when I was a kid, I know how quickly that question gets old.

"Me too."

We both know there's not much else to say, so we walk instead. She follows me, and we cut through my yard to the paved path down by the river. I resist the urge to point out my house, to show her how well I've done for myself. It would be mostly a lie anyway.

"So you still live here in New Hope?" she asks softly.

"I came back after undergrad."

"Anybody else stick around?"

I narrow my eyes at her. Does she already know my screwed-up history with the Thompson family, or is the question sincere? "Some of the guys from the team—Max, Sam, Grant. And all the Thompson girls except Krystal. She just moved to Florida with her boyfriend last month."

The mention of her old friends brings a smile to her lips and lights up her face, making her look like her old self. "Lizzy and Hanna are in town?"

"You should see if you can hook up with them before you leave. They'd love to see you."

She doesn't reply, but there's something about the way her face changes that tells me she's not going to seek them out. I wish I didn't need so badly to understand why. Cally didn't want to leave when her mom moved her away. She didn't want to leave her friends or her family. Didn't want to leave the life she had here. She was determined to keep in touch with us all, even talked about coming back here for college. She hadn't been gone but a couple of months when all that changed, and suddenly she would have nothing to do with any of us. Even me.

Arlen Fisher's cabin is along the river just off New Dreyer Avenue. The original road was closed in favor of creating some common green space for the new construction. This, of course, was code for putting some distance between the old rough neighborhood and the ritzy new one.

When I point to Arlen's house from the trail, she frowns. "It's really…small."

Her dad's a rough man. Simple to the extreme. His cabin sits in the trees just beyond the flood zone. It's small, no-frills, and falling apart.

"Are you nervous?"

She's slowed her steps, consciously or not. "I've only seen him a handful of times since we moved."

That surprises me. Someone would have told me if she'd been back, as there aren't exactly secrets in this town, but I would have expected that her dad took trips to Nevada to see all three of his girls. "Really?"

She shrugs. "It wasn't what we intended, but things just never worked out. You know my dad. He has other priorities."

I remember, vaguely. The man liked books and studying religious texts. He liked to spend his time meditating and his money visiting psychics and spiritual leaders. "That sucks."

"The road goes both ways," she says, and I don't know if she's reminding herself of her own responsibility to the relationship or his.

"How do your sisters feel about moving back here?"

She leans over and picks up a gnarled tree branch. It's as long as her legs, and its beautiful knots stand in contrast to the smooth skin of her hands. I already wish I had my camera.

"He sent me my ballet slippers," she says softly. "After he found out about Mom's death. I didn't even know he had them, and they showed up in this package—these tiny little slippers Mom and I had picked out together before my first lesson." Her lips curve in a smile. "I was only five, and I remember him telling me, 'If you want to be a ballerina, just believe you will be.' It was always that simple with him."

Once, it was that simple with Cally, too. I was drawn to her because that unfettered optimism radiated from her. After spending my formative years in my cynical grandmother's house, Cally was a breath of fresh air.

I look up at the house. The sun has dropped in the sky, and the little cabin looms darkly in the shade of the trees. "Are you ready?"

"I think so."

"Want me to wait here?" Again, I surprise myself. I should be itching to get away from her, from the reminder of what she did to me, but it all seems so long ago and unimportant under the pall of the crappy last couple of years. And next to the news of her mother's death, my old resentment seems downright trivial.

Her shoulders drop with her exhale. She's nervous. "Thanks."

She maneuvers through the trees and up the steep wooden stairs to the house. After knocking on the door twice, she turns the branch in her hands, waiting, fidgeting, while I wait in the trees. This whole thing should feel much more awkward than it does.

She knocks again, leaning forward this time to peek in the window.

Two minutes later, she gives up and heads down the stairs.

"Y'all looking for Fisher?" someone calls when Cally reaches me.

Cally perks up. "Yes. Do you know when he'll be home?"

I recognize Mrs. Svenderson from my grandmother's beauty parlor. She swats away gnats as she moves toward us. "Dunno when," she says. "He just left, so I 'magine it'll be a few days, least. Usually is."

I watch Cally as she digests this. Emotions flash across her face one by one—disappointment, sorrow, frustration, and finally anger, settling in around her jaw and eyes.

"Thanks. I appreciate you telling me."

"I thought you were too good to come visit your old dad," Mrs.

Svenderson says. "What's brought you here now?"

Cally gives a polite smile but doesn't answer the question. The old women around here don't beat around the bush. They figure life's too short, I guess, and ask what they want to ask.

"It's nice to meet you," Cally says, as if the woman didn't just insult her. "Thank you for your help."

When she reaches my side, we turn together and make our way back along the river.

"Did he know you were coming?"

"He knew." Again, anger flashes in her eyes, and it looks comfortable there, as if this Cally is angry a lot. The girl I knew wasn't like that, but a lot can change in seven years.

"Do you have a place to stay? Where are your sisters?"

"I dropped them at the little motel back by the highway. I wanted to make sure Dad was ready for us. They've had enough surprises lately."

What motel by the highway? "Wait. The Cheap Sleep?"

She shrugs. "Sounds about right."

Cally and her sisters certainly aren't living large if that's where they're staying. "You know people don't actually sleep there, right?"

She chuckles. I like the sound of it. It's not the girly laugh she used to have, but neither is it an adult's carefully crafted facsimile of a laugh. It's soft. Sweet. Honest. "We'll be fine. It's just for a few nights. Until Dad returns home and I can get them settled with him."

We walk in silence for a few minutes, the only sounds the rush of the river and our shoes scuffing against the paved path.

"Do you live around here," she asks, "or are you in town with your grandmother?"

When we cut back through my yard to her car, I nod to my house. "That's mine."

It's odd, seeing it through her eyes. I'm proud of the home I built—a two-story, brick behemoth with a gorgeous flagstone patio in the back—but as I watch her take it in, I'm almost embarrassed at the excess. Cally and her family never had much. In fact, they rarely even had *enough*. And now they're staying at the Cheap Sleep, and her dad is living in that dilapidated old cabin. Not much has changed.

She forces a smile. "It's beautiful. I'm very happy for you."

She steps away, but I grab her hand fast.

"Cally."

She turns to me, those big brown eyes, those perfect pink lips.

There are a hundred reasons why I shouldn't want anything to do with her, but I have two, maybe three days before she disappears from my life again. Maybe for good this time. I can't handle the idea of this being the end, and I'll be damned if I'm letting her stay at that shitty motel. "Why don't you and your sisters stay with me?"

She snorts. "You surely don't have room for us *and* your wife and two-point-four children."

"No wife. No kids. Just me and way too damn much space."

She shakes her head. "That's sweet of you, but we'll be fine. You've already done more than most would have." She walks to her car, slides into her seat, and pulls away without another glance my way, leaving me alone with my memories of strawberry wine.

chapter two

Cally

STRAWBERRY WINE.

I can practically taste it as I drive away from Will and back to the motel. It's the taste of my old life. Of careless teenage rebellion and first love, of starlit nights on the dock behind the old warehouse on Main. William and I would sit on the cool concrete and sip strawberry wine he snagged from his grandma's wine cellar (an impressive 500-bottle collection of Boone's Farm). We'd watch the moonlight play off the water and drink straight from the bottle. Sometimes we'd just look at each other. On cloudy nights, we could hardly see at all and had to let our hands do the looking—his thumb skimming across my lips, down my neck, under my shirt.

That was where I told him I loved him the first time. Where he splashed wine on my stomach and bent to lick it off. It was where he first unbuttoned my jeans and kissed his way down my body until he pressed his mouth—hot, wet, and so slow I wanted to die—right against the damp cotton of my underwear. And the night before I had to climb into the U-Haul with my mom and two little sisters, it was there on the dock that he kissed me softly, like I was this fragile thing he feared he might break. He ran his mouth down my neck and cupped my face in his hands and whispered, *"Hello."*

Strawberry wine, William Bailey, and a life so much simpler.

When I get back to the hotel, my fifteen-year-old sister, Drew, is sprawled on one of the two double beds, tinkering with her iPod, earbuds in her ears. She's wearing a white tank and cotton shorts that say "You Wish" across the back and show more of her ass than they conceal. Her long, dark hair falls over half her face like a curtain, hiding the features that look so much like Mom's.

"Did you find him?" she asks, lifting her head and popping out one earbud. "Dad better live in a big-ass house with a live-in cook and on-site spa."

I snort. "Okay, Pampered Princess."

"This so-called *hotel* is disgusting. Pretty sure they're renting rooms by the hour here, Cally."

If Extreme Bitchiness were a sport, my sister Drew has spent the last month training to be the world champion.

She's dealing with losing Mom. It's something I must remind myself of again and again. Instead of spending thousands of dollars we don't have to visit a shrink, who would tell us this is her way of dealing with her grief, I just need to accept it. I need to be patient until my still-bitchy-but-much-more-bearable sister comes back.

"He's out of town," I say. No need to tell her how unequipped the man is for company, let alone to take in and care for his youngest daughters. I couldn't see much through the little window, but my view into the old living room let me know there wasn't much to see. Books, books, books. Not even a fucking couch.

We'll figure it out. It's a mantra I've all but worn out over the last seven years.

"It'll be okay." God, I don't sound the slightest bit convincing. Even *I* am unsure about the wisdom of my plan. But what am I supposed to do? Move them into my crappy little apartment in Las Vegas with my three roommates? Let Johnny teach Gabby how to roll a joint while lecturing Drew on the acceptable price of a dime bag? Or worse, beg Brandon to take me back so he can take care of us all? *Fuck no.*

"Mom worked her ass off to get us out of this crappy little town," Drew says.

"So we're rewriting history today?"

"You really think she'd want you bringing us back here?"

I don't bother answering her. I'm sick of her painting Mom as the martyr she wasn't, sick of defending my decision to track down our father, sick of trying to explain that there's no money tree to harvest in order to allow her to keep living her old life.

"Whatever." Dismissing me with a roll of her eyes, Drew pops the earbud back in and snatches her cell off the end table. Her fingers fly across the screen, no doubt texting her friends back home about what a heinous bitch I am.

If this is what motherhood is like, God can strike my ovaries useless right here and now.

I spot Gabby in the corner, sitting on a battered wooden chair and peering out the window to the parking lot below. She's ten but she was born premature and her tiny frame and baby features never seemed to catch up, so she looks younger than she is. She looks up at me and gives me a sad smile, as if in apology for Drew.

My heart squeezes so hard and tight, my chest hurts and my lungs ache. I need those long, ragged breaths of a good cry and the bone-melting sleep that comes after. Every moment has been full since Mom died, and I haven't given in to the temptation since the funeral. Crying is a luxury I'm saving for a private moment.

"How about we order a pizza for dinner?" I force enthusiasm I don't feel into my voice.

"We had pizza for lunch." Drew rolls to her back, never taking her eyes off her phone.

She's right. In an attempt to lighten their sagging spirits today, I made a lunch stop at Chuck E. Cheese's. It failed miserably.

I ignore her objection—pizza is cheap and something they'll both eat—and look at Gabby. "Pizza and then maybe we'll order a movie on Pay-Per-View, what do you say?"

Gabby nods before returning her attention to the window and the parking lot below. What is she looking for? Or who?

The doctor said that there's nothing physically wrong with Gabby. *"She can talk, she's just choosing not to."* Then she recommended a therapist. Again.

I dig my wallet out of my purse and count the bills, even though I already know exactly how much I have. Or, more to the point, how much I don't have. I didn't anticipate my father not being here, and I'm out of money. All I have left is two singles, a quarter, two nearly maxed out credit cards, and a bank account wiped clean by Mom's funeral expenses. As it is, I'm going to need money from Dad just for the gas to drive home.

I pull out the Visa and grab the phone book.

Where the hell are you, Dad?

William

The morning sun is hot on my back as I knock on the door to room 132 at the Cheap Sleep and hold my breath.

What am I doing? Cally wants nothing to do with me, and she's leaving town in a few days. I should be calling Meredith, the granddaughter of my grandma's best friend since childhood. Meredith has everything going for her—the career, the family, the personality. Fuck, she's even gorgeous, and—judging by some of the texts she's sent me—a little dirty in the best of ways.

But I'm not calling Meredith. I didn't even respond to last night's text—a creative promise of what she'd do for me if I came to her place tonight. No. Instead, I'm here, chasing after Cally. Again.

My thoughts are cut off when she swings the door open. She's dressed in cut-offs and a tank and her hair is tied back at the base of her neck.

She freezes when she sees me. "What are you doing here?"

I lift the box in my hand. "Donuts?"

"Oh, thank Christ!" says a voice behind Cally. "If I have to eat another peanut butter sandwich, I'm going to retch."

A teenage version of Cally appears beside her at the door and snatches the box from my hand. She has Cally's dark hair and is dressed in far too little. Her short shorts and tank reveal more than they cover. I'm tempted to offer her my shirt to protect her virtue.

"Drew, don't be rude," Cally says.

I raise a brow. "Drew? Holy shi—shoot." Of course Cally's sisters wouldn't be the little girls they were when they moved away, but it's still a shock. Drew was in grade school when they left town and now she's got cleavage spilling out of her shirt.

Drew snorts. "You can say 'shit.' We're not babies anymore."

"Drew!" Cally scolds.

"Gabby!" Drew calls, ignoring her older sister and opening the donut box. "Cally's boyfriend bought us donuts."

"He's not my boyfriend," Cally says, snagging a square glazed donut from the box. "Don't eat too many. You'll make yourself sick."

"'You'll make yourself sick,'" Drew parrots.

Gabby's eyes light up as she looks into the box and draws out a chocolate croissant.

"You really shouldn't have," Cally says.

The little girl looks up at me with her big sister's killer brown eyes and smiles, and I know I couldn't regret this morning's impulse if I wanted to.

"Well done, sis. We're in town less than a day and you're already hooking up." Drew pushes her palms to the ceiling in a "raise the roof" gesture. "My sister is a player, man. Don't say I didn't warn you."

"Drew!" Cally says around a bite of donut. "Seriously!" Stepping onto the sidewalk with me, she pulls the door shut behind her. She puts her fingers to her mouth as she chews and swallows. "I apologize for Drew. She's just looking for attention."

"It's okay. I'm glad I could save her from the horror of another breakfast of peanut butter sandwiches."

She smiles at me, a patch of sugary glaze just below her lip. "Why are you here—really?"

Without thinking, I reach to brush away the glaze, and the space between us suddenly pulses thick with awareness.

Her tongue darts out to lick her lip and skims my thumb. "We can't do this."

"Why not?" I step forward, closing the small space between us, and slide my fingers into her hair so I'm cupping her face. It's so easy to touch her like this. Maybe it's stupid. Maybe I should stay far away from her. But I can't. And I don't want to. "Go out with me tonight, Cally."

"You know that's not a good idea," she whispers.

"You're leaving, I get that. I'm just asking for one night. You, me—" I smile because she's already turning her face into the palm of my hand, already as drunk on the memories as I am. "—and some strawberry wine."

chapter three

Cally

I SHOULD not go out with William Bailey. Nothing good can come of that.

I don't know how many times I've repeated these words to myself since he showed up at our hotel room this morning. Yesterday, I saw him and went from zero to lusty in one-point-five seconds, but I blamed his condition—sweaty, shirtless, generally mouthwatering in every way.

I didn't have that excuse this morning when he showed up looking so damn respectable in khakis and a deep blue polo the color of his eyes. With a freshly shaven jaw and those messy curls damp from his shower, he smelled of aftershave and soap. My panties didn't stand a chance.

So I'm still attracted to him. And he's still attracted to me. But that doesn't change what I did. And it doesn't make a date with him a good idea.

This is what I'm reminding myself of again and again as I push my cart through the produce section of the grocery store. This is what I'm repeating in my mind as I sip a cup of free grocery store coffee and catch myself holding the cheek he touched this morning.

"Oh my God! Cally Fisher, is that you?"

I'm getting sick of this reaction from random townies, but I plaster a smile in place and turn to the feminine voice asking the question. As soon as I spot the bouncing blond curls, my smile turns genuine and I screech. "Lizzy!" I throw out my arms and we run to each other, hugging like the BFFs we once were.

Her skinny arms squeeze me tight and she squeals. "I never thought I'd see you again! You disappeared off the face of the fucking Earth, girl!"

My throat grows thick, and I swallow back unexpected tears. As far as my former life here was concerned, I did fall off the Earth, and not for any of the good reasons. "I know. I suck."

Lizzy steps back and shakes her head. "Don't say that. You were entitled to live your own life. You needed to cut ties here in order to move on."

She's probably the only one who saw it that way.

I look around the grocery store, scanning the faces in produce.

"Hanna's not here," Lizzy explains, knowing I'm looking for her twin. "But I cannot wait to see her face when she sees you. We should totally surprise her."

"I'd like that." Again, I'm swallowing, and there's an alarming burning behind my eyes. I shouldn't have worried that the girls would hold my rare and overly brief communication against me. The Thompson girls are the best kind of friends—the kind who never made me feel less-than, never required me to pay my dues, never asked anything of me, actually.

Lizzy's green eyes light up. "Will you be here next week? We're having this giant end-of-summer bash at Asher Logan's place. It's going to be fucking epic."

I choke on my coffee. "Not *that* Asher Logan, though, right?"

She wriggles her brows and grins. "Yes, *that* Asher Logan."

"He lives here? In New Hope?"

"Right next door to my mama," Lizzy says, raising four fingers. "Girl Scout's honor."

I fold her pinky down, and she giggles. "Christ," I mutter. "I told my mom New Hope wasn't boring."

"And get this! Maggie's dating him. Practically living with him, actually, though she still has her old place by campus."

"Maggie is dating Asher Logan."

"I swear to God! And if she didn't deserve every ounce of his sweet, sexy ass, we'd hate her for it."

"Go, Maggie!" My smile drops away when I see Drew approaching us, arms crossed, a scowl on her face. "Drew, do you remember Lizzy?"

"Vaguely," she says in a bored tone.

Lizzy's jaw unhinges at the sight of my beautiful little sister. "Drew? No way! You're way too grown up!"

Drew rolls her eyes, no doubt sick of hearing those words from everyone we've run into. "They don't have any veggie burgers."

"Don't be rude," I warn.

Lizzy waves away my concern. "You're at the wrong grocery store if you want a good vegetarian selection. Go to Horner's by campus. They'll have everything you need. Fancier stuff for a fancier girl."

I wince. No doubt my picky sister would prefer the swanky high-end grocery, but I came here on purpose. Namely, I don't have cash to waste on designer veggie burgers. I also came for the free coffee but mostly for the prices.

"Thank God," Drew breathes, turning up her nose as she looks around the store.

She's become such a pretentious snob in the last few years. It was one thing when Mom was around to coddle her, but I'm sick of her acting like she used to live some posh life when that's never been the case. Given our circumstances now, I can hardly stomach her attitude. And when I think about the sacrifices I made so she could have the things she did—food, clothes, a roof over her head—I want to smack her.

Lucky for Drew, I'm only a shitty enough sister to think about smacking her and not enough of one to actually do it. I know she can't comprehend our situation. Truthfully, I wouldn't want her to.

"Oh my God," Lizzy squeals. "Is that little Gabriella?"

Gabby scoots to my side and leans away from Lizzy.

"I used to help babysit you, little stinker!" Lizzy says, clapping her hands. "My God, you're all so flipping dark and gorgeous. Where's your mom? How's she doing? Are you just visiting or back for good? So much catching up to do. We should—" Suddenly, Lizzy seems to register the horror on my sisters' faces and she cuts herself off.

"My mom passed away last month," I tell her softly. "I'm here to get the girls settled in with my dad."

"Gabby wants to wait in the car," Drew says, grabbing her little sister's hand and throwing a bitter look at Lizzy. "I'll take her."

"Jesus," Lizzy breathes as they walk away. "I had no idea. Are you guys okay? I mean, considering?"

"It was unexpected," I say, which is true. Mom had really shaped up her life. I can't say she ever let go of her precious orange bottles, but in the last few years she'd at least been a functional addict. Her overdose came out of the blue. "They're taking it pretty hard. The move doesn't help."

"I feel like a total bitch." Lizzy draws her bottom lip between her teeth as she watches my sisters push through the double doors to the parking lot. "I'm talking about rock stars and parties and you're here because you lost your mom."

I try to take a deep breath, but all this aching pressure in my chest keeps it shallow. "It feels good," I confess. "To talk about something fun for once."

"Well, it's next week. Seriously, you can bring your sisters if you want. Or you can come alone and drink yourself stupid. I'm cool either way."

Tempting. It would be nice to pretend to be a normal young twenty-something. I never got that experience.

"Give me your phone." She's already snagging it from where it was sticking out of my front jeans pocket. Before I realize what she's doing, her fingers are tapping buttons, and she's handing it back to me. "I just sent myself a text from your phone. Now we can get a hold of each other."

"Great," I say weakly. I know it would just hurt her if I tried to explain why I hesitate to do that. Keeping up with the people from my old life will only remind me of all the things I can't have. All the ways I've failed. I don't like to dwell on that shit. "I'd better get these groceries and get out to the girls."

As I walk away, I hear her call, "Think about the party!"

I pile my minimal groceries onto the belt at the checkout—peanut butter and off-brand wheat bread, ingredients for beans and rice, spaghetti, marinara sauce, bananas, apples. If my parents taught me anything growing up, it was how to eat cheap. I sprung for the fresh strawberries since they were on sale and Gabby's eyes got that sad, hazy look when she spotted them.

This will all have to go on the credit card, but it should be the last major expense before Dad returns. God, what I'd give to get into that house before then. No doubt it needs a good cleaning, and his piles of notes on the nature of the Universe or whatever else the hell it is he's always poring over probably cover every flat surface in the house.

I've already made long lists of the supplies I'll check his house for before leaving. I brought as much as I could—clean sheets for the girls' beds, some basic cookware, all their clothes and personal items. They weren't exactly living the high life with Mom, so the pickings were slim.

The clerk is ringing up my items when I hear someone call my name again. This time I know who it is and turn to a smiling William Bailey. His gaze is already at my feet, taking in my hemp wedge sandals and inching up my bare legs.

I really have no respect for men who do that elevator-look shit in public. So why is it that when Will does it, I want to strip for him and invite a repeat performance?

I'm trying to play it cool—to pretend the look in his eyes has no effect on me, but I think we both know better. "You're not used to girls telling you no, are you?" I ask with a raised brow.

He grunts, "You'd be surprised," then takes something from his pocket and hands it to me. "I saw Granny downtown, and she told me where your dad is. This is the number for The Center. I was on my way to the hotel to give it to you when I saw your car."

I take a piece of paper from his hand and stare at the number that will get me in touch with my crazypants, absent-minded, insert-twenty-other-shortcomings-here father. "Oh. Thanks." The fact that I'm disappointed Will isn't just here to talk me into that date? Ri.dic.u.lous. "What's The Center?"

"It's a Spiritualist camp a couple of hours from here."

"Spiritualist camp. Of course."

Behind me, the cashier is clearing her throat, trying to get my attention.

"Oh!" I fumble through my purse and pull out a credit card. "Here. Use this, please." The woman takes the card, and I turn back to Will. "Your grandmother knows the number to a spiritualist camp?"

He shakes his head. "No, not my grandmother. Granny—the Thompson girls' grandmother."

That makes a little more sense. I vaguely remember my father going to the woman for readings of some sort from time to time. "Well, I appreciate it."

"It's declined," the cashier says apologetically. "You want me to run it again?"

I close my eyes. That was only a matter of time. "Let's just try this one." I pull out my only other credit card and hold my breath as she slides it through the reader.

"Do you need some money, Cally?" Will asks softly.

The woman bites her lip. When she turns to me, she doesn't say anything. She doesn't need to. Her face says it all: Declined.

I can't look at Will. Mortification is climbing up my neck and into my cheeks, hot and red. "I'll pay you back."

I pick up my three bags of groceries while Will pays, and I want to crawl under a rock and disappear and a hundred other clichés all at once. When he takes the receipt, I head for the door, but he cuts me off and takes the bags from my hand.

"Let me."

"I can carry my own groceries."

"But then I can't show off my manly muscles and charm."

Oh, God. He's too freaking good and sexy, and I have a serious case of *want-what-I-can't-have*.

The ring of my cell breaks the tense silence of our motel room. A quick look at the screen shows an unknown number.

"Hello?"

"Cally?" It's my dad. I recognize his deep, scratchy voice. I called the spiritualist camp Will told me about and asked them to please have him contact me. I'm impressed it took him less than two hours.

"Dad? Why aren't you here?"

"Tell him he's earned Worst Father of the Year award already," Drew says.

I narrow my eyes at her and slip out of the hotel room so she can't add her two cents to our conversation.

Dad clears his throat. "Where are you?"

I squeeze my eyes shut. He's so absentminded. "The girls and I are in New Hope. Remember?"

"I thought you were coming on the tenth."

"It's the eleventh, Dad."

"No, it's not. It's… Oh." He clears his throat again. "Are you okay? Was the drive okay?"

"We're fine. When will you be home?"

I wait through the long silence. My father is a thoughtful man. Intelligent to a fault. When I was a child, time and again I'd ask a question and just when I'd be convinced he hadn't heard, he'd finally answer me. "I have a class tonight. Is it okay if I get in late? There's a guest speaker in from Seattle, and I don't want to miss this if I don't have to."

"That'd be fine. But Dad, are you really up for this? Raising two girls? Having them under your roof? Being responsible for them?" I wait. Listen. Wait some more. I hear him breathing and I wonder what he's thinking.

Finally, "It wasn't a responsibility I ever intended to give up. I'm glad to have my girls back."

Tenderness wells in my chest, spilling over, even as anger still boils in the pit of my belly. They crush together and make me feel childlike and helpless. Because despite all his faults, he's my father, and I love him. He means well, even if he falls short. I have to swallow back emotion before I can speak. "I'll see you tomorrow, then?"

"Yes. I'm sorry I wasn't there, Cally. I won't let you down again. I promise everything is going to be fine."

"That's good to hear," I whisper, and whether I should or not, I kind of believe him.

"Holy shit, Dad. Nineteen seventy-two called and it wants its house back."

Inside and out, the house cries for maintenance, and Dad has an explanation for every shortcoming. From green shag carpet that needs replacing (*"I had it professionally cleaned before I moved in."*), to the gutters that are full and falling off the house (*"With the pitch of this roof, we don't really need gutters."*), to the barely functional kitchen (*"That's what the hot plate is for."*).

I met Dad at the house midmorning, setting the girls up with a movie and some snacks at the motel so I could get their rooms pulled together here.

After Mom left Dad and took off for a "better life" (oh, sweet irony), Dad quit his job at Sinclair University, sold my childhood home, and went all *Eat, Pray, Love* on his life. The girls were young, so I don't think they care that Dad doesn't live in the old house, but they *will* care if they see they're expected to live in a madman's hovel.

"Did you do *anything* to prepare for them?" I ask, peeking into the bedroom the girls are supposed to share. "You've known for a month they'd be moving in with you."

"What do you mean?" His question is followed by a long coughing fit. His third in the ten minutes I've been here.

"We have to move these bookcases out of their bedroom. Little girls don't need their bedrooms filled with *The Gospel of Sri Ramakrishna* and the *Tao te Ching* and whatever else you have piled on those old shelves."

"That's my collection of religious texts signed by spiritual leaders from around the globe. There are over two-hundred autographed books. I think they'll find it cool."

I gape at him. *Crazy. Pants.*

"You think they'd mind?"

I grab a book at random to prove my point. "*Learning From Your Past Lives: Enlightenment through Deep Meditation.* Yeah, that'll make a nice bedtime story." I prop my hands on my hips and stare at him. He starts coughing again. A violent, angry cough.

"Okay, okay," he says when the fit passes and he's catching his breath. "I can move them to the attic."

"Have you talked to a doctor about that cough?"

He nods. "A healer." Then another coughing fit.

I raise a brow. "A healer or a *real* doctor?"

"I don't like Western medicine. You know that."

"You don't *like* it? You sound like you're ready to cough up a fucking lung, but you don't *like* it?"

"I'm working with a very talented healer. I just need some time to meditate on our healing mantra and—"

"No! Uh-uh. You are not leaving your health in the hands of a fucking *mantra*." He flinches at my second use of the f-bomb, but I don't even care. I need him to hear me. "Jesus, Dad, you're responsible for two girls now. Don't you get that? They *need* you."

"I see your mother's skepticism finally rooted itself in you."

The little girl still living somewhere inside me flinches at those words. I was once so special to my father because I, too, believed in the magical things he did. I, too, believed everything happened for a reason, wishes came true, and good would always overcome evil.

Part of me wants to be his special princess even now. And even though I don't believe any of that crap anymore, part of me wants to, just so my father will be proud.

Fuck. Shit. Damn. "I want you to see a doctor on Monday before I leave. I want you—"

"Okay."

"—to take care of yourself. What?"

"I said *okay*," he says softly.

Maybe I should just pack up the car and take the girls back to Vegas with me. If I thought I could make a life for them, I probably would, but I can see it in his eyes—my dad is ready to do right by his girls. And I know New Hope is a better place for them than my world will ever be.

"Thank you," I say softly. Then I grab a box and start packing up books to take to the attic. Tonight, I'll call my boss and tell her I won't be back until the end of the week. If I'm going to make this house a home for those girls, I have my work cut out for me.

chapter four

Cally

I NEED to get back to the hotel, but instead I'm sitting on my dad's front porch, looking up at the stars through the trees and listening to the river run beyond them. The house may be shit, but I'll give him credit for the location.

When my phone rings, I'm so sure Drew is calling to ask when I'll be back that I don't even look at the screen before taking the call. "Miss me?" I ask with a smile.

"More than you can imagine." That voice is definitely not Drew's.

Cold dread steals through me at the sound of the deep, familiar voice. "Brandon? Is that you?"

"Guilty."

Fuck. I swallow, preparing to tread carefully. "What a surprise. How did you get this number?"

"Baby, you know you can't hide from me."

"I wasn't trying to." Not a complete lie.

"I miss you," he murmurs, dropping his voice to that low whisper he used to use in bed. Four years later and I still remember.

"Surely you've found someone better than me by now." I force a smile to my face as if he can see me.

His low hiss slithers through the phone line and then I hear a hard *clunk,* as if he just threw something against a wall. "Jesus, Cally. You know I don't want anyone else." His voice softens, the anger floating away as quickly as it came. "You're my girl."

I don't reply. There's no response I could live with that won't just piss him off.

"I thought you'd come to me when your mom died. I know you need money. Your sisters need money. Let me help."

At what price? "We're fine," I lie.

"I blame those college classes, making you think you're less of a woman if you take money from your man."

You're not my man, I want to scream. But it doesn't matter. Brandon has only been back in Vegas a couple months, and soon he'll remember I'm no longer his "type" and he'll find someone who is. In the meantime, I just need to let him feel like the one in control.

"Do you have everything you need?" he asks softly. "Whether you're with me or not, I don't want you going without."

"You've already done enough."

"I'd do even more. For you…." Again, that low whisper. "Damn, I miss you girl."

"What about Quinn? Don't you miss her?" God bless that girl. Finding out about her visits with him gave me the perfect excuse to cut ties while he was gone. Or cut them as much as I dared.

"Cally, baby, please."

I look up at the stars. When did I lose sight of mine? My father raised me to believe in magic, in wishes, in beautiful destiny. And then life went to shit and destiny played second fiddle to just getting by.

"Come see me when you get home. We'll talk about what we can do for your sisters. We'll talk about us."

"Okay," I lie. I won't go to him willingly again. Not if I'm left with a choice. But if I say no, he'll think I'm playing hard to get, and that will make him want me more. "Goodnight, Brandon." I end the call before he can reply.

I catch my breath in the darkness, trying to let the adrenaline fizzle out and my heart rate slow. Just the sound of his voice makes me crave a hot shower and a scouring pad. Or maybe just the touch of a man who makes all the ugly go away.

I scroll through my sent texts to find Lizzy's number. I punch it in and hold my breath while I wait for an answer.

"Cally!"

My chest warms with the enthusiasm in her greeting. "Hey, Liz. I was wondering if you had William Bailey's phone number."

William

The gym is nearly empty tonight except for Max, who's working behind the counter, and Sam, who's spotting for me as I attempt to channel my frustration into the weights.

My phone buzzes, and I open the latest text from Meredith, detailing exactly what she'll do with her tongue and certain parts of my anatomy.

Our grandmothers have been doing their best to set us up, and I'm beginning to think I made an epic mistake by sleeping with her. I thought we were on the same page, though. We both wanted something casual. Companionship. A good time.

Or so I thought. But these texts are becoming more frequent and when I was at her place last week, she slipped and asked how soon I wanted kids.

I'm about to throw my phone back down when it buzzes again with another message from her.

"Meredith?" Sam asks.

"None other," I mutter. I tap out a quick excuse and toss my phone down.

"Why do you suddenly seem so uninterested? She's fucking hot. And smart. And she's got her shit together."

"She's getting too serious. I think she's going to want something... long-term."

Sam lifts a brow. "So complains the Mayor of Commitment-Land?"

"Shut up," I growl. "That's not what I want right now."

"Hey, I heard Cally Fisher's back in town," Max calls from behind the counter.

"Cally Fisher?" Sam asks. "You shitting me?"

I grab a pair of forty-pound dumbbells. "Yeah, I saw her already."

Max grunts. "Did you tell her to fuck off?"

I drop the weights and turn on him. "Don't."

Max lifts his palms up in surrender. "Message delivered and received, man, but you do remember that she totally burned you, right?"

How could I forget? "It doesn't matter anymore. That was a long time ago."

Sam chuckles. "Who knew she could still have a hold on you, what, six years later?"

"Seven," I mutter, dropping down to the bench to rest my head in my hands. I swear my mind hasn't stopped spinning since I spotted her lost outside my house.

"You still want her," Sam says softly. It's not a question.

Max heads over to join us. "Is she sticking around?"

"Her mom died. She's here to move her sisters in with her dad, then she's heading back to Vegas."

"That sucks," Max says.

One look at my eyes, and Max is backing up. "Fuck. And I thought you had it bad for Maggie."

My phone buzzes again.

"Meredith again?" Sam asks.

"Probably."

Before I realize what he's doing, Sam scoops my phone off the ground and reads my text, his eyes going wide.

"That shit's private," I protest, but I really don't care. There's nothing worth protecting about my relationship with Meredith. But then Sam lets out a low whistle that has me whipping my gaze back up to him.

"'This is Cally,'" he reads. "'Is your offer still good for tonight?'"

I snatch the phone away from him, half convinced he's screwing with me, but sure enough, Cally's message is staring back at me. I punch the *call* button without hesitation.

"William?" I would recognize that sweet voice anywhere.

"Cally?"

"Yeah. I hope you don't mind. Lizzy gave me your number. I didn't want to call in case it was a bad time."

Max smirks, but he and Sam head to the other side of the gym so I have some privacy. We'll give the assholes credit for that much at least.

"Of course it's not. Is everything okay?"

The line is silent for a few beats too long, and I look at my phone to make sure it didn't disconnect. Then finally, she says, "If you seriously don't hate me, I'd like to go to dinner with you tonight. That would be... amazing."

"Can I pick you up in an hour?"

"Okay." *Pause.* "William?" I love the way my name rolls off her tongue. She takes my very corn-fed, middle-America name and makes it sound almost exotic.

"Yeah?"

"Could we go for dinner somewhere outside of New Hope? I just remember how people talk and I don't want that."

There's more to it than that, but I'm not going to push. Not now. "I know just the place. I'll see you in an hour."

Cally

"You look cheap," Drew says from behind me as I take in my muddled reflection in the old mirror. "Do you really have a date, or are you planning to stand on the corner and give five-dollar blow jobs?"

I spin on her. "Watch your mouth, missy! You think Mom would want you to talk like that?"

She lifts a brow, unimpressed by my wrath, and returns her attention to her cell phone.

With a long, deep belly breath, I turn back to the mirror. She's right, of course, which just pisses me off more. I brought clothes suitable for cleaning, unpacking, and sleeping. Nothing for a date with the sexiest man I've ever met. And as much as I tell myself it doesn't matter, that's just a bunch of crap. I was forced to open a box of Drew's clothes and borrow her black cotton dress—a "favor" she only allowed when I promised I would send her money for a new dress. But Drew is shorter than me and less curvy, so something that looks sweet and sophisticated on her makes me look like a floozy showing more leg and cleavage than the showgirls on the strip. I'm tempted to call Lizzy and see if she has a dress I can borrow, but Will's going to be here any minute, so there's no time for that.

Someone squeezes my hand, and I look down to see Gabby giving me a half smile. I don't know if I've seen her smile all-out since Mom died. I miss her smile. I miss the sound of her voice.

Reaching onto her tiptoes and behind my head, she pulls the hair tie from the base of my neck so my long, dark hair falls free, then she places her hand against my cheek and nods her approval. She might not be talking, but most days she communicates with me one hundred times better than Drew does.

I pull Gabby into a hug and take in the sweet bubblegum scent of her hair. When I release her, Drew is staring at us and, for the split second before she can hide it again, there's sadness in her eyes.

"You sure you guys will be okay?" I ask.

Gabby squeezes my hand, and Drew nods, averting her eyes. "You deserve to have a little fun too."

My breath catches with surprise, and that need to cry is back. *Damn it.* I shove it down. "Thank you."

Drew lifts a shoulder. "I can tell you like him. Anyway, he's hot."

I grab a pillow and throw it at her. "Hot and too old for you!"

She laughs and throws it back at me. "Yeah, but which one of us is going to be living here?"

"I don't care how hot he is, if he touched you, I'd cut off his balls."

Something flickers in her eyes, a secret caught peeking from the hidden corner of her mind. Even though I haven't lived under the same roof as the girls since I was sixteen, I've remained their primary breadwinner and been involved in their lives. My role as surrogate mother isn't a new one. And yet there's so much I don't know about her. I want to fix that, but there's a rift between us that I don't know I can heal from a distance.

From the outside looking in, people are probably most worried about Gabby. But me? It's Drew who keeps me up at night. Gabby's going to be okay. I believe that. But Drew is just old enough that she can really get herself in trouble if that's what she wants to do.

I swallow hard, pushing back the fear and sadness and locking it away for another time. "I'm going to wait outside. Slide the deadbolt and the chain behind me. I'll text you when I get back, and you can let me in."

Drew nods and pops her earbuds back in, and Gabby blows me a kiss.

I push myself out the door before I can change my mind and I'm greeted by a night of glittering stars. The stars in New Hope are brighter and more plentiful than anywhere else I've ever been. When I was a little girl, I would look out my bedroom window each night and pick my favorite one and only then would I make a wish. My father taught me to believe in the magic of wishes and destiny, and I was such an adoring daughter that his words were my scripture and the starry night sky became my temple.

When we moved to Vegas, Drew was eight, and she told my mom she felt sorry for people who lived there because weren't enough stars to go around. Mom laughed and said you don't need stars when your wishes had already come true.

She thought Rick was her wish come true. That was why she took us there, away from my dad, away from New Hope. She met some guy online, hooked up with him a few times while telling Dad she had to travel for "trainings" for work. Then she served her husband with divorce papers and took her daughters to live with a complete stranger who she thought was her everything.

We were there less than a month before she realized Rick wasn't the man she thought he was. He was a controlling drunk who liked to put his hands on my mom and sometimes me and the girls. We left his million-dollar home and found ourselves a couple of rent checks away from eviction and a homeless shelter, but it was the right decision. For all the mistakes Mom made, for all the decisions I wish she handled differently, I'm proud of her for leaving that man.

A black BMW pulls up in the spot before me, and William steps out, wearing dark dress pants and a grey button-up Oxford. The sight of him flips a switch in my body and I'm instantly buzzing with awareness.

"Hey, beautiful," he says softly, and with one slide of his eyes over me, all my concerns about this dress fizzle away.

chapter five

Cally

THE LITTLE tapas restaurant north of Indianapolis is the perfect setting for a secret date with this man who makes me forget myself. There's candlelight and soft music, and we're sitting in the corner at a booth that puts us at a little round table sharing the same curved seat.

We're eating brie and fresh fruit, seared ahi tuna, and miniature crab cakes, and already coming to the bottom of our first bottle of wine.

"So, what are you doing these days?" His voice has gone deeper and husky, and for a minute I'm so tied up in the sensual pull of the sound of his words that I don't actually register what they mean.

I blink when I realize he's staring at me expectantly. "Oh, I…I'm a massage therapist?" I hate that the answer makes me uncomfortable. In most contexts, I'm proud of what I do, but William knew my mother. I resist the urge to get defensive and explain that she may have taught me to love her trade, but I don't get big tips she did for the reasons she did. Not that I have any room to judge her anyway. I have my own secrets.

"Is that a question?"

I smile and shrug. "I don't know. I like what I do, but there are always people who assume the worst." People in New Hope. People who have already made up their minds about me and my family. "What about you? Do you still like photography?"

"I do. I teach it over at Sinclair."

"You're a college professor? Seriously?"

He grins. "I landed a fellowship after I finished my MFA. I like teaching, but I'd rather actually be a photographer than teach other people how to be."

"You were always so talented," I say softly. "I'm glad you didn't leave that behind."

"What about you? Did you go to college?"

"I got my massage certification at a community college and I've taken a few classes since, but I haven't managed to finish any kind of degree." I won't any time soon, either. I need to work as much as possible and send money to Dad to help with the girls.

Reaching across the table, William catches my fingers under his. "Why did you call, Cally? What made you change your mind?"

Why *am* I here? Because I want him? Because I'm trying to forget Brandon? Because I'm lonely as hell and needed an adult to talk to?

"I guess that's as much a mystery as why you would want to be here with me. After... Should we just acknowledge the elephant at the table and talk about how I stood you up for your own prom?" I let out a breath, relieved to finally say the words to his face. "I'm sorry. I've always been sorry. I hope you know that."

He drops his gaze to my mouth. "Come here."

Biting my lip, I slide around the booth so I'm next to him. The lights are so low, I can barely make out his expression, but I don't need to in order to feel the heat between us. Is it in my head? Can he feel it too? Whatever it is—hormones, memories, the knowledge that this is temporary and I'm leaving soon—the pull between us is magnetic, and I let my bare thigh press against the soft fabric of his pants.

"That's better," he whispers, his hot eyes on me.

"I think so, too."

He lowers his head and glides his lips over my neck in a movement so sweet, so simple, my breath leaves me in a rush. "I'm supposed to be pissed at you," he whispers. "You broke my heart."

"Then why aren't you?"

"When I saw you again, there was no room for my anger. I want you too much."

Under the table, his hand settles against the inside of my knee, making little circles that send my heart racing and turn my muscles to jelly. "Me too," I admit.

His fingers trace an invisible line two inches up the inside of my leg, and I clench my thighs together instinctively, trapping his hand between my legs.

"I can stop," he says in a whisper.

"No," I breathe. I want the opposite, and I force myself to relax, and my legs open to the exploration of his hand.

"You look amazing in this dress. I love the way it shows off your legs, but it just makes me think of having them wrapped around me."

I bury my face in his neck and moan softly, remembering the way he used to touch me. He smells amazing, and his whisper-soft exploration of my thigh sends tiny shivers of pleasure through me.

His hand slides higher until his fingertips reach the edge of my panties. I almost squeeze my legs together again—not because I want him to stop but because I want his hand there so badly, touching me, exploring me, his fingers sliding into me.

"What do these look like?" He traces down the satin center of my panties.

Oh, God. By some miracle, I'm already ready for his touch. I haven't been this turned on this quickly since…since William.

His knuckles brush over me, lightly pressing the soft fabric against my swollen clit.

He opens his mouth against my ear and draws my earlobe between his teeth, nipping and sucking. My eyes flutter closed. I want to fall into the pleasure that's spinning like a cyclone around every nerve ending, and I'm almost afraid of how quickly he has me falling into it.

I rock into his hand instinctively. "Touch me."

"Tell me," he whispers. He makes wicked little circles on my panties. "What do they look like?"

This desire clawing at me is madness. At this moment, I would do anything to get him to slide under the barrier between us. "They're black satin."

"Mmm, satin. I can tell." He rewards me by rolling his fingers against the fabric in question.

Holy shit.

"What else? How do they look?"

Under the table, I cling to his forearm as if I'm afraid he might escape. "They're string bikinis with a little bow at each of my hips."

His hand leaves that pulsing, aching spot between my legs to explore the string over my hip, leaving me ready to cry out or beg or both.

"God, I bet these are gorgeous on you. If I had you alone, I'd stand you in front of me in nothing these panties and I'd untie them with my teeth."

Yes, please.

I can hardly breathe. I want what he's describing. More. "Have you thought a lot about getting me alone again?" Drawing back a bit so I can watch his expression, I watch his eyes and wait for the answer I need to hear.

"Every second since you showed up on my street."

"Me too. And before."

Heat flares in his eyes. The intensity of his gaze would scare me if I didn't already trust this man with every inch of my being.

He presses his mouth against mine as his hand returns between my legs. It's not a gentle kiss. It's hard—punishing and demanding—and I need it. I could lose myself here, in this kiss that is equal parts desire, anger, and regret. I could forget who I am, what I've done, and become the stroke of tongue against tongue, become the pleasure of his hand working between my legs as I moan into his mouth.

He breaks the kiss and leans his forehead against mine. "You feel so damn good." His hand moves slowly, smoothly.

How can he affect me so much more than any other man I've ever been with? He's always been the standard by which all other men have been measured and come up short.

I shouldn't be here with him. I gave up my right to this seven years ago. I take a long drink of my wine—seeking courage and permission for this evening suspended outside of time and heartbreak. One night. One indulgence.

I lift my hips off the seat, seeking out his touch.

"Do you want more?" The words are so low they're more a vibration against my ear than a sound.

"I'm leaving in a couple of days. I can't stay." And that's the only reason we can do this at all.

His teeth nip my ear again, suck at the lobe before he speaks. "That's not what I asked, Cally."

Outside my panties, the pad of his thumb is resting on my clit with nothing but the promise of the pressure I need. When his hand leaves me, I hear my own gasp of protest.

"Come home with me tonight."

I squeeze my eyes shut. After weeks of looking after my sisters, I need to be something other than a resented stand-in mother. Even if only for a couple of hours in this man's bed. He deserves the night I once promised him. *I* deserve it. But I shake my head. "I can't."

"Then tell me to stop." The rough pads of his fingers toy with the thin ribbons at my hips. With his free hand, he places a sliced grape to my lips, and I take it, only briefly letting my lips brush his fingertips. His eyes flash—hot and hungry. "Tonight is yours. Whatever you want."

"This," I whisper, rolling my hip into his touch.

Then he tugs, and he releases the tie on my panties. His hand snakes around to the other hip, and he grins at me as he frees that side as well.

"Lift," he whispers, and before I realize what he means to do, he's slipped my panties from under the table and tucked them in his pocket. He flashes me a small smile as he sips from his wine glass.

My panties are in William Bailey's pocket.

"You intending to give those back?"

"Not a chance." But then, instead of heading straight for my newly bare girly bits beneath the table, he cups my face in his big hand and brushes his thumb across my cheek. "Memories have this amazing way of changing on us, and I had myself convinced you couldn't have been as beautiful as I remembered. I was idealizing you."

I can't reply. The heat in his eyes alone is enough to make me want to crawl into his lap. Add the way he's been touching me, and in this moment, I am his.

"I was right about one thing," he whispers.

"What's that?"

"My memory got it all wrong."

"It did?"

"You're so much more beautiful than I remembered."

Our lips touch again and I will myself to memorize every second of this kiss. The soft brush of his lips before he opens his mouth over mine, the patient sweep of his tongue as I open for him, the way he tastes—a potent cocktail of wine and regret.

I don't even realize his hand has left my face until I feel the possessive wrap of his fingers around my thigh. Then, as he slides to points farther north, I have to break our kiss to catch my breath.

"Jesus," he hisses as his fingers reach my wet heat.

I almost cry out when he takes my swollen clit between two fingers.

"You're so wet," he whispers against my neck. "So damn wet."

"I—William…." I have to fight to keep my volume down, to keep from moaning.

He's touching that swollen, sensitive spot in a slow and gentle rub that has me rocking into him.

"You want to know what I'd do to you if you came home with me tonight?"

I'm weak. I want to know, need to hear. "Yes."

"I'd get you naked because you have too goddamn many clothes on right now. Then I'd start with your amazing breasts. Remember how I could get you off just by kissing your breasts, sucking those beautiful nipples?" He brushes my taut nipples with his free hand and even through my dress and thin bra, the contact is enough to make me gasp. "Answer me, Cally."

"Yes," I breathe. His fingers have slowed their movement under my dress, as if he knows how close he is to getting me off and he wants to wait.

He moans appreciatively. "I'd start there. My tongue and lips and teeth on your breasts until I've memorized every curve and dip, until you're begging me for more—" He removes his hand from between my legs, "until you come for me."

"William."

"I'll get you there, baby. I swear. But not yet." He slides his hand farther up my dress and circles my navel. "Do you want to know more?"

God help me, I do. I want to know it all. And then maybe when I'm back in Las Vegas and wishing I could have him, I'll shape his words into my very own fantasy. My very own souvenir of my *what-if* life. "Please."

"Then I'd kiss you here." He pinches my navel piercing. "Damn, I bet this looks so sexy on you. When did you get it?"

"After I moved."

He draws back, his eyes hot on mine, his jaw hard. "For a man?"

"No. I got it when I was missing you."

He moans into my ear then fans his hand out to my waist. "I'd have to take my time there then. I'd run my tongue from hipbone to hipbone, then turn you over and lick down your spine." He slides his hand across my hip and under my ass. "When I got here," he says, squeezing, "I'd have to see if you're as sensitive here as you are everywhere else. Your ass is so incredible, and I can't forgive myself for neglecting it when I had a chance. I'm dying to bite you *here*."

He pinches my ass, and my breath draws in sharply. I shudder in his arms and feel his smile against my neck.

"Would you be ready for me then?" As he asks, he returns his hand between my legs, and I find myself scooting to the edge of the seat, parting my thighs to give him better access. I don't just want him to touch me. I need it. Like water. Like air. I *need* to feel William's hand between my legs because right now I am nothing but the pulsing ache of my arousal, and it's the fucking best I've felt in months.

No man I've ever touched could touch me the way Will does. It's like he has some sort of ability to intuitively know how I'm feeling.

Even now, sitting at the back of this candlelit restaurant with the wait staff milling around us, he doesn't rush in his movements. His fingers slide over me, alternately teasing and touching, working anticipation in equal measure against the pleasure.

"What else would you do?" I bite back a moan. "If we were alone?"

"I'd drop to my knees," he whispers. "And I'd cup your amazing ass in my hands as I tasted you."

It hurts, sitting here, listening to this, wanting it, knowing I can't let myself have it. Knowing that tonight, this moment, is all I get.

I curl my nails into his forearm, and he groans in my ear.

"But for now," he says, "for now I'll settle for touching with my fingers what I want to taste with my lips." He slides two fingers inside me, curling them as his thumb rubs my clit. "That's what I want you to think about next time you touch yourself."

I shudder, the pressure and pleasure building. "William," I whimper.

"Because next time my dick is in my hand, I fucking swear that's what I'll be thinking about. You. Naked. The taste of your pussy as you come against my tongue."

Dear God.

I have to bite his neck to muffle my moan as my orgasm hits, hard and fast.

chapter six

William

THE CAR is quiet on the drive home, and when I reach for her hand, she lets me take it. I have to remind myself that she's leaving. That this—the sweet silence of our touch, her soft fingers twined through mine—this isn't the new normal. I don't get to keep her. I don't get to finish what I started at the restaurant. She's leaving.

When we pull up to the motel, she doesn't rush from the car, so I turn and press my lips to hers. At first, I think she's going to pull away, but she opens under me slowly, and what I intended to be a brief good-bye kiss leaves me hard and breathless, and her clawing at my shirt and half in my lap.

We lean our foreheads together and catch our breath.

"When are you leaving?"

"Tomorrow? Day after tomorrow maybe? Dad's home. I just want to get the girls settled, but then I need to get back for work."

There's nothing I can say to get her to stay. I'm not even sure I should want her to. Tonight wasn't real after all. Reality wouldn't have let me touch her in in public like that. Reality dictates that I stay away from her, that I hate her for what she did to me. Or, at the very least, that I want nothing to do with her.

But tonight wasn't reality. It was like visiting a memory. And it was perfect.

I walk around to get her door. The moment she steps onto the pavement, I have her pressed against the side of the car, my hands in her hair, my knee between her legs, pressing our bodies as close as possible. Because touching her in the restaurant only made this need for her grow, and now I want her more than ever.

She kisses me back, clings to me, hand fisted in my shirt. Her mouth and hands match the desperation of my own, closer and closer, as if she wants to disappear into me.

I want more. I want to put her back in the car and take her to my house, take her to my bed. Because if tonight is the only stolen moment we get, I don't want it to end.

But despite all that, I'm the one who breaks the kiss. I'm the one who pulls away. Looking at her doesn't make it any easier. She's so fucking beautiful it breaks my heart. Flushed cheeks, swollen lips, thick lashes fluttering as she opens her eyes.

If I'd forgotten who and where we are, if I'd forgotten that she's no longer the girl I once loved, the look in her eyes brings me back. The girl I knew would have had nothing but love and desire in her eyes. But I see pain there now, pain and weariness edging away her desire.

"What happened to you?" I whisper.

"What do you mean?"

Swallowing, I trace the edge of her jaw. "You've changed. There's something…darker about you now."

Sadness washes over her face. "I regret so much. I should have been with you and I shouldn't have…." She shakes her head and looks up at me through her thick lashes. "You should hate me."

Impossible. "I've tried." I force a laugh, but it's hollow. "I don't know how."

Her lips tilt into a ghost of a smile. "You're too damn good, William Bailey, and I don't deserve as much of you as you've given." She grabs my hand and kisses the rough skin of my knuckles. "Thank you for tonight. It was amazing."

I kiss the corner of her mouth and squeeze her fingers in mine.

"I should go in," she says. "I'll never forget this. Goodb—"

I press a finger to her lips before she can say our once-forbidden word. Because I can't bring myself to hear it. "Don't ruin tonight with that word."

She closes her eyes.

"Sleep well," I whisper.

She slips away, heading toward her room and leaving me feeling empty. "Sleep well," she calls over her shoulder.

I watch her disappear into her room, and then I look up at the moon and stars we once wished on together. They make me feel lonelier than ever. Because she may no longer be the girl I once loved, but she's the woman I want.

Cally

When Gabby was six and Drew was eleven, I pawned a pair of three-carat diamond earrings and took the girls to Disney Land. We didn't stay at the fancy resorts and we couldn't buy all the cool souvenirs, but the girls didn't care. We packed up the car and drove to a cheap motel, setting an alarm so we would be at the park gates right at opening. Maybe it wasn't the smartest thing to do with the money. There were a thousand other ways we could have spent it. There was definitely a voice at the back of my mind that said this was why rich people think poor people make their own problems. But the look in Gabby's eyes when she saw Minnie Mouse for the first time made it worth it. Even Drew teared up as Goofy wrapped his arms around her and spun her around.

At Gabby's parent-teacher conference two months later (where I was standing in for Mom, who was "sick"), the teacher confronted me about it. Was that really the wisest use of our limited funds? Didn't I understand that we were two months behind on our share of classroom supplies? Think how many pairs of shoes I could have bought the girls with the money we spent on our park passes.

I stared at my lap and took every judgmental word from her lips. But it didn't matter what she said because, for one day, I got to show my little sisters that there really are magical things in this world. I got to prove to myself that the entire world wasn't as shitty as it had felt for the three years under Brandon's rule. That was worth a thousand years of school supplies and a hundred pairs of new shoes. Maybe I'm a little bit like my father in that way—willing to sacrifice practicality for a little magic.

As we pull up to Dad's house, I wonder if any of that has stuck with them or if they've lost faith in their world. I throw the car into park and turn to Drew, whose eyes have gone wide and horrified in the passenger seat.

Thunder rolls in the distance and heavy storm clouds hang over the house, making it look even more depressing than it did in yesterday's sunshine.

"It looks worse than it is," I say softly. "A little TLC, and it'll be just fine."

She climbs out of the car and slams the door behind her. The sound echoes through the car.

I turn to Gabby in the back. "It'll be an adventure."

Her bottom lip trembles and she's twisting her hands in her lap. She was three when we left and the couple of times she saw Dad over the years weren't enough to create those bonds a child deserves to have with a father, especially if he's going to be her primary care provider. Of course, she hasn't said a word about any of this, but she doesn't have to. It's all written on her face.

I climb out of the car and open her door, offering her my hand.

We twine our fingers together and follow Drew to the door—Drew, who's decided to take the disinterested tack and is already glued to the screen of her phone.

Dad pulls the door open before we even climb on the porch. "Welcome home. I was wondering when you'd get here. You girls hungry? I made some chili?" He's speaking too fast—a rare occurrence for my father—and his words trip over each other.

Drew glances up from her phone but doesn't answer. Gabby squeezes my hand.

"Chili would be great," I answer, leading the way in the house.

I'm relieved to see that he's straightened up the place a bit. The kitchen counters and little table are clear of papers and books, and he's set out red disposable bowls at each of the four seats, a metal spoon and glass of water next to each.

Gabby and I sit down, and Drew joins us, her jaw tight.

"Phone," I remind her, and Drew slides it into her pocket with a roll of her eyes.

We sit quietly as Dad serves us the thin, red soup he's calling chili. We stare at our bowls.

"Did you make this?" I pick up my spoon, preparing to set a good example for my sisters.

"Yes. I hope it's okay. I'm not used to cooking for anyone but myself."

"What's in it?" Drew asks, poking at it with her spoon.

"It's…vegetarian." Dad clears his throat. "Tomatoes, beans, onions, green peppers, okra."

Drew drops her utensil. "I'll pass."

"*Vegetarian*," I growl.

"*Okra*," she growls right back. She crosses her arms over her chest and leans back in her chair.

"Thanks for thinking to make us lunch, Dad," I say, attempting to salvage these awkward beginnings. "That was thoughtful." I make myself take a big bite, keeping my face neutral as I chew and swallow.

Next to me, Gabby slowly lifts her spoon to her mouth. She blanches slightly when the soup hits her tongue—the still-crunchy vegetables and slimy beans make for an odd combination of textures—but she's a trooper and smiles at Dad before slowly taking another bite.

"So, what grade are you girls in now?" Dad asks between bites of his own soup. I've never seen him so nervous. For the first time I'm realizing that the girls aren't the only ones suffering a major life upheaval. "Drew, you must be in, what, seventh grade by now?"

Drew shoots me a look, as if our father's cluelessness is entirely my fault.

"She's in high school, Dad. Drew will be a sophomore. And Gabby will start fifth grade in the fall."

Dad looks taken aback by this information. "You've grown up so much," he says, almost to himself. Then he turns his gaze to his soup and we finish our meal in silence.

I make a mental note to get money from Dad to go grocery shopping for some basic foodstuffs. Drew will likely starve before eating okra. She may be a vegetarian, but she shouldn't be mistaken for someone who actually eats vegetables.

After our meal, I show the girls to the room they'll be sharing, and for Drew's sake, I try to see it through her eyes. Old pea-green shag carpet, mattresses on the floor that I've already made with their sheets and blankets from home, rickety little end table between the beds.

"This is worse than the brothel of a motel you had us staying at," she says under her breath.

"It'll be better when we move all your stuff in."

She snorts. "Sure. The lipstick on the pig didn't do it, so let's try some mascara."

"Drew, I need you to *try*." I feel Gabby at my side, grabbing my hand. "This situation will only be as good as you let it be."

"Good?" Her voice shakes and she throws her phone on her bed. "What in the *fuck* is good about any of this? I lost my mom and I have to live with this guy who never cared enough to visit more than a handful of times or, I don't know, *call* on my birthday. I had to leave my friends and my home. I hate this house. I hate this town, *and I fucking hate you.*"

I stagger back as she twists the dull blade in my heart. "What do you want me to do?" Tears roll down my cheeks because I'm not heartless and I hate what I'm asking of them. "I'm serious. Please tell me, because I don't know what to do."

Beside me, Gabby squeezes my hand. Then she speaks. It's the first word I've heard from her lips since I found her squatting on the floor next to Mom's dead body.

"Stay."

chapter seven

William
Seven Years Ago

"SHE'S NOT taking my calls." I throw the phone against the locker room wall. It hits with a sharp *crack*. Brand fucking new phone ruined. I'm not even like that. I don't lose my temper over shit. But Cally left, and I'm not even myself anymore.

At first it was okay. We talked all the time. I sent her a new cell since her mom missed the payment on her old one and it got shut off. We shared the mundane details about our days. We texted. We made plans for prom. I sent her emails with the web links about the little cabin I booked. We traded text messages about the strawberry wine I snuck from Grandma's basement. We whispered late until sunrise about our first night together. And I confessed how I can't stop thinking about what it's going to be like to finally slide inside her.

Those stolen moments weren't enough, but they kept me sane. And now I don't even have that much.

Max and Sam exchange a look. They've been holding their tongues where Cally's concerned, but I can see they're done with that.

"Man," Max says, "you're about to start college. It'll be awesome."

"Maybe you should just...let her go," Sam says. "Be young. Date around."

I set my jaw. "Right. Sure." But they don't fucking understand. I don't want to date around. I want *Cally*.

I drag a hand through my hair. My stomach burns. She's been ignoring my calls, blowing off my texts with occasional vague responses about being "busy." The last time I did get her on the phone, she was distant, not saying much, not bothering to laugh at my jokes and making excuses to get out of the conversation before it even began. "I sent her plane tickets to come home for prom. That'll help. I shouldn't have gone so long without seeing her. Prom will fix things."

"Long distance is hard when things are good," Max warns. "It's no way to fix a relationship that's broken."

"*We're. Not. Broken.*"

Sam shoves his hands in his pockets. "Are you sure she's still coming?"

"Of course she's still coming. She hasn't said otherwise."

The guys both nod and exchange those damn knowing looks again.

"She's not cheating on me," I mutter. They haven't said it, but that's what they're thinking. They're thinking I'll be better off without her. But they don't know Cally like I do. They don't understand how she gets me like nobody else, how she fills the aching hollow places that I've had since Mom and Dad died. "She wouldn't cheat on me."

"Okay, man," Max says.

"Of course not." Sam slaps my back. "Is there anything we can do?"

Their kindness pisses me off. They wouldn't drop the subject so easily if they believed she was being faithful. "Just…leave me alone for a while."

After they're gone, I grab my phone from the floor. The glass is shattered, making a starburst on the screen that reminds me of the girl I'm too afraid to admit I've lost.

William
Present Day

Another blast of thunder rattles the glass in the gallery windows, and I'm fucking glad. Rain pelts the back deck and hits the river with a vengeance. The day is gray and the weather violent. It matches my mood.

Soon, Cally will take the girls to her dad's and then she'll leave town. Maybe forever this time. Or maybe she'll be back often, since her sisters are here now. The hope is almost worse than the despair.

I slam my palm so hard against the glass, it stings. "Fuck."

"Well, hello, sunshine."

I don't bother to turn toward the sound of Maggie's voice. I'm glad she's working today. She can cover the gallery so I can get the fuck out of dodge and blow off some of this steam. A run in the rain might help. Or a bottle of whiskey.

"I'll make coffee," she calls, and then I hear the click of her heels on the stairs as she climbs up to the kitchenette in the loft.

I drop my head and lean against the cool glass. I want to go back to Cally's hotel and beg her not to leave. I want to taste her again, just to make sure I won't forget the flavor of her lips, to touch her one more time so I remember the sound she makes when she comes. I want to drown in the feel of her hair and the softness of her skin until the bad shit washes away.

And at the same fucking time, I want to fight with her. I want to call her out on what she did to me seven years ago. I want to make her understand how much she screwed me up.

Maggie's footsteps sound above and before I know it, she's back down and shoving a hot mug of coffee into my hands. "Drink before I have to put you down," she scolds. "I left a very sexy, very willing man in bed to talk fall exhibition with you. If you're going to be a grumpy ass, I'll go right back out that door and spend my morning screwing his brains out."

"I'm so glad we've reached a point in our relationship where you can be so open," I mutter, though truthfully, I am.

She returns my scowl with a smile. "I know. Isn't it special?"

I watch her sip from her coffee, her red hair flying in loose and wild curls around her face. In the last two months since she worked out everything with Asher, she's been happier than I've ever seen her. I wouldn't have thought it was possible, but she's even more beautiful when she's happy.

I'm so fucking glad we're past those awkward early days after she chose Asher over me. We got there faster than I expected. Not so long ago, I wanted Maggie more than I wanted anything else. Or I thought I did. It's so obvious we shouldn't be together. I didn't want a life with her. I wanted to save her from my screwed up past and save myself from my guilt. There's a big fucking difference. We would never have worked. I think Maggie understood that, but me? I hold out for the dream. Maybe Cally taught me that.

"Who's the girl?" she asks, peering into the dreary day. "Is this about that Meredith chick? She was here looking for you the other day."

Meredith. *Crap.* "Why do you assume there's a girl?"

She lifts a brow and snorts. "Because. You're Will. With you, it's always a girl. Usually a broken one or a forbidden one."

I guess I earned that. "Cally Fisher's back in town."

She whistles, low and smooth. "As in, your high school sweetheart?"

"That's the one."

"And you've seen her?"

I don't answer, but the truth must be in my eyes because Maggie steps back and holds a hand to her chest. "Holy shit, Will. You slept with her? How fast do you *work*?"

"As if I'd tell you."

"I thought you were taking a break from relationships?"

"I am," I growl, my jaw set tight. Two failed engagements in as many years is more than enough reason to step back from the dating scene for a while. Not that my feelings on the matter have slowed my grandmother's attempts to set me up with Ms. Right.

"So Cally's back in town. You still have feelings for her, but you didn't sleep with her—though, clearly, you did more than have a nice little chat. And now you're trying to convince yourself not to dive headlong into another super-intense relationship. Especially one that's doomed to failure because she dropped you like a bad habit. Is that about right?"

"There's no danger of a relationship. She's not staying."

"Oooh. That explains the mood."

"I guess."

"I remember when she left," Maggie says, looking thoughtful. "She screwed you over. Why would you even want anything to do with her?"

"I know."

"Did she ever explain?"

"Explain what?"

Maggie narrows her eyes and crosses her arms. She's not going to tolerate me being obtuse today.

"Explain why she broke up with me via text message the night she was supposed to come back for the prom? Why she sent back the cell-phone I bought her so I couldn't get ahold of her anymore? Why she was fucking another guy when I tracked her down in Vegas?"

Maggie lifts a brow. "Yeah, something like that."

"No," I growl. Thunder cracks and shakes the entire building. "I didn't ask."

"Because you don't want to know?"

I shove my hands in my pockets and walk away from Maggie. She understands me too well, and I'm not sure I want to be understood right now. I just want to be dark and broody and pissed off. And yet I answer anyway. "I didn't ask any of those questions because I knew she wouldn't spend any time with me if I did. I wanted her too much to risk that."

"Oh. My. God. You're still in love with her."

I drag a hand through my hair and avoid her eyes. I don't know what I am. "I see her for the first time in seven years, and I want her back so damn badly—despite all logic. She's here and she's beautiful and she owns a piece of me I'd forgotten I even had." I lean against the wall and sink to my haunches. "She was in town and *lost*. Of all the places she could have been lost, she found herself right in front of my house."

"I can see how that might suck, but…." She trails off.

Maggie doesn't get it. "*Cally* used to tell me that destiny would bring us together again and again, that she was mine. What are the chances of her showing up on my street? In front of the house I built?"

She looks skeptical. "She didn't know you lived there?"

"No. I don't think she even wanted to see me, but there she was. And now…what? Am I supposed to just let her go?"

"Do you really want me to answer that?"

I swallow hard. I wouldn't want to hear it from most people, but I trust Maggie. I nod.

"Yes," she says softly. "You need to let her go."

"Goddammit."

"Listen to me. You are quick to give and quick to love. You want to share your life with someone. I get that. You want marriage and the family you didn't get as a kid. I get *that*. But that's why you need to let her go. Because you need some distance to figure out how you really feel about her. Right now you're flying high on nostalgia. You need to know if you can forgive her before you ask for more."

I drag a hand through my hair and nod. I know she's right.

"I remember what everyone said after she dumped you," Maggie whispers. "I remember the rumors."

"They were rumors," I growl. "Nobody knew."

She shrugs. "But what it they're right? What if the guy you found her with was the reason she broke up with you? What if she cheated on you? What if she was in Vegas, sleeping with some older guy, while you were here, waiting like the good boyfriend you were? Can you really get past that?"

I stare at her. Because this is Maggie and of all people, she knows just how much I'm willing to forgive.

"Not me," she whispers. "I know you forgave me, but that was because you were trying to save me. That's not the case with Cally. Everything is different with her. I'm not asking if you can forgive just anyone. I'm asking, can you forgive *Cally*?"

She's right. There's a difference. I'm not sure it makes sense, but it's true.

"Let her go, Will. As a favor to yourself. If all that destiny crap is real and you're meant to be together, she'll be back. Right?"

I hang my head. Because she's right.

"Just let her go."

chapter eight

Cally

NEW SCHOOL, day one. Drew walked, since the high school is only a couple of blocks from Dad's. I offered to walk with her but she rolled her eyes and accused me of trying to make her the laughingstock on her first day at a new school, so I let her go on her own.

Now it's Gabby's turn, and my stomach is a mess with worry. Aside from her one-word request last week—*Stay*—she hasn't spoken. I already had a meeting with the school counselor and exchanged emails with her teacher. Everyone assures me they'll work with her, but I hate that I can't be at school with her to see for myself. My only reassurance is that at least I'll be here. Here in New Hope, living with Dad for the foreseeable future.

My boss at the spa back in Vegas has agreed to hold my job until the first of the year. I fought so hard to get into a position where I could support myself, and that job is an important part of the equation—great tips, decent salary, benefits. I need the income to help Dad support the girls. I need the income so I don't have to rely on Brandon again.

Would I have quit if my boss weren't willing to work with me? Probably. Gabby needs me, so I'll do what needs to be done. I always have.

We drive to the elementary school. It's only about a mile and we could walk, but it's a hot day and I don't want Gabby feeling self-conscious in sweaty clothes.

I offer her my hand as we approach the building. She shakes her head, reminding me that despite currently having the speech patterns of a toddler, she is in fact ten years old and doesn't need her big sister holding her hand.

We walk through the front and head into the building. Once we get to the heavy oak door to her new classroom, she stops me, her hand squeezing my wrist.

"I have my cellphone," I tell her. "I'll be looking for a job all day, but you call if you need anything."

Worry is written all over her face, and I find myself questioning our move for the hundredth time. I didn't have a home for them in Vegas, so I assumed they'd be better here. I assumed I'd be able to work and send Dad part of my monthly check. But now that part of the plan is gone. What if I was wrong? What if uprooting them from their lives after Mom's death was the worst thing for them? And now that I've chosen to stay, what if I can't find a job?

Finally, Gabby squeezes my wrist again, takes a deep breath, and heads into the classroom.

When I turn around, I see Lizzy Thompson. She's practically glowing, her smile is so bright. "Lizzy! What are you doing here?"

"Student teaching!" She rubs her hands together. "Well, it doesn't actually start for a few weeks, but Mrs. Monroe said I could come meet the kids for the first day of class and I just found out Gabby's one of the students. This is going to be great!"

Relief swamps me. "I'm so glad you'll be in there."

She squeezes me into a tight hug and whispers, "She'll love it. Have some faith."

"I know." I shrug. "This is what parents must feel like, huh? I think I'm more nervous than both the girls today."

"They'll be fine. But you? You look like you need some stress relief, and I know just the thing." She grins. "I'll text you the details."

"Stress relief" sounds like code for "party," and I don't have time for that right now, not with finding a job and working on Dad's house. I don't want to seem unfriendly, though, so I return her smile. I can always let her down after the invitation comes. "Okay. Thanks."

I'm heading out the front door when the secretary from the front office calls my name. She's a tiny little thing with a gray bob and a sweet smile. "You're Gabby Fisher's sister?"

"I am."

She presses an envelope into my hand and drops her voice low. "Your father's textbook rental check bounced."

"Oh." *Shit.* "I'm sorry about that. He can be kind of...absentminded. I'll have him...um...move some funds and write a new check."

Her smile suggests she knows there are no funds to move. "There's paperwork in that envelope for assistance. You just have your father fill it out, and Gabby's textbooks will be taken care of. I also included the application for free lunch."

Of course. Because the Fishers always need handouts. Nothing changes. I force myself to thank her before rushing from the building.

I'm unlocking the car when I hear someone call my name. I pin on my smile before turning.

"Cally Fisher, right?" the woman repeats. I don't recognize her. She's gorgeous and sophisticated in a black pencil skirt and a button-up pin-striped shirt, her long, blond hair pulled into a low ponytail.

"Yes, that's right." I offer my hand. "And you are?"

She drops her gaze to my hand and then brings it back to my face. "I'm Meredith Palmer. Owner of Venus Salon?"

She still hasn't taken my hand. Feeling like an idiot, I tuck it back into my pocket. "It's nice to meet you," I manage. This woman may be smiling, but coldness radiates off her. For whatever reason, she doesn't like me.

"I saw that you were interested in working as my massage therapist."

I shift uncomfortably. I already know where this is going. "I was looking into it."

"Yeah." She straightens her shirt and repositions that plastic smile. "But you see, we're not that kind of establishment, and I would rather watch my business *wither and die* than have someone like you giving—" she lifts her hands and makes air quotes, " —'massages.'"

William

Tuesday morning brings sunshine and clarity. Maggie's right, of course. I need to let Cally go. Not that I have a choice. She'll leave town soon—hell, maybe she's already left—and I'll forget there was ever a woman who owned me, body, heart, and soul, as much as she did.

I turn on the gallery lights and start up the computer. Maggie will be in soon, and she can watch the floor while I take care of some paperwork in my office upstairs. I need to finish the grant proposal for the downtown arts event and hopefully finish the syllabi for my fall classes.

When I unlock the front doors, I find Cally waiting on the sidewalk.

"William?" She blinks at me, as if she can't figure out why I'd be here. I'm wondering the same about her.

"Good morning." God, she's beautiful. She left down her silky, dark hair today and it's like a curtain over half her face. I clench my fists against the temptation to touch it, tuck it behind her ear to reveal the smooth skin of her cheek, kiss her lips.

I should send her away quickly. When she's looking at me, I can't lie to myself about being at peace with letting her go.

"I'm here about some rental space? Do you know the owner?"

"Rental space?"

"Yeah." She raises onto her toes and peeks into the gallery over my shoulder. "God, it's such a gorgeous place. Do you mind?"

I step back and motion her in. "By all means."

Her eyes are wide as she surveys the space and studies the art hanging on the walls. First, she approaches a work done in pastels. A child's face is lit up with laughter as she squeezes a large male hand between both of hers. "Wow." Cally's mouth drops into a perfect circle of awe.

"Maggie Thompson did that."

"Who's the child?"

"Her name is Zoe. She's Asher Logan's daughter."

"Asher Logan has a daughter?"

"Yeah. She lives in New York with her mom most of the year, but she spent most of July here. She and Maggie were inseparable." I shake my head, remembering the look of pure contentment in Maggie's eyes when she brought Zoe around. "Maggie and Zoe might not share any blood, but they were meant to be mother and daughter."

"She loves her. You can see it on the canvas." She moves to the next wall and stops at the five-by-two-foot panoramic of the New Hope River.

I'd taken a photograph from the same spot every week for a year, then I'd digitally merged the images together so they appear to be a single photo. The seasons change by the slightest degrees from left to right.

She lifts her fingers to the placard with my name just below the photo. "You made this. It's amazing."

My heart is pounding. Cally in my gallery. Cally looking at my photographs. Cally close enough to touch.

She spins toward me and sinks her teeth into her bottom lip.

I shove my hands in my pockets, temptation three inches away.

"Good morning?" someone calls from the front door.

Maggie stands just inside the gallery, her brow wrinkled with worry as she takes in Cally and me standing together.

Cally jumps back when she spots Maggie. "I'm just here about a room Lizzy was telling me about."

I shake my head. I already forgot about that. I was so absorbed in watching Cally appreciate my gallery—so absorbed in watching *her*—that I lost focus.

I turn to Maggie. "Can you handle things down here for a bit?"

"No problem. I was going to do inventory today while it's slow, then later I need to talk to you about my schedule for the fall."

"Of course." I turn to Cally. "Follow me upstairs?" I head into the loft, where I feel her watching me as I pour myself a mug of coffee. "Want one?"

"Sure."

"Cream or sugar?"

"Cream if you have it."

Opening the little fridge, I pull out the cream and add a dash to her coffee before handing it to her. "How's that?"

Her eyes close as the first sip hits her tongue and that soft, mewling sound slips from the back of her throat, reminding me of our night in the restaurant and turning me *way* the fuck on. "God, that's good."

"Jesus, I thought I was special for making you moan like that, but now that I know coffee can render the same results, I might need to check my ego."

Her cheeks flush and she shoots a look toward the stairs then back to me. "Hush!"

"Maggie doesn't care."

"Yes," Maggie calls from the showroom floor below, "yes, Maggie does care."

I bite back a grin and motion Cally toward my office, closing the door behind us so we can have some privacy.

"To be fair," she says, "you make a damn good cup of coffee and I've been subsisting on instant crap. Powder creamer and all."

"Instant? Damn, you must have been hard up."

Her eyes connect with mine for a minute, and the heat there clears up any doubt in my mind that she was left wanting as much as me after our date.

Let her go, I remind myself.

"I'm looking to rent a room for massage therapy clients, and Lizzy said there was an apartment above the gallery she thought would work great. Obviously you work here too? Do you know the owner?"

"You're looking at him."

She drops her gaze to her coffee. "I was beginning to suspect as much. Lizzy could have mentioned that."

"I'm glad she didn't." We both know Cally wouldn't be here otherwise. Maybe that was intentional on Lizzy's part. "So you're staying?"

"For a couple of months, yes."

"What changed your mind?"

She crosses her arms and her face turns sad. "My sisters. It was foolish of me to think I could just drop them at Dad's house and they'd magically feel at home." She shakes her head. "And the house is a disaster. Not dirty, really, but a mess and not maintained or updated. I took a shower there this morning and the water pressure was so bad it took ten minutes to wash the shampoo from my hair. So I'm staying, helping get the house in order, helping my father figure out how to be a dad. It'll be okay."

"So you're going to start up a massage business while you're here?"

She shrugs. "I need money, and it's what I do. Lizzy gave me a couple

of leads on spas by campus that might be looking for someone, but—"
She hesitates for a minute, choosing her words. "Nothing worked out."

"Wouldn't the money be better on your own?"

She shrugs. "Established businesses come with built-in clientele. Kind of a shortcut, which makes sense since I don't plan to stay."

"My friend Meredith owns a salon, and I think she was looking for a new massage therapist." I'll call in a favor. God knows Meredith has made it clear enough that she wants to see me again.

"Meredith Palmer? At Venus Salon?"

"Yeah, that's her."

"She's not interested in hiring me."

"What? Why?" She lifts her gaze to meet mine, and I get it. Meredith knows about Cally's mom. The rumors. "I can talk to her. I'll explain."

She puts her hand on my arm, stopping me from getting my phone. "Please don't." She forces a smile. "It's probably best. Once I have a client list built up, the money is much better on my own. I'll find a space to rent."

"*That* I can help you with."

She sinks her teeth into her bottom lip. "How often are you here?"

"Often enough."

"I think we both know this would be a bad idea so—"

"Hold that thought." I motion back to the hallway.

She follows me across the little kitchenette and reception area to the other side of the upper story that holds a small apartment.

For a few weeks after my second failed engagement, when I was just opening the gallery, I spent a lot of nights here to escape the big, empty house and all my ruined plans. Now the apartment sits unused for the most part.

I pull my keys from my pocket and unlock the door, flipping on the lights as we head in. "There's access from the outside, too, a balcony out back, and a stairwell down the side of the building. Your clients wouldn't have to go through the gallery, though they're welcome to."

She nods, but she's frowning.

"What's wrong?"

She turns a slow circle, taking in the furnished living area and small kitchen. "It's just really nice, but it's too much."

"Would you be living here, too?"

"No. I'll stay with the girls. I just need a space to work."

I motion her toward the bedroom. "I thought this would be a nice space for you," I say, flipping on the lights in the small bedroom. "Honestly, I've become accustomed to using this apartment for a quick shower when I don't want to run home. I'd give you a deal if you wanted to rent only this space, and I'd make sure to stay out of your way when you had clients."

She nods as she looks around the room. Like my office, this room has a set of floor-to-ceiling windows that overlook the river and let in tons of light. "Lizzy was right. This would be perfect."

"Then why do you sound so disappointed?"

"It's not a good idea for us to work this close."

Despite all reason, I can't help but smile. "I can't think of many ideas better. You don't even have to pay me upfront. I know money's tight now. You can pay me once business picks up." I sound desperate. Maybe I am. I want to be close to her, to have her close to me.

She shakes her head and looks at me, bewildered. "I'm not in a position to say *no* to that, so…thank you."

I grin. "You'll take it?"

Slowly, she returns my smile, but hers is shakier, more tentative. "I'll take it." She pauses a beat. "William?"

"Yeah?"

"Thanks for not assuming the worst. About the kind of massage business I'll be running, I mean. Thank you for understanding I'm not my mom."

"You'll never be like her, Cally. You're too good."

A crash echoes off the walls as her coffee cup slips from her hands and shatters on the floor, coffee splashing all over her legs.

"Oh," she whispers. "I'm so sorry."

I run to the kitchen for some towels, and when I return, she's on her knees, collecting shards of coffee mug. Her hands are shaking.

"Hey." I sink to my haunches, dropping the towels and taking one of her hands in mine. "It's no big deal."

A tear spills onto her cheek. "Mom wasn't bad. She just did what she believed she had to do."

"Aw, shit." I gather her against me, and she cries, big, body-shaking, silent sobs that leave my shirt wet and me feeling like the biggest asshole on the planet.

chapter nine

Cally

AFTER I recover from my little meltdown, I rush from the gallery as quickly as I can without running. I need to put space between me and William. It felt too good to cry in his arms, to have him stroke my hair and murmur apologies he doesn't owe me.

Once I'm outside, I go around the building and sink onto a bench, dropping my head into my hands. I take deep, calming breaths.

Everything's going to be okay. It's all going to work out.

That space is perfect. So perfect. The apartment's tiny kitchen and living room would make a comfortable waiting area for clients. I would set out herbal teas and bottles of water on the kitchen's granite island. Clients could sit with me on the couch and chat about their concerns with their bodies. And the massage room? Those windows overlooking the river give it a unique ambience I would bet nowhere else in town can match. I'd set up the room with minimalist luxury, and my clients could look out those windows as I gave their massages. Not to mention how ideal the location is. What says "high class" more than an art gallery? And even though my business wouldn't be a part of the gallery, people would connect the two in their minds, instantly earning me the respect I'll need in order to escape my mother's reputation.

It's perfect. And I should probably walk away. Because I already want William too much, and I can't have him. If he knew the truth, he wouldn't want me anyway.

Someone sits next to me, and I look up to see Maggie Thompson, her red curls framing her frown. I remember being jealous of her when Will and I were dating. She's a couple of years younger than me, so it's not as if he seemed interested in her *romantically* back then, but I knew how she felt about him. She would have been maybe fourteen when he and I were together. But he was always very protective of her. Of all her sisters. And now she's working for him. Interesting.

I sit up and force a smile. "Hey, Maggie."

"Hey." She toys with the pendant on her necklace. It looks like a piece of shattered glass, and the sunlight dances on its surface. "Do you think renting that space is really a good idea?"

"Probably not." I should see about commuting to Indianapolis. Maybe I could find a position at a spa where I wouldn't be working under the shadow of Mom's reputation. But that would mean gas money, and I'd have more hours away from the girls. I've always wanted to work for myself, but I've never had the luxury of being able to walk away from the benefits of working for a large company. This may be my only chance.

"But you're going to do it anyway?" she asks.

"Sometimes the bad idea is still the best option you have."

She narrows her eyes and studies me as if she understands this. Most people wouldn't. "And what about Will?"

Even in the hot August sun, I rub the chill from my arms. I don't want to talk to Maggie about my relationship with William—despite the fact that she's been here while I've been away. Or maybe because of it. I don't want to talk to anyone who knows that I broke his heart. I'd rather pretend that didn't happen. *Real mature.* "What about him?"

"You're staying in town for awhile. Are you going to get back together with him?"

"I— It's—"

"None of my business?" she asks with a raised brow.

I let out a breath. "Yeah. Pretty much."

She looks out at the river, and I'm relieved to have those scrutinizing eyes off me. "You can't pick up where you left off, Cally. William's not the same person he was when you lived here before. He's been through a lot."

My life, on the other hand, has been a freaking walk in the park. *Right*. "I'm not trying to pick up where I left off. You don't need to worry about that."

"But you slept with him?" Her gaze is back on me now.

"What? No. Did he tell you that?"

Her shoulders drop and she shakes her head. "No, he didn't, but I can tell something happened between you two to get him all hung up on you again."

I push off the bench. Nothing's fucking changed. People in this town still believe Will is a saint and I'm just a dirty poor girl who must have tricked him somehow to make him fall for me. I wonder if Will ever figured out that's why I wouldn't have sex with him. There were some who assumed I was easy, who thought sex was the only reason a good-looking young man like him would be with a girl like me.

Maybe, once, I might have felt the way they did. Although I respected him too much to think he was using me for sex, I didn't understand why Will would want me when he could have any girl in our high school. I didn't understand why he went against his grandmother's wishes and dated me when there were dozens of prettier, smarter girls from better families. Girls his grandmother would have been happy to see him with. Girls his friends wouldn't tease him for loving.

But I'm older now and I know my worth. Funny how low I had to sink to learn it.

"I appreciate your concern," I finally say, choosing my words carefully. "But I think Will can take care of himself."

"I'm just looking out for a friend."

"And that's all he is to you? A friend? You're sure about that?"

She flinches then her face hardens. "Don't pretend you know me or what I'm about."

"Fine. But return the favor." I turn on my heel and walk away, my anger growing with each step. Because I didn't ask for this. If Will is "hung up" on me again, it's certainly not because I encouraged it. And yet, I know I'm not angry with Maggie. I'm angry with myself.

Cally
Seven Years Ago

The restaurant is a little on the dark and dingy side, but it's close to the apartment, and I wouldn't have to take the bus or use Mom's car to get here. I head straight to the bar to ask the hostess if I can see the manager.

The waitress looks me over and shakes her head but does as I ask.

There's a silver-haired man sitting at the bar, looking me over as if assessing the value of a horse. I'm tempted to ask him if he'd like to check my teeth when a short, stocky woman comes out from the back.

"Hello—" I pause. Her name tag says *Manager*. No name, just *Manager*. "Hello, I'm Cally Fisher." I stick out my hand, and the woman takes it with the enthusiasm of a person picking up a piece of chewed gum. "I was wondering if you had any positions available for servers. I have some experience, and I'm a hard worker."

"How old are you?" she asks, hand propped on her hip.

"Twenty-one," I lie. Because no one wants to hire a waitress who can't serve alcohol.

She snorts. "Yeah, me too."

"I really need a job. My family—" I cut myself off, not wanting to sound too desperate. "I could really use a break. I'll do anything. You won't be sorry."

She crosses her arms over her chest. "I need a hostess. Nights and weekends, minimum wage, no tips. Take it or leave it."

Minimum wage. That won't be enough, but it will have to be for now. Because even a little is better than nothing. "Okay."

"Come back tomorrow and fill out your paperwork. You can start this weekend." Then, as if dismissing me, she turns on her heel and walks away.

"Looks like it's your lucky day," the man says.

I force a smile. "Yeah. I guess so." I don't want to sound ungrateful, but minimum wage isn't going to get me far. "Maybe I can work my way up to server, right?"

He shakes his head and pulls a business card out of his pocket. "I'm not talking about some crummy hostess job. I'm talking about the fact that I'm sitting right here."

I unconsciously step back, away from him, away from his greedy and calculating gaze.

He shrugs and tosses his card on the bar. "You need money? I can help. A little loan. Work it off or pay me back. Whatever. No big deal."

I eye the card, afraid to touch it. "Work it off doing what?"

"Don't worry so much. This is what I do. Help people."

I don't need a flashing neon sign telling me this man is bad news. I already know it. I swallow hard and take another step away. "I appreciate your offer. But I'm okay."

He smiles. Not creepy, not in a leering way, just a genuine smile. He throws some money on the counter and shakes his head. "Your funeral, sweetheart."

What does that mean? I watch him leave the restaurant and only after the glass door floats closed behind him do I pick up his card. *Just in case,* I tell myself, tucking it into my purse.

When I get home thirty minutes later, I expect to find Mom stoned or crashed on the couch. She's been hitting the Vicodin pretty hard since things didn't work out with Rick.

But she's not sleeping. She pacing and antsy and in a *mood,* which is way worse.

"Did you know there's a fucking waiting list to stay at the only decent women's shelter in town?" Mom throws the phone across the room, and I hear a crack as it hits the wall. Her eyes are bloodshot and she's chewing on her thumbnail again.

"I got a job," I tell her, sitting on the edge of the bed. "At that restaurant down the block."

She shakes her head, eyes watering. "It's too late. They're gonna throw us out if we don't have two months' rent by the end of the weekend. Landlord did me a favor letting us move in with nothing, but now he wants his money. We're gonna be on the streets."

I tell myself it's the Vicodin talking. Or rather, the lack of Vicodin. She goes just twenty-four hours without, and the worst-case scenarios start. It's never as bad as she thinks. Though it has been getting much worse, and I'm starting to get worried.

"Let's go home, Mom. Why are we even staying here? We can move back to New Hope."

She laughs but it's not my mother's laugh. It's a frightening, nearly maniacal sound. "You think we'll be better off there?"

"Yes! We'll move back in with Dad."

"Your father is off in India, finding his inner peace or some shit. We sold the house, remember? Aside from your boyfriend and a bunch of judgmental assholes, what's waiting for us there?"

I squeeze my eyes shut. We should have never left. We should have never come here. Dad taught me that all you have to do is believe things can be better, and they will be—*the power of manifestation*, he called it. But I've been believing so hard since we moved here, wishing so hard, I'm wrung out. He said it was that simple, but he couldn't even keep food on the table. He couldn't even save his marriage. What else that he taught me was a lie?

chapter ten

Cally

I'm GOING to Asher Logan's house. The thought makes me want to pinch myself and jump up and down all at once. I was planning to stay home, but Drew found out I was declining a party at Asher Logan's house (apparently his brand-new single "Unbreak Me" is *amazeballs*). She told me she would disown me if I didn't go and tell her all about it. So, twist my arm, I'm gonna party with a rock star.

And his girlfriend, who may or may not hate me.

Fuck it all. I could use a night out. Drew and Gabby had a good day at school, Dad's cough is getting better after a five-day course of antibiotics and some breathing treatments, and I used Dad's credit card to get some minimal supplies for my massage studio. All in all, I'm feeling *okay* about where my life is going.

When I turn onto Asher's street, I'm surprised to see there aren't many cars here. I don't know what I expected. Lines of Mercedes and Cadillac Escalades? There's a blue Mustang at the front of the drive and the Charger Lizzy said was hers, but other than that, only a pickup, a couple of sedans, and a yellow Ducati across the street.

I park along the road so I won't be blocked in if I decide I need to jet.

A hard tap on my window yanks me from my thoughts and makes

me jump. Hanna pulls the door open, eyes bright, smile covering her whole face.

"You're really here!" she squeals, wrapping her arms around me before I can get out.

"I told you!" I hear Lizzy say.

"I had to see for myself!"

I push lightly against her embrace. "You're kind of squishing me, Han-Han."

She releases me and steps back to let me climb from the car.

"Dang, girl!" Hanna runs her gaze over me. "You left an average pretty girl and came back a freaking vixen!"

"Isn't she hot?" Lizzy says.

I feel myself blushing. I was pretty awkward during my early teen years, usually hiding in boxy T-shirts and behind my thick mop of hair. Brandon is the one who taught me how to dress for my curves and long legs. He even hired someone to teach me how to apply makeup with a modicum of skill. These, I suppose, are the souvenirs I get from a relationship I'd otherwise rather forget.

"Such a hottie!" Hanna agrees.

"She's a goddess."

I turn to the unexpected deep male voice and find myself facing William Bailey. Since we're going to be working in the same building, I guess I should get used to running into him, but I'm not sure I'll ever get used to the heat that fills me when he looks my way.

He takes in my tattered jeans and fitted black mesh top, making me extra grateful the boxes of clothes my friends shipped from my apartment arrived today. Even so, his careful perusal is worthy of a slinky formal gown, not some outfit thrown together to hang with old friends.

My cheeks are blazing by the time he returns those blue eyes to mine. Hot blue eyes that remind me of candlelit corners, sweet wine, and his calloused fingers on my thigh under the tablecloth.

"Hey, Cally," he says. "Good to see you again."

"Are you coming to the party, Will?" Hanna asks.

He shakes his head. "No, I just stopped by to get something from Maggie."

"You should stay," Hanna says softly. "It's going to be a good time." There's something tentative about the way she makes the offer, and I'm pretty sure I'm missing something.

"Thanks, but I have plans." His lips tilt into a half smile as he slides his gaze over me again before crossing the street. "See you around, Cally."

Just when I thought William Bailey couldn't get any sexier, he throws his leg over the Ducati and pulls on his helmet. The revving engine settles into a purr and, with a wave, he shoves off, and he's gone.

"Holy sexual tension, Batman," Hanna says.

"Yeah, after that we're going to need to cancel the party," Lizzy says. "There was so much tension between you two, it left *me* hot and bothered."

"What was that about?" Hanna asks.

I turn back to the girls to see them eyeing me expectantly. "What?" But I know the flush of my cheeks gives me away, and if they had any idea how hard my heart is pounding…

"Mmm-hmm," Lizzy says.

Then Hanna says, "You two were always so cute together. He needs someone like you, Cally."

Someone *like me*? They don't even know who I am anymore.

"He is such a good guy," Hanna adds, "and the last year has been shit for him."

"What happened last year?" I ask.

Lizzy nudges her. "Not now."

Hanna waves away my question. "Lizzy's right. That's for another time. Let's go inside and lust after Maggie's boyfriend."

"Are you going to tell me how she came to date Asher Logan?" I ask, following the girls to the front door.

"She went skinny dipping in his pool after Will and Krystal's reception," Lizzy says.

"Lizzy," Hanna hisses.

Lizzy winces. "Shit."

I blink. "Wait. Will and Krystal? Like, your older sister?" Then the rest of her sentence sinks in, and I shake my head. "Reception?" Didn't he say he wasn't married?

Lizzy looks forlorn, and Hanna's biting her lip, but neither gets to answer before the door flies open.

"Cally?" Maggie's wan smile falls from her face but she quickly remembers herself and pastes it back in place. "Good to see you."

Lizzy nudges me toward the door. "Let's move! This tequila isn't going to drink itself!"

William

"Nice of you to finally join us, Willy," Grandma says as I slide into a chair at her giant pine dining room table.

"I had to close up the gallery and run a few errands." I know it's useless trying to talk her out of the coming guilt trip, but old habits die hard.

She surprises me with a kiss on my cheek. "It's alright. You're a hard worker, and I'm proud of you."

I narrow my eyes at my grandmother. The woman doesn't pass up an opportunity to lay on a guilt trip unless she wants something.

"There's someone special joining us tonight."

So that's why I'm off the hook. There's nothing Grandma likes more than finding eligible young women for me, and I'm sure Cally's return to town will only make her redouble her efforts.

I look around the table but only see Grandma's friends.

"She's in the kitchen, making us a fresh pot of coffee. Why don't you see if she needs any help?"

"Easy on the matchmaking, okay?" I peck Grandma's leathery cheek and head to the kitchen, pretending I don't hear my grandmother's friends whispering, "At least she's not a Thompson," as I go.

About once a week, I meet Grandma and her friends for a couple of hours of Texas Hold 'Em. I'm under the impression that other people's grandmothers get together to do something respectable, like play Bridge and drink tea, but the old ladies in New Hope prefer poker for their nightly games and whiskey in their coffee. When I'm lucky, I get to enjoy the game with ladies whose skills at the table shouldn't be underestimated. When I'm unlucky, the little biddies use the opportunity to set me up with some unsuspecting great-niece/granddaughter/cousin's step-granddaughter once removed. It's only been worse since things didn't work out with Krystal.

In the kitchen, a tall, jean-clad blonde is filling the coffee carafe with water. Her eyes widen when she sees me and she puts the pot down and holds up her hands. "I'm so sorry. I had no idea you were going to be here."

I wave away Meredith's concern. "It's fine. Don't worry about it."

"I just don't want you to think I'm pushing myself on you. I heard your old girlfriend is back in town, and you probably don't want anything to do with me."

I cross my arms. "You *heard,* or she wanted to work for you and you turned her away?"

A rush of pink moves up her neck and blooms in her cheeks. "She told you?"

I shrug. "It came up."

She dries her hands on a towel and sighs. "I'm not a bitch, you know? But my business means everything to me, and I had to make a hard decision."

I'm not sure the decision was that difficult, but I can hardly be upset about it. Not when the result puts Cally so close to me. "It's going to work out after all. She's renting the apartment above the gallery, and she'll run her business out of there."

Her lips form a perfect circle of surprise. "Are you sure that's a good idea? People will think you approve of what she does."

My jaw tightens. "What do you mean by that?"

She lifts her chin. "I mean, her mom gave twenty-dollar hand jobs in her massage parlor. Maybe worse. Whether it's fair or not, people are going to assume like mother, like daughter."

I have to give Meredith credit for putting it out there like that. Most people tiptoe around the rumors. Regardless— "That's bullshit."

"Of course it is." She frowns. "Total bullshit. But people believe what they believe. It could really hurt the gallery. Just think about it."

I cross to Grandma's liquor stash beside the sink and pour myself two fingers of brandy. I shoot half of it back without tasting it. "I've thought about it. And my mind's made up."

"You're a good guy. She's lucky to have you."

I shake my head. "It's not like that," I say, then I toss back the rest of the brandy.

"I promise I had nothing to do with tonight," she says softly. "In fact, I'm a little embarrassed, but you know how Grandma and her friends go rogue in their matchmaking efforts. When I found out Cally was back, it was obvious why you started blowing me off. I don't want to be in the way."

And the Asshole of the Year award goes to *me*. I drag a hand through my hair. "I didn't mean to blow you off. I thought we were keeping things casual." Fuck. I even *sound* like an asshat.

Her cheeks bloom red again. "This is so embarrassing. I thought…I mean, when we seemed to get along so well."

Dammit. "I never meant to give you the wrong idea."

She holds up her hands. "It's totally my fault. I just hadn't wanted anything serious and then you…." She shakes her head. "See? Totally embarrassing. But no harm, no foul, right? I mean, we're on the same page now, and you can carry on with Cally without worrying about me."

"I'm sorry, Meredith."

"Don't be. Please. I owe *you* the apology." She drops her voice to a whisper. "I've been too much of a coward to tell my grandmother you're not interested, and I just want her off my back for a little bit, you know? I really hope you don't mind. I promise to tell her soon."

"So here we are." I take the carafe and finish preparing the coffee. "I don't suppose it would help if I told you that you can do better than me?"

Her cheeks flush. "I think we both know that's not true."

She's really pretty, but her red-tinged cheeks only have me comparing her to Cally, which isn't fair since all I've been able to think about for days is the way Cally responded to my touch in the back of that restaurant.

I press the brew button on the machine and pour myself a cup of coffee from the thermos on the counter.

"Grandma just wants great-grandbabies. And you know what? Things not working out between us was good for me."

"It was?"

"I realized I just need to do it."

I raise a brow. "Do what, exactly?"

"I've decided not to wait on babies," Meredith says in a rush. "So, even though I'd really like it if we could still be friends, it's probably good that you won't be around much. I don't want my store-bought sperm to get jealous."

I choke on my coffee. "I'm sorry?"

She pours her own cup of coffee and smiles. "It's the twenty-first century. I don't need a husband to start a family. My mom gets it, and when I have the heart to tell her, Grandma will too."

"Of course, but you're young." She's only a couple of years older than me, maybe twenty-seven. "Why the rush?"

Something like sadness draws down the corners of her eyes. "Sometimes you just know you're meant for something, and you go after it despite the logic."

"I can understand that."

The machine beeps, and we work together preparing a tray of mugs, coffee, cream, sugar, and whiskey. At my waist my phone buzzes a text alert.

"So what about you and Cally?" she asks. "Are you two working things out?"

"It's complicated." I pull my phone from my hip and smile when I see Cally's name on the screen. Maybe she's decided to stop avoiding me.

"I hope you can work it out," Meredith says. "She's a lucky girl."

I open the text and can only blink at the screen.

Just a week ago, we were at the restaurant and you were touching me under the table.

"Let me guess," Meredith says. "Mrs. Complicated?"

"You could say that, though I'm not sure our relationship has progressed to anything as official as *Mrs.* yet."

"You want more?"

I don't answer, but the truth must be in my eyes because she snags the phone from my hand and slides it into the pocket of her jeans. "What are you doing?"

"Helping you. If you want more from *Miss* Complicated, don't reply."

I fold my arms. "Isn't that a little childish?"

She shrugs, flashing me a grin over her shoulder as she strolls back in the dining room to join the card sharks. "Deal me in this hand?"

"Willy, what about you?" Norma calls.

"I'm in," I say and prepare myself to hand over my pride and my money to a bunch of old ladies.

chapter eleven

Cally

THIS MORNING is doing a fantastic job reminding me of the reason I stay away from tequila. No, make that *three* reasons.

1) Lack of moderation. My first shot gave me that fuzzy warmth in the pit of my stomach. The second had me feeling lighter and more carefree. By the third, I was definitely dancing, though I have no idea if anyone turned on any music. And then there were more shots. I just don't remember how many more.

2) Fuzzy memory. Pretty much everything after the third shot of tequila is fuzzy. A patchwork of unstitched memories—lots of pieces missing, no clear order.

I might have tried to get Asher Logan to sing to me.

3) Impulsiveness. I vaguely remember sending Will a text message… or two? (See reason two.) I'm scared to look and see exactly what I wrote, but I'm pretty sure I have to. Maybe I could lie and say Lizzy and Hanna got ahold of my phone?

I brace myself against the counter and take a tentative sip from my mug of coffee. Sliding my phone from my pocket, I open my text messages and click on Will's name.

Not just one sent message. Not two. *Four.* Four drunken, desperate, horny girl text messages. I lower my pounding head to the counter and whimper.

"Feeling good this morning?" I'm hung over, and Lizzy's voice is bright and perky enough to put the *justifiable* in *justifiable homicide.*

I crack open one eyelid and peer at her. "Don't talk to me."

"Don't be bitchy just because you drank too much." She pulls my phone from my fingers. "Did he ever write back?"

I lift my head. "You knew I was sending those? Jesus, Liz, you're supposed to have a girl's back when she's drunk."

She snorts. "I did have your back. God, after you told me about the restaurant, I did the only thing a real friend would do. I handed you your phone and tried to get you laid."

"I told you about the restaurant?"

Maggie and Hanna walk into the kitchen, heading for the coffee. "Sweetie, you told *everyone* about the restaurant," Maggie says.

My cheeks fill with heat. I wouldn't have thought embarrassment was possible with my head pounding this hard. "That is…mortifying."

"It wasn't too bad," Hanna says softly. "I mean, you didn't go into graphic detail about your orgasm or anything."

My face is on fire. "You're not helping, Hanna."

"You did tell us all about your panties, though," Lizzy says. "Now I want some like that. So fucking hot."

Asher walks into the kitchen and wraps his arms around Maggie, pulling her back to his front before whispering something in her ear.

I look at Lizzy and Hanna. "Are they always like that?"

Hanna leans on the breakfast bar and props her chin on her hands, sighing. "They're even worse when they think no one is looking. We're all jealous. Liz and I told him he has to find us our own rock stars, but so far, nothing."

Lizzy frowns at my phone. "I can't believe he never wrote back. Most guys would have been knocking down the door to take you up on these offers. And this last one?" She whistles low and looks at me with a raised brow. "You are creative, I'll give you that." She shows the phone to Hanna, who takes it and cocks her head while reading.

"Wow. That's… You can actually…? And he never showed up? I wonder if he's in the hospital somewhere."

I snatch my phone back, then wince as pain ricochets through my head at the sudden movement.

"More than likely, he knew she was drunk," Maggie says softly, eyeing me. "Will's a good guy. He doesn't take advantage."

I rub my temples. Last night it became clear to me that Will has a history with both Maggie and her oldest sister, Krystal. Of course, no one wanted to talk about it, but I filed away the information. This is New Hope, after all. If I put my mind to it, I won't have to go far to find someone who knows the whole story and wants to gab.

"Maggie's right," Hanna's saying. "Call him today, sober, and I'm sure he'll be all yours."

"I don't want him to be mine."

Lizzy snorts. "*Bullshit*. The tequila-addled brain doesn't lie."

"It's a bad idea. I'm leaving in a few months—*max*."

Maggie is frowning at me, worry lines creasing her forehead.

Hanna puts her hand on my arm. "You were always the one telling us to keep an open mind and an open heart. You were the one convinced that if we just believed, good things would come into our lives. What happened to that girl?"

She sold out for a paycheck. "It's complicated. Being with Will would only hurt him in the long run."

"Then leave him alone." Maggie steps toward me. Asher touches her arm, but Maggie shakes her head and he backs off. "All Will wants in this world is to get married and make a family of his own. He might be attracted to Cally, but if she knows she won't give him that, she should stay away."

Hanna and Lizzy are looking at their hands, and Asher's eyes have gone sad. There's definitely more to this story than I've been told.

"I agree." My phone buzzes, and I take it back from Hanna to see a text from Drew.

Gabby had nightmares all night and I had to climb in bed with her, and dad made some sort of tofu-nugget sausage for breakfast that smells like roadkill. If you come home without an Asher Logan autograph on your boob, you are no longer my sister.

"I need to go."

"Don't rush away because of some silly texts," Lizzy says. "Asher's going to make us breakfast."

It isn't the texts that have me running. It's the reminder that some sexy texts sent to an old boyfriend are the least of my worries.

"But before I go…." I grab a Sharpie from the basket on the counter. "Maggie, is it all right if I have your boyfriend sign my chest?"

William

I don't want to wake up. I want to snuggle in closer to Cally and breathe in her scent while I sleep the day away. Then when I do wake up, I want to do it slowly, exploring her body with my hands and mouth before I bother opening my eyes.

Except she doesn't smell right.

I wrap my arm tighter around her waist and pull her closer. She must be using a different shampoo. She still smells good but more like perfume and less like…Cally.

But fuck sleeping, I'm hard just thinking about having her this close to me. I've been dreaming about her since she came back to town. About holding her. Touching her. Sliding inside her.

I fan my fingers under the waistband of her jeans, and she moans sweetly…

Only it's not Cally's moan.

My eyes fly open and I jerk upright in bed. Not my bed. My childhood bedroom at my grandmother's house. And it's not Cally next to me, it's… *Fuck.*

Meredith rolls over and smiles, peering at me from under half-closed lids. Then her eyes snap open and her face is masked with horror as her hands drop to investigate her clothing.

We're both fully dressed in the clothes we were wearing last night, and she appears to be as relieved by that as I am.

She tentatively lifts her hand to her head then grabs a pillow to press over her face.

"When did we start spiking our coffee like the old ladies?" I ask, rubbing my shoulder.

"When they were half drunk and kicking our asses," she mutters behind the pillow. "We decided it was giving them an edge."

"Rookie mistake," I mutter.

She lifts the pillow and peeks at me from under the corner. "We didn't? I mean…you don't think we…? Will Cally be upset?"

I shake my head. "We didn't do anything but sleep."

"I don't know if that's true," she mutters, sitting up.

"What do you mean by that?"

"I definitely woke up to someone groping me."

I drag my hand over my face. "I thought you were Cally."

The more I wake up, the more I remember about last night. It was Grandma's idea that we stay over, and we came to my room, laughing about how she was probably planning for us to conceive her great-grand-child.

We had fun. Meredith and me. I'm remembering how much I like her. She's funny and carefree and smart. Last night she stood up for herself when the old ladies were giving her a hard time about her series of love life foibles.

She didn't push herself on me. She even asked questions about Cally. About our history.

Cally.

She texted me last night, and Meredith didn't think I should reply. "You still have my phone?"

She pulls it from her pocket and tosses it toward me on the bed.

I pull up my text messages and see that I missed three more messages after the first. I blink at my screen.

"Is she mad you didn't text back?"

My stomach pitches and twists in a mix of worry, nerves, and boyish giddiness. "She must have been drinking," I say, more to myself than Meredith.

"Is she okay?"

"I think I'll go find out." I run a hand through my hair and attempt to smooth my clothes. "Can I get you anything? Coffee? Breakfast?"

"I'm good. Go get your girl."

"Thanks for being so cool about everything, Meredith."

She presses the pillow against her stomach and gives me a sad smile. "It's nothing."

I decide to drive over instead of call, but when I pull up to Arlen

Fisher's house, I'm suddenly questioning my plan. What did I think I was going to do? Point at the last text and say, *This one, pretty please?*

Drew and Gabby are sitting in camping chairs out on the front deck, Drew's eyes on her phone and Gabby looking out toward the river.

I climb off my bike and head toward the house, but I haven't even hit the deck when I can hear Cally's voice—loud, angry.

"You had two thousand dollars in the savings account yesterday. Where did it go?"

I can't hear her father's words, just the deep murmur of him speaking.

"You're kidding me! A *guru*? You don't *need* a guru. The girls *need* textbooks. They *need* lunch. Stop giving your money away to some fraud promising things he can *never* deliver." *Pause.* "Kids are expensive. And this house is falling apart." *Pause.* "So, what? You're just going to meditate your way to a better net worth? You *have* to get a job and you have to stop spending money on this bullshit."

"Dad dropped two grand on one-on-one counseling with his guru," Drew explains. "He wants to be enlightened or something stupid like that. And now Cally's mad because we can't afford the uniform for me to be on the cheerleading practice squad. Never mind that I don't want to be a stupid cheerleader. I only did it at home because my friends did. I don't have friends here."

More murmuring from inside. Then Cally, her voice less angry: "Well, you should have known better. Mom was never good with money."

"Translation," Drew drones, "Mom was a druggy."

I swallow, wondering what Cally would think if she knew I was here, hearing this.

"How many fucking autographed spiritual books do you have? Sell a few of those and beef up your checking account." *Pause.* "You're writing a book? Show me a big-ass contract from a real fucking publisher and I'll believe it. Call the college and get a *real job.*"

More murmuring.

"We should have stayed in Vegas," Drew sing-songs.

Cally: "If *politics* are the worst you have to face to put food on the table, you're one lucky bastard. Get over it." Then we hear the clack of footsteps, and she's pushing out onto the deck, the door slamming behind her.

She doesn't even see me. She's studying her shoes, her chest heaving. I can't tell if she's crying or just angry. I open my mouth to announce my presence, but Drew beats me to it.

"You have company."

Cally's head snaps up and her eyes widen as she spots me. "William."

"Cally."

"Did you hear all…. *Shit.*"

"Can we talk?" I ask.

She looks to Drew, then Gabby.

"We're *fine,*" Drew says, shooing us away.

Gabby nods, giving me a half smile and a little wave of her fingers.

Cally draws her lower lip between her teeth, her brow wrinkling as she studies the girls.

Finally tearing her eyes from her phone, Drew says, "Go give your boyfriend a blow job and maybe he'll buy us a nice dinner."

Cally draws in a sharp breath, but before she can speak, Gabby says, "Behave!" It's one word, but it's clear and strong, and it wipes the rage off Cally's face. Drew's jaw drops.

Cally presses a kiss to Gabby's hair, then heads down the steps toward me.

"Wanna get out of here?" I nod to my bike, wanting to give her the break the strain around her eyes says she desperately needs. "We could go for a ride."

She shakes her head and tucks her hands into the pockets of her jean shorts. "Can we just walk?" She points to the gravel lane that meets up with the paved jogging path along the river.

"Sure."

It's a beautiful day, unseasonably cool for late August in Indiana and a nice break from last week's heat. Sunlight reflects off the water and makes her dark hair shine.

"I guess you're here about the texts I sent? I can only apologize. I had a little too much tequila."

I am, but that seems trivial in light of the argument I just overhead between her and her father.

"Do you need money? I can loan you—"

"Please don't. I already owe you for the groceries and the space for my massage studio." She looks out at the river. "We'll figure it out. We always do."

I let it drop—for now—and we walk in silence.

"You could do something for me," she finally says.

Anything. "What's that?" We wander onto a little dock and pause to look out at the water.

"See if there are any adjunct positions open at the college? Dad could use the work. Philosophy, religion. Anything like that. You know he's qualified."

"I'll make some calls, but don't get your hopes up. The fall semester starts on Monday, so they probably have all the classes covered."

She lets out a long, slow breath, her shoulders falling. "Right."

"I'll put in some calls. There are always temporary grant-funded positions he could consider for the short term. Research, maybe?"

"I appreciate it. I really do." She turns and wraps her arms around me and buries her face in my chest. "I'm lucky to have you."

I hug her back, pulling her close. God, I love the way she feels in my arms. Her hair is silky soft against my nose and I inhale deeply.

As if suddenly remembering herself, she stiffens and pulls away. "Sorry about that."

"Hmm…about those text messages…."

She grins and hits my stomach with the back of her hand. Her cheeks blaze red with her blush. "And here I thought you were going to let me off the hook."

"Maybe for the first three, but that last one isn't something a guy forgets."

She drops her gaze to the wooden planks of the dock. "I guess this is the part where I tell you that nothing can happen between us."

"I don't think we've been reading from the same script," I mutter.

"You haven't asked me why I didn't come to prom. You haven't asked why I ended things."

A crane spreads its wings and glides low over the water. "I figured you would have already told me if you wanted me to know." But my stomach folds over brutally at the reminder. Even seven years later, the memory still hurts.

"Can you promise not to ask me?" Her voice is so soft, and she's studying me.

"If I asked, would I want to know the answer?"

She shakes her head and her eyes fill.

"You know my mind is going to answer the question anyway. I've had seven years to imagine what happened. The answers I've imagined have run the gamut. I've been pissed and worried and then pissed all over again. If you think *not knowing* is better, you're wrong." Stepping forward, I cup her face in my hands. Her eyes are moist but determined, and her cheeks are dry. I've thought about Maggie's words a lot in the last few days. "I think you'd be amazed what I've been able to forgive of people, Cally. And none of them have been you. If you slept with someone while we were still together…," I trail off as she closes her eyes.

"Don't," she whispers.

The light from the midday sun warms our shoulders, and the painful silence of regret wraps us in its barbed embrace.

Nothing can be done about the past, and I don't need to know what happened to forgive her.

"I promise," I say quietly.

chapter twelve

Cally
Seven Years Ago

A DRIVER picks me up after dark. I was told to wear something classy. *"A black dress will do. Don't be afraid to show a little ass."*

I tell myself I don't know what's going to happen. I tell myself not to jump to the worst possible conclusion.

I climb into the limo in a black skirt and matching button-up blouse, and I'm greeted by the man from the restaurant. Anthony.

"Hey, sweet thing." He runs his eyes over my body so slowly, my stomach churns.

When I broke down and called him for the money, I was only trying to keep my sisters off the streets and put some food in the fridge. He met me at the restaurant and gave me cash. For two weeks, everything was okay.

Then, yesterday, one of his guys showed up outside my apartment, looking for me to pay my debt with interest. I didn't have it. I still don't.

I swallow back my fear. "I'm sorry I don't have your money yet. I thought I could pick up extra shifts but then the girls both got sick and—"

He cuts me off with the wave of his hand.

"I've given you everything I can." Even as I say the words, I know they're ridiculous. There is no A-for-effort when it comes to owing money to men like this.

"I appreciate that you're trying to save your family from living on the streets, sweetheart. But your minimum-wage job isn't gonna cut it." He laughs, as if this is some big joke. "The longer you try to get by on pennies, the further behind you fall."

"We can go to a shelter," I whisper. "I'll get Mom to clean up first so they won't call CPS. Or...maybe I should just let them put my sisters in foster care." I don't mean the last. I won't let that happen. I can't.

He leans back in his seat, studying me. "That doesn't take care of the matter of money you already owe me."

I bite my lip and taste blood. "What do you want from me?"

His eyes leave my face and drop to my breasts, and I don't even care. He's been looking at me like that since the beginning. I hate him and his eyes on me make my stomach churn, but I'd let him look at me all day long if it would just make this all go away. "You work for me now. I have a client waiting."

"Please," I whisper. "I'm a virgin. I can't sell my body."

He claps his hands together. "Now, that's what I thought. Best news I've heard all day."

I can't allow my brain to process what that might mean.

Anthony narrows his eyes at me. "You don't have to have sex tonight, sweetheart. We'll give him a taste, but no intercourse, you hear me?" He tucks my hair behind my ear, and a shudder rocks through me. "We're going to save that for now. It's too valuable."

They drop me at one of those fancy high rises where the man at the front gets permission from the tenant before letting you up. The high security does nothing for my peace of mind, and as I am led to the elevator, I feel like everyone is staring at me, like everyone knows exactly why I'm here. My stomach knots.

When the elevator doors slide open, a servant greets me and ushers me into the condo. It's beautiful with sleek contemporary furnishings and a marble floor. And the moment I step inside, I want to turn around and leave.

He takes me to a room at the back of the condo where the ceilings are vaulted and the walls are covered with bookshelves. The man sits behind a polished desk and motions for his servant to leave. He's attractive, probably in his mid-thirties with dark hair and striking hazel eyes, and he's obviously wealthy. The kind of man my mother throws herself at. What could he want with me?

"Close the door," he says softly.

I force myself to do as he asks. This isn't real. This can't be happening.

Moving from behind his desk, he settles into a winged back chair. "Come here." He crooks a finger at me.

My feet move slowly. One step. Two.

"Take off your shirt."

My hands shake as I obey, sliding the black plastic buttons free from their holes, telling myself it doesn't count if he doesn't touch me. This isn't real. No worse than a peeping tom looking in my window. I let the shirt slide from my shoulders and fall to the floor.

"Your bra."

Goosebumps break out on my arms, making my hair stand on end. I close my eyes as I reach behind my back. I think of my sisters.

"Now look at me," he says.

I force my eyes open and look at him. As I watch him run his greedy eyes over me, revulsion rises like bile in my throat. But not even my revulsion is as strong as my determination.

Shifting his hips forward in his chair, he pops the button on his slacks and pulls out his dick.

I back up a step. "He said no sex," I mumble stupidly.

My phone rings in my purse. William's ringtone.

"Not tonight," he says. "But soon. I can tell I'm going to like you. So you. What are you? Sixteen?"

"Yes."

"That's just perfect. You're going to do great."

The bright happiness of the ringtone is so sharp against the misery of this moment. My life with William feels so far away now. I was too much of a "good girl" to give myself to Will. And I'm supposed to suck a strange man's dick for money that's already gone. I ignore the call and drop my purse to the floor.

"It's okay, sweetheart." He stands up and crosses to me, his dick protruding between us.

I hate him for making me stoop to this. I hate myself for making the decisions that brought me here. I've spent so many years trying not to be my mom, and I've never felt so low as I do right now. Never so pathetic.

"You do a nice job and I'll bring you back." He tucks my hair behind my ear and smoothes it down. "You're beautiful, and I'll take care of you."

I'm trembling as I drop to my knees in front of him. My stomach heaves.

"That a'girl."

My phone rings again. William. As if he knows and wants to save me from this.

My chest shakes and my cheeks are damp with tears. I said I'd never stoop to my mom's level. I said I would never allow myself to be sold. I've spent years being proud about that. So fucking self-righteous.

I snatch my purse off the ground and grab my shirt and bra, running from the room. I thought I was better than Mom, but as I run to the elevator, I feel lower than ever because she did what she had to do. And I *can't*.

William
Present Day

"I just scheduled a massage for tonight," Max says, taking a sip of his beer. "I'm really looking forward to it."

I retrieve my cell from my pocket and pass it to him. "Would you like to call and cancel it or do you want me to do it for you?"

Cally's been working out of the apartment above my gallery for over three weeks now. She's been a consummate professional where I'm concerned, greeting me when we pass in the apartment kitchen, asking all the appropriate small talk questions while still managing to avoid having any meaningful contact with me.

Max eyes my phone, his lips twitching. "It's just a massage. Has she given you one?"

"Not since she was sixteen. Cancel it."

"Man, you've got it bad."

"Fuck yeah, I do." The smell of stale beer and onion rings is enough to turn my stomach off my lunch. Even so, I prefer this scene to the bars closer to the university, where I'm all too likely to run into my students.

"So, do something about it."

I set my jaw. "Hell, why didn't I think of that?"

"You're not on your A-game, man. She has you frazzled. You're not even seeing the obvious here."

I sit back in the booth and stare at my friend. Because he's right. Cally's been avoiding me and I've been waiting on her, rather than making my own move. "You know, I *could* use a massage."

"That's my boy," Max says. "You can take my spot. Tonight. Six p.m."

Cally

I have a fifteen-minute break before my next client arrives, and I collapse onto the couch in the apartment's living-room-turned-waiting-room. We've started leaving the door between the gallery's loft reception area and the apartment open to encourage gallery visitors to check out my specials and encourage my clients to exit through the gallery.

Through the door, I can see Will sitting on the couch in the reception area, peering into his laptop. He does that a lot, I've noticed, choosing to work in the common space instead of his office, but he leaves me alone.

For three weeks, I've been taking clients in my little studio and avoiding him as best I can. But between giving massages and the horrible couch I'm crashing on at Dad's, I'm too exhausted to worry about limiting our exposure to each other tonight. The man might be a magic panty disintegrator, but the way I feel right now, he could make my panties dance the merengue against my girly bits and I still wouldn't be interested.

"Busy day," he says. He closes his laptop and heads toward me. He taught today and he's still wearing the button-up Oxford, the top unbuttoned, his sleeves rolled to his elbows.

"Lizzy and Hanna had their mom tell all the women at the country club about me and my introductory prices. And I'm doing this refer-three-get-one-free deal." I shrug. "It's working. People are finding me."

He rocks back on his heels. "I'm just impressed that you've had re-peat business already. How many massages do people need in less than a month?"

I roll my head to the side so I can look at him while we talk. I'm not about to waste the energy to lift it. "I'm good at what I do."

He tucks his fingers into the pockets of his jeans, his shoulders look-ing impossibly wide. "I remember."

My cheeks flame to life. My mother had taught me massage when I was young, and I liked to practice on Will when we were dating. Of course, what started as my hands on his body usually ended as both of our hands and mouths *everywhere*. "Please don't use my techniques at sixteen to judge my talents now," I say. "I swear, I've grown remarkably more skilled over the last seven years."

He grins and runs those hot eyes all the way from the roots of my hair to the tips of my tennis shoes. "So have I."

Panties disintegrated.

I push off the couch, mentally preparing myself to find the energy for my last client of the day. "I'm going to have to ask you to leave," I say as sweetly as possible. "I have a client in a few minutes."

Will unbuttons his dress shirt and slings it over the side of the couch. Before I can ask what he's doing, he grabs the hem of his undershirt and tugs it over his head, leaving me staring at his gorgeous, solid chest.

What was I saying? "I have a client," I repeat, more for myself than for him.

"I know." He shuts the door between the apartment and the gallery. He turns back to me before unsnapping the button on his jeans and ex-posing another half inch of that soft, golden trail that travels down his belly. "You want me to take it all off, or should I leave on my boxers?"

William. Naked. Sexy stomach. My hands on William's stomach. My mouth. My tongue. I can't even…. "What?"

He pushes his jeans from his hips and steps out of them. "I'm your six o'clock."

"You're my—" He's wearing dark blue boxer briefs that hug his mus-cular thighs, and my panties might as well be dancing for as much as my girly bits are standing at attention.

"Cally, you keep looking at me like that and I'm going to find a new use for that massage table."

My eyes snap up to his. He's grinning that boyish grin, and I am swamped with the desire to shock him. To slide my hands down the flat of his stomach and lower until that smile falls away.

I roll my shoulders back. I am a professional. Pride myself on it and demand my clients treat me as such. That's not going to change tonight. I clear my throat. "I'm going to step out for a minute. You may undress to your comfort level and lie on the table under the sheets." Then I pretty much run from the apartment. *Right. A professional.*

Maggie is washing coffee mugs in the kitchenette, and she bites her lip when she sees me.

"You knew about this?" I hiss, crossing to her and scooping up my appointment book. "I thought my appointment was with…."

"Will's buddy Max?" she asks with a raised brow. "I don't think Will was going to let that happen. Guy code or something."

Dammit. "I've massaged many beautiful men. William's no different."

"Mmm-hmm."

"I've massaged *William* before," I say stubbornly.

She tries to stop her grin. "How'd that turn out for you?"

I spin on my heel and stomp back into the apartment and to my massage room, where I knock on the door twice before cracking it. "Are you ready?"

He's lying between the sheets face down. I usually start face up, but this will be easier. "I don't know. I thought I was getting a massage, but you look like you're ready to beat me."

"Sorry. You're not that lucky," I mutter. The sound of his chuckle brings a reluctant smile to my lips.

I prepare in my typical way, lowering the lights, adjusting the volume on the music, rubbing oil on my hands. When my hands touch his back, I expect instinct to take over. I have no problem separating my touch as a professional massage therapist from my sensual touch. There are people who struggle with that—that's why some don't enjoy massage and others think it implies something sexual. They believe that every touch between adults is sexual. Add in the naked or nearly naked factor and they totally squick out.

For me, it doesn't matter if my client is male or female, attractive or unattractive. The minute I begin a massage, my touch is therapeutic and all the other stuff falls away while I think about muscles and connective tissue and healing.

I know this isn't going to be the case with William the second I touch my hands to his lats. First of all, he's a moaner. Again, not something that normally affects me in the slightest. But with every touch, I am hyper aware of who I'm touching. This isn't just a massage. It's part of this long, drawn-out game of mental foreplay he's brought me into.

His body is amazing. I've seen a lot of bodies, and I appreciate them all as beautiful in their own right, but if I had to pick out a male body that was most beautiful to *me*, it would be William's. He works it hard. Not many adult men can say they're in better shape than they were in their high school football days, but Will definitely is.

"You're tight in your lower back." I apply pressure to the point and close my eyes against the sound of his moan. I wonder if he moans during sex? Did he moan when we made out as teens? How could I forget something like that? "You should come to my yoga class at the gym. It'll get this loosened up for you."

"Is that where you go when you leave here on Thursday nights in those tight little black pants and tank tops?"

"Yeah." I move up his back to the muscles over his shoulder blade. "This job is pretty hard on my body. I need yoga to keep my muscles from cramping up."

"And yoga involves a lot of watching you bend yourself in pretzels and stick your ass in the air?"

"Watching the *instructor* would probably be more appropriate."

"I can promise you, my eyes would be on you. Appropriate or not. And I don't think I should be in public while I witness that," he says, and I press a little too hard into the ridge under his shoulder blade. "Ouch!"

"Behave," I mutter. I soothe the area with gentle strokes and resume my massage.

chapter thirteen

Cally

I GROAN at the sound of my alarm and roll over to turn off my phone. Waking up is equal parts painful and welcome. The first night on the couch wasn't so bad. But after a few weeks on this Salvation-Army-find, I'm greeted every morning with an aching back and a sore neck, and now I hate it so much that sleep deprivation is less torturous than lying on the damn thing.

Dad has been helping herd the girls out the door in the mornings, but I've realized I enjoy spending a little time with them until they take off for the day. I'm at my massage studio until eight some nights, picking up the clients who like to come in after work, and sometimes I only get to see the girls for an hour or so before I make them go to bed.

My sleep was more restless than usual last night. I dreamed about William, him moaning in my ear, my oil-slicked hands running over his hard muscles. I made it through the whole massage without giving in to any of my...*baser urges*, and I got out of there as soon as I could. But after last night's dreams, I'm pretty sure I need to head into the gallery early and make good use of the fancy showerhead in the apartment's bathroom. Of course, sometimes Will showers there, and if I ran into him in the shower—

I push myself up and shake my head, trying to make my unwelcome fantasies scatter.

I'm hardly off the couch before Gabby is opening the door to the bedroom she shares with her sister. She flashes me that sweet smile before heading toward the bathroom. She's been talking more. Just a little here and there, but her teacher told me she'll answer questions sometimes in class, and the general sense of despair seems to be lifting off her shoulders.

The squeak of the old pipes and spray of the shower carry through the door. Satisfied that things are moving in the right direction, I decide to start a pot of coffee before waking Drew. My father has given up all "mind-altering substances," which apparently includes caffeine, so I had to buy my own coffee, but luckily I found his old pot in the attic and I don't have to settle for instant anymore.

After filling the pot and pouring the water into the reservoir, I add grounds to the filter and hit the switch to start it brewing before heading in to wake up Drew. There's no need to rush when the house only has one shower.

"Drew," I call, knocking softly on her bedroom door. "It's time to get up."

"No," she calls back. "Go away."

I crack the door and peek in to see her with the covers drawn up over her head. "You have thirty minutes to take a shower, dry your hair, and get dressed. If you don't want me sending you to school in your pajamas, get out of bed."

"I'm not going," she says, her voice muffled from behind the blankets. "You didn't finish high school. I don't see why I have to."

"Because I don't want you to have to do everything the hard way like I have." I sigh. To say that Drew "isn't a morning person" is a dramatic understatement. "Get up and I'll let you borrow my clothes."

She rips the covers down and glares at me, as if I just hurled insults as her instead of promising something she's been begging for.

"Come on, Drew. It'll—"

I don't get to say any more because my words are cut off by the sounds of Gabby's shrieks, and Drew and I both run into the bathroom to see what's happening.

"Oh, my God!" Drew screeches when I open the door. "That's so gross! I fucking *hate* this place."

I let her stomp away and try to hold back my own shudders of disgust. Gabby is standing on the edge of the tub, clinging to the shower curtain, eyes wide and focused on the floor.

I hear my dad's heavier steps behind me but I'm still too horrified to move.

"What's going on?" he asks, sleep slowing his words.

I swallow hard. I have to fight every instinct to climb on top of something—anything—and get my feet off the floor. "Dad," I say, impressed with how calm I'm able to keep my voice. "You have a rat."

William

"So," Meredith says. "What happened with Cally? Did you *uncomplicate* things?"

We're jogging along the river together this morning. Before Cally moved back to town, Meredith and I went running a few times a week. In retrospect, I can see why she may have thought our relationship would evolve into something more, so I've been finding excuses to cancel. When she texted me last night to see if I wanted to join her, I agreed. I'm a lot more comfortable about our friendship since we cleared the air during poker night with the grandmas.

"Things are still complicated," I answer. "Epically so. I had to endure a thirty-minute lecture from Grandma when she found out Cally was renting the space above the gallery for her massage studio."

"Ouch. You should have seen that coming, I guess."

She's right. I love my grandmother and like to tell myself she's only looking out for me, but sometimes she's so damn judgmental I can't understand how she's the same sweet woman who made me fresh chocolate chip cookies every Sunday afternoon while I was growing up.

"What's Grandma going to think when she finds out you and Cally are dating?"

I point to the turn and we follow it up the street to double back toward my house. I don't know what I expected to happen during the massage last night. Did I think she'd pick up where we left off seven years ago, where "massage" was code for heavy make-out session? The only thing that changed after an hour of her hands on my body was that I wanted her even more than before and she seemed more anxious than ever to get away from me. "I'll worry about that when she's finally willing to spend more than five minutes in the same room with me."

She slows to a walk, so I do too.

"I'm sorry," she says. "Do you mind?"

"Not at all. Are you okay?"

She nods and fans her hand in front of her face. "Yeah, I'm fine. Just a little under the weather."

"We don't have to run. Let's just walk."

She flashes me a grateful smile. "Thank you. I guess it's a good thing it's hot today since I have a cold shower waiting for me at home."

"Why's that?"

"Water heater broke. The guy's coming out to fix it tonight, but until then I'm roughing it."

I frown. "Why don't you just take a shower at my house?"

Her face brightens. "Hot water? Seriously? That would be awesome."

"It's no problem at all. I have plenty to go around."

We walk in silence for a bit, and my mind instantly wanders back to Cally, to her hands on me during my massage, to the way she's been avoiding me, to her eyes on my body when she thinks I'm not paying attention.

"Can I ask you a question?" Meredith asks.

"Of course."

"How long are you going to wait around for her?"

It's one of those questions I shouldn't honor with an answer, not with my complicated relationship with Meredith. But maybe she deserves the truth. "I'll wait until I have every reason to believe there's no chance for us."

Cally

I've only seen William's house the once, but it's bigger than I realized that first day in town, barely hinting at the *Mc* in McMansion. I knew he had a sizable trust fund, but judging by his house alone, his parents left him even more than I thought.

I press the doorbell before I can chicken out. I feel like I'm taking and taking from William and I hate asking for more.

I wait for a moment, listening for movement. I'm about to walk away when the door swings open.

"Holy shit." The words slip out of my mouth before I can stop them and my mouth goes dry at the sight of the man before me.

"Cally? What are you doing here?"

Fresh-from-the-shower William Bailey in nothing but a pair of gym shorts and all the muscles a girl's hands could ask for. His blond curls look darker wet, and he still has beads of water on his bare shoulders. Lord have mercy.

He blinks at me, and I realize I haven't said anything. "Hey," I say softly, "I need a favor."

"Come in." He pulls the door open wider.

I follow him into the house and try not to stare at the rivulet of water running down between his shoulder blades. "You caught me just out of the shower. Make yourself at home. I'm going to run upstairs and get dressed."

Please don't. "No problem."

"There's coffee in the kitchen. Want me to grab you a cup before I run up?"

"No need." I shove my hands into the pockets of my work scrubs. Too damn tempted to touch. "I'll just follow my nose."

The corner of his mouth pulls up in a lopsided grin. As his eyes scan the length of me, something flutters wildly in my stomach. "I'm glad you came by, Cally."

Then he's jogging up the stairs, and I'm alone in his expensive house, feeling like I'm sixteen years old again. The memories of waiting for him in his grandmother's living room are not my favorite. She would eye me disapprovingly and ask passive-aggressive questions about my parents. She knew them both and approved of neither. Such was my adolescence.

I follow the smell of coffee and have to bite my lip against the instinct to whistle when I step into his kitchen. Dark wood contrasts sharply with the shiny stainless steel appliances and cool stone counters. Sunlight pours from a bay window on the far wall and splashes against the polished wooden table in the breakfast nook.

I find the coffee pot tucked in a little alcove next to the refrigerator and a mug in the cabinet above. I fill it with shaking hands. There's no way I can drink this. Not with the riot of nerves making a mess of my gut.

Why am I so nervous? Because I'm going to ask him a favor, or because I'm alone with William in his house?

I'm not the girl I was when Will and I were together. Not much makes me nervous anymore. But *he* does. Being so close to something I want so much and can't have does.

Settling into a chair at the breakfast nook, I take in his gorgeous backyard. Lush, green grass, flag stone patio, all bathed in delicious early-autumn sunlight that reminds me of my childhood and tempts me to indulge in *what-ifs* and *might-have-beens*. What if I had never taken money from Anthony? What if Mom had never made us move? What if I had taken that plane home for his senior prom?

It's hard to remember that I was once the one who believed so strongly in destiny. In us. I believed the Universe would find a way to bring us back together.

I squeeze my eyes shut and wrap my hands around my mug, willing the warmth to soothe my uncharacteristic nerves.

"You didn't have to sit in the dark." William's voice startles me, and the room fills with light.

"Your home is beautiful. I imagined you in a house like this."

"You imagined me, huh?" He pours himself a cup of coffee and settles into the seat across from me. "What else did you imagine?"

His hair is a mess of wet curls and his black tee stretches across his shoulders and over his sculpted pecs. He didn't have those muscles when we were teenagers. Not that he didn't have a nice body, but the good-looking boy has developed into a jaw-dropping man. And I want him.

It's nice to want things. Something I'm frequently telling Drew.

"I imagined you married with a couple of kids."

The pain that sweeps over his features at my remark reminds me to find out more about what happened with him and Krystal. Had Lizzy said something about a wedding reception? Was he divorced? And how did Maggie figure in to all of that? So many questions I have no business asking when I'm not willing to answer similar ones about myself.

"No wife or kids yet. But don't bring it up around my grandmother. She's doing her best to remedy the situation."

That makes me smile. Maybe his grandmother never was much of a fan of mine, but I always respected her for the way she raised and loved her grandson. She would have done anything for him. We all deserve someone like that. "How's the old lady doing?"

"She's great. She's gonna outlive all of us."

I grin. "That's good to hear." Then, because I want to get it over with, I blurt, "I need a big favor."

"Sure. What is it?"

"I want your permission to move the girls into the apartment for a couple of days. There was a—" I take a breath and shudder, "—a *rat* in the bathroom at Dad's house this morning. I can't make them sleep there until we get an exterminator out."

He frowns. "How's that going to work? There are three of you, and the only bedroom has your massage studio set up in it."

"It'll have to work. We'll make it work somehow. Seriously, they flipped out. I just can't make them stay there until it's taken care of. I'll pay you more rent for use of the whole apartment, but…." God, I hate this. The IOUs I have out with Will are really adding up, and I hate owing people. "It might be awhile. I can't afford a hotel."

"Of course, Cally, but I think you're missing the obvious solution here."

I tense. "What's that?"

He waves his hand, gesturing to the space around us. "This house. I have more than enough room to take you all in for a few days. Longer if you need. Move in here with the girls and have the exterminator come out, but you can also use the time to get the carpets changed and do the painting you wanted to get done."

I'm speechless. I don't deserve anything from this man, and yet he keeps giving. "We couldn't impose on you like that."

"It's no imposition."

I tear my eyes away from his and look out into the yard, trying to remember my childhood here in New Hope, our rundown little house in town, never enough money and too many girls under one roof—just Mom, Dad, my two little sisters and me, wishing for a better life. They were good days. We just didn't have the perspective to understand it then. "I'm only agreeing because I think it's best for my sisters. If it was just me—"

"I know, I know. If it was just you, you'd stay far away from me and my hot body."

A giggle slips from my lips. "True story."

"I'm happy to help, and not just with this. Let me help you out at your dad's. I was really hands-on when I built mine, and I'm not without skills."

I stomach flips. "So you keep reminding me."

Tension, heat, and awareness pulse between us as our gazes tangle.

"Do you have a hairdryer?"

I jump at the sound of the unfamiliar female voice and turn to see Meredith standing in the kitchen in a terry cloth robe, her wet hair falling around her shoulders as she towels it dry.

"Sorry." She wrinkles her nose and draws her shoulders around her ears. "I hope I'm not interrupting."

Will pushes away from the table and stands. "Cally, you've met Meredith. She owns Venus Salon."

I force a shaky smile. What did Will tell me about their relationship? They're "friends"? Friends who shower together? I nod at her. "Meredith."

"Good to see you, Cally." Her smile lights up her whole face, and if I hadn't been there, I'd never believe this is the same woman who told me she'd rather have her company wither and die than let me work for her.

Will shoves his hands into his pockets but he looks perfectly at ease with both of us standing in his kitchen at the same time. Perfectly at ease about the fact that she's way too close to him for my peace of mind.

"There's a hair dryer under the sink in the guest bathroom."

"Great! Thanks!"

I wait until she leaves before speaking. Even then, I'm sure to choose my words carefully. I don't want to sound jealous or spiteful. I might feel both, but I have no right to. "Maybe the girls and I should just stay in the apartment after all."

"What? Why?"

"You're kidding me, right? You really think your girlfriend is going to want your ex and her little sisters living with you? And Jesus, how long have you been seeing her anyway? Does she know only a month ago you were feeling me up in public?" The words spill out of me before I can stop them. So much for choosing them carefully.

Will's lips curl into a grin and he slowly closes the distance between us until I have to lift my chin to meet his eyes. "You're jealous?"

I shift and my breasts brush his shirt. "Of course not." *Liar, liar, pants on fire.*

"Meredith is a friend. We went running together this morning and I let her use my shower because her hot water heater broke."

"How convenient." I lift my chin. God, I can feel his heat. "She wants you. And I bet money she didn't need help finding the hair dryer. She just wanted me to know she was here. Naked. She *wanted* me to be jealous." I sound like a child throwing an irrational tantrum and I can't help myself.

"Hmm." His eyes drop to my lips. "Well, now you know."

"I'm not saying you can't date her. I mean, date who you want. It's none of my business. I just want to know what I'm walking into if I move in here for a few days."

"No, you're right." He toys with the ponytail at the base of my neck and tugs lightly, drawing me closer until I'm pressed against him and his eyes are on my mouth. Until *I. Want. More.* "She was totally trying to make you jealous. You should definitely get even by making out with me."

Just like that, all the tension knotting between my shoulder blades releases and laughter bursts from my lips. "You jerk." I put my hands to his chest and shove him back a step. "Don't make fun of me."

He shakes his head and runs his eyes over me. "I would never joke about something so serious."

chapter fourteen

William

"Oh. Em. Gee." Drew's eyes go big as she walks into my house. "*This* is what I'm talking about. Cally, you've been holding out on us. Making us live in that shithole while your boy here can give us the Ritz?"

She steps into the two-story entryway and spins a little circle, and I am so damn glad I convinced Cally to bring them here. I invited her father to stay as well, but he's not as sensitive to rodents as his daughters, and he said he wouldn't be comfortable taking advantage of my hospitality. Not the case for Cally's little sisters. Drew is looking around with the wide eyes of a child on Christmas, and Gabby's grin stretches from ear to ear.

"I'm glad you like it," Cally says to Drew, "but we're not staying long."

"*Like* it? You know, I think I was born to be rich. There's a pampered princess somewhere who really wishes she could live in that rat-infested cabin of Dad's and right now she's enduring her evening pedicure and facial. I was switched at birth."

"Hush," Cally says. "Your life is not that terrible. Will, do you want to show us where the girls will be sleeping? I'll bring in their suitcases."

Cally and the girls follow me upstairs, and I show Drew and Gabby the room they'll be sharing. The house has four bedrooms but one is set up with all my camera equipment and computers, so it's not fit for company.

"Your sister will in the room just down the hall if you need her."

"Not to be ungrateful or anything," Drew says, "but let's simplify things and put me in her room from the start. We all know Cally's going to end up in your bed anyway."

Cally's cheeks flame red. "Drew!"

"She's welcome there anytime," I say, "but we'll let her make that choice, okay?"

Drew just looks back and forth between us for a minute before shaking her head. "I don't get you two."

Cally avoids my gaze and studies the hardwood floor at her toes. "That makes two of us."

After we get the girls settled into their room, I show Cally to hers. "I apologize if the bed's not very comfortable. It's my old bed from Grandma's."

Something flashes in her eyes. Memories of what we used to do in that bed? Regrets about what we never did? "It has to be better than that couch I'm sleeping on." She rubs her forearm then digs her thumb into the palm of her hand.

"Are you hurt?"

She drops her hands to her sides as if she hadn't realized what she was doing. "I'm just sore from giving so many massages today. Sometimes my hands want to lock up at the end of the day." She shrugs. "It's normal when I'm putting in this many hours."

I take her hand and start working my thumbs into the muscles of her forearm, starting near her elbow and massaging my way down to the palm of her hand. As I apply pressure to the pad of her thumb, her eyes flutter closed. A low, barely audible moan slips from her lips.

Evening sun slants in the back window, spilling light across her face. She's so damn beautiful. The thick smear of her dark lashes across her cheek, the sweet curve of her lips. I could kiss her now. I could pull her close and put my lips on hers, slide my hands down her sides and curl my fingers into her hips as I seduce her with my mouth.

I could do all that. I want all that. But I want her near me more, and I know kissing her will scare her away.

"Cally."

Her lids flutter open and she blinks at me. We stand like that, staring at each other in the warmth of the evening sun, two people reorienting themselves after getting lost in a moment.

"Oh, God!" Drew's irritated tone snaps us both to attention. "Seriously, just give me this room and move her downstairs with you."

Cally

Brady's. Beer. Pool. Girl time. Tonight.

Grinning at Lizzy's text, I drop the paintbrush I was using on the front door and tap out a quick reply: *You have something against complete sentences, Miss Teacher?*

Bite me. <-- Complete sentence.

Minutes later, her cherry red Charger pulls into Dad's gravel drive, saving me from contemplating the painfully long list of repairs that need to be done to the house. Drew might not need the glam she says she wants, but even so, a couple of gallons of paint aren't going to cut it. While working here today, I realized the roof is leaking, causing God knows what kind of damage in the attic. Then when I was out on the back deck, I noticed a rotten board cracked under one of the girl's camping chairs. The place is a hazard and a money pit. At minimum, he needs a new stove, a new deck, and a new roof. None of those things come cheap.

Lizzy and Hanna climb out and survey the house.

"Ouch," Lizzy says, wincing. "Is that place…sanitary?"

"It's not *that* bad," Hanna attempts. "Maybe with some fresh paint?"

"It needs more than paint," I mutter.

"How's your dad's job search going?" Hanna asks. "Any luck?"

"He managed to find a part-time research position working for a faculty member at Sinclair."

"Oh, that's great!" Hanna says.

He needs something more, but I don't share any of that with my friends. They're worried enough about me without me piling it on.

Lizzy spins on me. "I can't believe you moved in with William and didn't tell us."

I shuffle back. "I didn't realize I needed to keep you updated."

"Save it for the margaritas," Hanna tells her sister. "Some conversations require tequila."

The bar is more crowded than I expected for a Wednesday night, but that makes the girls happy. I objected to the possibility of more tequila, so they've ordered us a pitcher of beer and staked out a booth by the pool tables, where they're scoping out the unsuspecting townies.

"Are you following me?" The question comes from right by my ear, and I have to resist the urge to lean into William.

"We got here first," I say. He brushes the hair off my neck, and I stand stock still and attempt to pretend I'm not affected by his touch. "I think that means *you're* following *me*."

The girls' eyes widen at the sight of Will.

"I see you brought your posse," Lizzy says, looking over Will's shoulder.

Will smirks. "I think you've already met my friends Sam and Max."

I was so focused on William, I didn't even realize he wasn't here alone. The guys slide out of a booth on the other side of the bar and join our little meet-and-greet. I recognize them from high school. Like Will, time has been good to them. They're both ridiculously handsome. The dark-haired one is in jeans and a fitted blue T-shirt that calls attention equally to impressive pecs and an amazing pair of baby blues. The other sports a dark polo and khakis. But neither of them is anywhere near the level of nuclear hotness that is my William is in a button-up white Oxford, sleeves rolled to his elbows, jeans hugging his narrow hips.

My William. Dangerous thinking.

"I don't know if you remember Sam," Will says, nodding to the one in the polo. He points his thumb toward the dark-haired one. "Or Max."

"It's been a while," I say.

"Good to see you again, Cally," Sam says, making me drag my eyes off Will. "How's your temporary roommate treating you? He doesn't drink out of the milk carton, does he?"

"He's a great host, and it's *very* temporary."

"Go finish your drinks." Lizzy shoos them toward their table. "We need some time for girl talk."

The girls slide into our booth, and Hanna sighs heavily.

"What's that about?" I ask.

She tucks a long, dark lock behind her ear and shakes her head.

"She's got a crush on Max," Lizzy explains. Hanna jabs her elbow into Lizzy's side, but Lizzy ignores her. "Can't say as I blame her. You could bounce quarters off the boy's ass."

"He has no idea I exist," Hanna mutters. "He's only had eyes for Lizzy since he came back to town and opened that gym."

Lizzy frowns. "I never would have gone on that date with him if I'd known Hanna liked him. I dropped him the minute I found out."

"Does he know how you feel?" I ask. Hanna looks nauseated just talking about it.

"God, no!" Lizzy snorts. "Are you kidding? Hanna doesn't tell guys when she's interested. She'd rather hide and tell herself she doesn't stand a chance. Which is stupid and a lie."

Hanna shakes her head. "What would he want to do with me anyway? He's an athletic trainer who runs his own health club, and I'm a fat girl."

"Hanna!" Lizzy and I say in unison. Hanna is bigger than her twin, plush and curvy with long dark hair, whereas Lizzy is tiny and lithe with blond curls. They look nothing like twins, but they're both equally beautiful.

Hanna shrugs off our protest. "It's *true.*"

"You're fucking gorgeous and any guy would be lucky to have you." Lizzy's face is drawn into a fierce scowl, daring Hanna to disagree.

"Time to change the subject, please," Hanna whispers into her beer.

Lizzy presses a kiss to her sister's forehead then turns to me. "Half the town is buzzing about you moving in with Will. I'm sure we had to find out from our *mom*. Why didn't you tell us?"

"Maybe there was nothing to tell?" The girls both stare at me like I'm trying to sell them land on the moon. I shrug. "What?"

"Sweetie," Hanna says, "there is so much heat in that boy's eyes when he looks at you, we can still smell the smoke. And now you're *living* with him?"

"You slept with him, didn't you?" Lizzy says, grinning. "We need details."

I cast a quick glance over my shoulder to make sure the guys can't hear. "I didn't sleep with him."

Lizzy's jaw drops. "Why not?"

"I screwed up with him once already," I whisper, holding up one finger. I add the second. "And I'm leaving after Christmas."

"You're really not going to sleep with him?" Lizzy's tone is more appropriate for talk of torturing kittens and killing puppies.

"I'm *really* not going to sleep with him," I growl.

"Will or no Will," Lizzy says, just as Will approaches our table, "I'm going to get you laid."

William

Cally's cheeks blaze and she shoots a lethal glare at her friend, then levels it at me, daring me to say something.

I bite back my smile. "A true friend, indeed."

Lizzy's gaze swings around to me and she bursts out laughing. "I had no idea he was there. I swear."

"What's going on over here?" Max strolls over to the table and runs his gaze over Lizzy. The guys want to hang with Cally and the twins tonight, and frankly, I'm game. I just want to be close to Cally.

We end up piling into a big booth together, me and Cally shoulder to shoulder on one side and Sam and Hanna on the other with Max and Lizzy pulling up chairs to the end, and before I know it the girls are all laughing and drinking and I'm sitting silently, nursing my beer and thinking how good it feels just to be *close* to her.

My phone buzzes in my pocket and I pull it out to see I have a text from Meredith.

Wanna get together for a drink tonight?

I key in a quick reply. *I'm hanging with the guys. Maybe another time?*

I look up from my phone and catch Cally watching me. "Sexting with your girlfriend?"

Max tips my phone down so he can see the screen. He groans. "Meredith? Girl can't take a hint, can she?"

Cally stiffens next to me, and Lizzy pipes up with, "*Meredith?*"

"She's a friend."

"Will's grandma set them up," Max says. "They went on a few dates and now she sends Will dirty texts day and night."

Shit. "We're just friends now."

"Dirty texts? How dirty?" Lizzy asks.

"*So* dirty," says Sam.

"Dirtier than the drunk texts Cally sent from Asher's party?" Lizzy asks.

Cally's eyes go wide. "Lizzy!"

"What drunk texts?" Sam asks. "Damn. Seriously, Will's phone gets more action in a day than mine has seen all year."

Lizzy winks at Sam and pulls out her phone. "What's your number, cutie?"

Cally's already gone stone cold next to me, and she's studying the table top like it explains the meaning of life.

I grab her hand and drag her out of the booth.

"What are you doing?" she asks.

I pull her over to the jukebox and drape her arms around my neck. "You're doing me a favor. I don't want to talk about Meredith right now, and when it comes to her, the guys are like a dog with a bone."

"Oh."

This isn't a slow song, but I don't care. I want her head against my chest, her body close to mine. She looks amazing in nothing more complicated than a little black tank top and jean shorts that show off her long legs. The second I walked into Brady's and saw her standing there, I started thinking about how much I want those legs wrapped around me, her nails digging into my back as I make her come.

"Do you exchange dirty texts with all of your *friends*?" she asks, her voice dropping low and lethal.

"We dated a little bit before you came back. It was supposed to be casual, but she ended up wanting more."

"I'm sure most girls around here would love a chance for more with you."

A Nine Inch Nails song kicks on, and I smile. "You remember this?"

Her eyes widen, her pupils dilating. We used to lie in my bedroom, listening to this album. We'd talk. Me about my controlling grandmother and her unreasonable expectations, Cally about her crazy father, her disappointing mother. We'd dream about going to college together and moving away, about a better life for her—she wouldn't have to worry about getting her sisters fed and to sleep at the end of the day—about an easier life for me—I wouldn't be expected to live up to every dream my grandmother ever had for the son she lost too soon. Then we'd explore each other, our bodies young and eager, our hands and mouths tentative as we learned together where and how to touch.

I lead her to the back corner of the bar and press my palms against the wall, pinning her in.

"What are you doing?" she asks in a whisper.

"This." I drop my mouth to hers before she can protest, and my hands move from the wall into her hair.

She doesn't hesitate and her mouth is greedy under mine as she kisses me back and wraps her hands around my biceps. I draw out the kiss, knowing damn well there are people watching, knowing damn well how fast news travels in this town. I want them to see. I'm ready to send the message that Cally is the only woman I'm interested in.

"I've spent the last month thinking about touching you at the restaurant," I whisper against her ear. "As long as I can remember the sound of you coming, you don't have to worry about any other woman laying claim to me."

"Speak of the devil," she mutters, looking over my shoulder.

"Who?"

"Meredith, and if looks could kill, you'd be holding a corpse."

I barely register her meaning, too busy burying my nose in her hair, trying to memorize her scent. It's something equal parts sweet and tempting.

Meredith is here. And if I'm not a dick, I'll release Cally and go talk to her. And yet, maybe Cally was right about Meredith laying claim to me.

Pressing my hand against Cally's back, I fan my fingers until two dip into the waistband of her jean shorts and under the silky smooth material of her panties. She draws in a breath and snuggles closer.

I'm tempted to brush my fingers over her and tease that sensitive skin of her lower back, tempted to whisper something wicked in her ear. But I don't. I just move my hips to the music, savoring the moment until the song ends.

Her dark eyes hold arousal and sadness and so much I don't understand. "I'm going to go back to the table," she whispers.

I nod but I don't follow her. I need to catch my breath, to get my head right.

I head to the bar and order a beer. Within seconds, Meredith has joined me. She leans against the bar and frowns. "I thought you were out with the guys."

She's smiling, as if she's trying to make it a joke, but the hurt is in her eyes. Meredith is sweet and pretty and sexy, and if I had any sense at all I'd be chasing her instead of a girl who once shattered my heart.

But Meredith isn't the one I want.

"Cally and her friends were already here."

"You should have told me she was here with you. Now I feel like an idiot for showing up."

"What did you think would happen if she wasn't here?"

She drops her gaze to her hands. "We were good together. I just…I just want you to remember that."

"This isn't fair to you, Meredith. You should find someone who deserves you."

She frowns, her carefully painted lips drawing into a pout. "You said you didn't want anything serious, and I didn't believe you because everyone knows that you want to get married. You want to make a family. It's part of who you are. Only, you were telling me the truth. You didn't want anything serious. At least, not with me. Those rules don't apply to Cally."

"Meredith—"

"No." She holds up a hand, cutting off my explanation. "Don't. We're just friends. That was the deal." She shakes her head and tucks her purse under her arm. "I'm not a bad catch, you know? Your grandma loves me, and things were going great between us. But suddenly you're pushing me away because Cally's back, and Cally… Cally's not even staying. She's heading back to Vegas in a few months. Add to that the fact that your grandma can't stand her. Never could. Never mind that she dropped you without a thought back in high school."

"That was a long time ago," I growl.

She shrugs. "People don't really change, Will. Not much. I hope you know what you're doing. I don't want to see you hurt."

chapter fifteen

Cally
Seven Years Ago

I'M HEADED to work when the dark SUV slows alongside me and the window rolls down. A man pokes his head out and smiles at me, a sick, calculating smile. I don't recognize him, but I know without asking that Anthony sent him. His nose is crooked, as if it's been broken a few too many times, and his dark hair is slicked back with too much gel. He looks so much like a stereotypical movie bad guy, I almost want to laugh. Only there's nothing funny about the way he's looking at me or the fear tearing through my stomach.

"Your little sisters sure are cute," he says.

I freeze in my tracks, my feet glued to the sidewalk.

"That little one, she sure does like the swing at Tyson Park. And the older one, she's got potential. A couple years and think of the things she could do." The man grins. "Boss said you can either work off the loan or your sisters can do it for you."

A chill whips through me, sharp and angry. "No."

"Anthony doesn't do second chances, sweetheart. It's your lucky day. The client you ran out on took a special liking to you. He wants to see you again, requested you personally. You couldn't have played it better, actually. That one likes a little bit of the chase, and now he won't take any of the boss's other girls. Only has eyes for the sweet dark-haired virgin." His laugh is more like a cackle. "We'll pick you up tonight. No fuck-ing around this time." He doesn't wait for an answer before his window slides back into position and the car pulls away.

I don't bother going to work. What's the point? I head home and stare at my phone, trying to figure out what will happen if I call the police. They'll help me. I won't have to go to that man again tonight. I won't have to do the unspeakable things I'm sure to have to do. But what will happen to my sisters? And how long can the police protect me from Anthony and his men?

So I shower and change and wait for Anthony's car to pick me up.

When my phone rings, William's name looks at me from the screen of the phone he bought and paid for to keep us together. I send the call to voicemail and steal two pills from Mom's secret stash.

Cally
Present Day

"You little lying, hooky-playing twerp!" I growl as I tap out the text to Drew: *Where are you?*

I burst into William's house looking for her. After I walked Gabby to school, Drew's truancy officer called to let me know that Drew wasn't in her first class. Was she sick today?

I caught her playing hooky once before, and if she's doing it again, I'm going to ground her for a month. If she thinks she's going to get away with skipping school just because I'm working all the time, she's got an-other thing coming.

I storm up the stairs, my anger growing as I burst into the room she and Gabby share. The room is unoccupied. Empty.

"Drew! Where are you?" I head back downstairs, not bothering to quiet my tear through the house. William was already gone when I left with the girls this morning—heading to the gym to squeeze in a work-out before opening the gallery. I avoided him after getting home from Brady's last night. I shouldn't have let myself dance with him. It felt too good to have his body close, his breath on my ear. By the time he kissed me, I was already too far gone to make a sensible decision.

After hitting the family room and the kitchen, I still haven't found Drew. I'm starting to worry when my phone buzzes with a text from her.

I'm at school.

"No," I grumble. "You're a liar."

Then the shower kicks on down the hall, and I'm darting toward the Master before I think about it. His shower is one of those with shower-heads on three walls and Drew has been chomping at the bit to try it out.

The door to his bedroom is open and I'm more incensed with every step. William has done so much for us, and this is how she thanks him? Skipping school and using his freaking shower?

I open the door to his bathroom and blink when Will's running clothes greet me in a neat pile by the door. I freeze, staring at the rum-pled pile of cotton, remembering the look of his sweat-slicked skin when he comes off a run.

Move, Cally.

But I can't.

Then I hear a long and low groan come from the direction of the shower and what I see when I lift my head has my heart racing and my breath going shallow.

Drew isn't anywhere to be seen. Only William.

Behind the steamy shower door, he stands under the spray, one hand braced against the tile and the other...*oh, hell*...the other wrapped around his shaft as he moves over it in long, even strokes.

His body is gorgeous—broad shoulders tapering to narrow hips. Hard, sculpted muscles that I want to touch with my hands, taste with my tongue, and test with my teeth.

From the angle he's standing, with only five steps and the steamy glass between us, I see more than I should and so much less than I want. I need to take these feet—the ones that are glued to the bathroom tile—and put them in reverse. I need to back myself right out of this bathroom and figure out where Drew really is. Or hell, maybe I need a shower of my own. A really cold one.

But what I really want is a better view. I want to see the expression on his face as he works himself over. I want to see the ripple of his muscles as he strains against the need to come. I want to open the shower door and—without a word—drop to my knees and replace his hand with my mouth.

Just the thought of it has my legs unsteady. Who knew the thought of giving a blow job could turn me on so much? With anyone else it probably wouldn't, but this is William, and my heart slams in my chest as I imagine filling my mouth with him, his hands in my hair as I take him deep, his ass flexing under my hands.

The thought is more than enough to turn me on. It's almost enough to get me off.

He groans again, longer, lower, deeper this time, and I know this is the moment I have to make my decision. Either get the hell out of dodge or muster up enough courage to join him.

As much as I hate to leave, I'm too much of a coward to stay. I stumble back. My heel hits the trash can and I jump. My hands fly out to the sides to catch my balance and my arm whacks the sink as I go down.

The next thing I know, Will is out of the shower, dropping to his haunches in front of me. Worried. Naked. Dripping wet. "Are you okay?"

"Yeah. Fine. I was…." *Wishing I was brave enough to join you? Fantasizing about sucking you off?* "Looking for Drew." My eyes drop involuntarily to the erection still standing strong between us. I have never wanted to taste something so badly in my life.

"Cally." He clears his throat, and I lift my eyes to his face. He's smirking. "She's not in here."

Tonight, maybe tomorrow, I'll probably think up a genius smart-ass retort, but right now the capacity for speech seems to be escaping me.

He offers his hand, and I take it, trying very hard to keep distance between our bodies as he helps me up. I should go, but I'm caught under the spell of those hot blue eyes.

He traces my jaw with his fingertip, moving from behind my ear down to the tip of my chin before touching his thumb to my lips. "Join me in the shower?"

I swallow. Hard. Whisper, "Tempting."

He groans, low and long and so much like the sounds he was making when I caught him stroking himself in the shower that it takes everything in my power not to strip down, follow him under the spray, and act out every second of my fantasy. Then he dips his head so his lips brush my ear. "Having you watch me while I stroked myself in the shower was one of the hottest experiences of my life."

A tiny thrill dances down my spine and blossoms, wild and nervous, in my belly. Lower. "You knew I was here?"

Again with the low groan, but he presses closer this time, the hard length of his erection pressing against my belly. "I was already thinking about you. Thinking about how badly I wanted to take you in the shower. Thinking about touching every inch of your body with my soapy hands. Thinking about making you come like I did at the restaurant, but this time you could cry out as loud as you want. You have no idea how much I want that."

It's my turn to moan. My body is alive with pulsing sexual energy as if we were hours into foreplay. The wild nerves dancing in my gut play on the unwelcome arousal churning beneath. His breath against my ear sends shivers down my spine. Need and desire spiral low, and I know that if he slid his hand into my panties now I'd be slick, ready.

I lift my hand to his face. I can't resist. He didn't shave this morning, and his cheek is rough against my palm. I slide my hand into his wet curls.

"I don't know what you're scared of, Cally." He brushes my hair out of my face and behind my ear. "But I won't push you beyond anything you're ready for. Just tell me what you want. Tell me what you need."

I press my lips to his. He tastes of toothpaste and fresh water, and when our mouths first touch, he stays perfectly still. I brush my lips over his once, twice, three times.

My fingers trace the edge of his jaw, then the top of his shoulders. I explore the firm muscles of his chest. He doesn't move. Doesn't touch me. When I finally reach his abdomen, my fingers find the V of his hip-bones, and he draws in a sharp breath.

"Cally," he whispers.

I let my lips find his. He kisses me back softly, tentatively, as if he's afraid I might run away. Maybe that's fair, and maybe I should, but right now I'm his. I'm not going anywhere.

He tucks a lock of hair behind my ear and runs his thumb down my cheek, and I decide I don't care about before or after. I decide I'm going to do something stupid and wonderful right *now*.

William

Cally's in my bathroom, touching me. I am all too aware that I'm naked and aroused. All too aware of what I was doing before she attempted her clumsy escape.

Her eyes flick back south again before she catches herself and pulls them back to my face, tongue darting out to moisten her lips.

I could press her against the wall. I could talk her into what we both want. But before I can make a move, she glides the palm of her hand against the flat of my stomach and fans her fingers until they're brushing the base of my cock.

"Jesus," I hiss. I lift my hands to touch her, then clench my fists and drop them to my sides.

"Let me touch you," she whispers. Her fingertips dance along the underside of my erection. "No strings. No expectations. Just let me do this for you. Please."

"Cally." Her name is a whisper and a prayer, but she's already dropping to her knees.

She runs her hands down my body and wraps one around my cock in a movement so sudden and so unexpected, I have to steady myself on the vanity. My heart pounds wildly in my chest and I want to close my eyes and sink into the fucking amazing sensation of her hand sliding over my dick, but I won't. I can't bring myself to miss a second of Cally on her knees before me, her lips parted as she looks up at me through those thick lashes and strokes.

"I've wanted to do this for so long," she whispers. Then she touches her barely-parted lips to the head of my cock and sweeps her tongue along the underside. When she opens her mouth over me and takes me deep, I can't resist touching her anymore and my hands find their way into her hair.

Her soft moans fill my head as she slides her mouth over me, sucking me deep before pulling back and repeating the motion. When her hand slides up the inside of my thigh to cup my balls, my fingers tighten in her hair and I have to fight the instinct to rock into her, to press myself deeper into the heat of her mouth.

She squeezes lightly on my sac and then, when I don't think it's possible for her to take any more of me, she slides her lips down my shaft, taking me in nearly to the root. Then I can't take it anymore. My dick so deep in her mouth, her hot tongue curling around me, and that sexy ass moan makes her lips vibrate just barely against me.

I tug gently at her hair. "Baby." She doesn't pull back but somehow takes me another fraction of an inch deeper. "Sweetheart, I'm gonna come."

My words only seem to steel her determination and she adds just enough suction that I can't hold back. I knot my hands in her hair as I release into her throat. Hard and fast and so intense I'm almost worried about her.

Pulling her to her feet, I lean against the wall to catch my breath. I hug her against me. "You're so fucking amazing," I whisper.

Her lips, pink and swollen and apparently my true Kryptonite, curl into a smile before she can bite it back. "Thanks."

I reach for the hem of her shirt and she stiffens. "What is it?"

"Fuck. *Drew.*" She squeezes her eyes shut and presses her palms against my bare chest until I step back.

Only then do I hear the music down the hall. Before I can ask what's going on, Cally's headed in that direction.

I reluctantly pull on some jeans and try to come to terms with the fact that I'm not going to be getting her naked any time soon. By the time I join her in the living room, she and Drew are already facing off, arms crossed and bodies tense in nearly identical stances, faces drawn into nearly identical scowls. I would laugh if I didn't think it would get me hit.

"I don't see why high school is so important." Drew is saying, "You didn't finish and you're doing fine."

"*Fine?*" Cally says. "What about my financial situation seems *fine* to you?"

"You would be fine if you stayed with Brandon. He used to buy you stuff and take care of you. What's so wrong with that?"

Cally's hands are balled into fist at her sides, and tension has made her posture stiff. "That's your great plan? Find some guy to take care of you?"

"It's better than what Mom did for her clients. It's better than what the people at school say you're doing."

I can see the moment the words register with Cally. Her shoulders sag and she sinks into the couch and leans forward, elbows on knees, head in her hands.

Drew's face falls, regret wiping her expression clear of its former bitterness. "I don't believe what they say. I know that you don't... I'm just...." Her gaze shoots up to meet mine, as if I might be able to take her words back for her.

Cally lifts her head. "Drew, go to your room, please." There's something unsaid between them. Old promises drudged up by a strained relationship.

"I'm sorry," Drew whispers, then she runs past me and up the stairs.

I cross to the couch and sit next to Cally.

She takes my hand before I even offer it. "I shouldn't have moved them. I should have had Dad sign custody over to me. I could have talked him into it. We would have figured out...something."

"She's at a tough age. She'll be fine. She just needs more time."

She nods, tugging her bottom lip between her teeth. "She's pissed at me because she wanted to sleep over with this new friend this weekend. I told her she had to work on Dad's house with me instead."

"You're working on your dad's house this weekend?"

"The exterminator is done, so...yeah. We can't stay here forever."

They could. I wouldn't mind.

She shrugs. "Anyway, I think Dad misses them."

"What all are you doing at the house?"

"Not as much as I want. Everything is so expensive. But we can paint and deep clean. Don't worry. We'll be out of your hair in no time." She shakes her head and pushes herself off the couch. "I have to get that pipsqueak back to school before my first client."

"Cally," I call, stopping her when she hits the first stair. "You're not in my hair at all." *Please stay.*

"Just in your bathroom." She bites back a smile. "Sorry about that."

A groan I hardly recognize rumbles up from my chest. "I'm not."

chapter sixteen

Cally

WHEN I climb out of the shower, the house is still. The last of the home-work is finished, dinner put away, the television turned off. The giggles from the girls' room have quieted.

I pull on my robe and wrap my hair in a towel before heading to my room, stalling at the staircase halfway there. He's down there. Maybe tinkering with his photos on his laptop, maybe sitting in the living room with his feet up, grading student papers. Maybe taking a shower of his own. My eyes float closed as I conjure up the image of him under the spray, muscles taut as he strokes himself.

Maybe he's in bed. Maybe he's thinking of me, of my mouth on him this morning. Maybe he knows I'm thinking of him.

I pad to my room, closing the door quietly behind me—for privacy or to put another obstacle between us?

Over the last few nights, I've found myself heading back downstairs after the girls go to sleep at night, just hoping I might run into William in the kitchen. I love the way his eyes roam over me every time we're in the same room, as if he's trying to memorize me, and I find myself craving those moments, looking for them.

I could throw on some clothes and go down to find him, but I won't.

Not tonight. Not when the girls are in the house and I'm so close to giving in to temptation. Every day I'm realizing it's not a question of *if* I'll acquiesce the attraction between us. It's a question of *when*.

My phone buzzes, vibrating against the nightstand, and when I pick it up, I see William's number on the screen.

"Hey there," I whisper.

"How was your shower?"

"Wonderful. Hot. Long. Water pressure to die for. Much needed."

His hum of approval carries over the line and rumbles through my body, vibrating through my core and settling between my legs. "You could have taken it down here. You'd like my shower."

"And have it ruin me for all other showers?" I grin and plop onto the bed. "Hardly."

"I had a good time hanging out with you and the girls tonight." His voice drops low, seducing me with treble alone. "I like having you around, Cally."

I like being around. "I owe you so much for all of this. I really can't thank you enough."

"You're welcome. It's been my pleasure."

The silence rises up between us. It's not an empty silence, eating up space in our conversation. Instead, it's this loaded silence, charged with attraction and unfulfilled desires. Fantasies. Memories. Unspoken secrets.

"Remember our phone calls after you first moved away?"

"I remember."

"Lock the door, Cally."

"Are you trying to keep me in or keep yourself out?" Even as I ask, I turn the lock on the handle.

"You don't have to worry about me coming up there."

"I don't?" Why am I disappointed?

"No, sweetheart. Your sisters are up there, and when I'm finally inside you, I want to hear you scream."

My knees turn to jelly, and I sink onto the bed.

"The lock is so you won't be interrupted while I'm listening to you touch yourself."

"William." His name comes off my lips like a plea.

"I left you something on the dresser."

"Wine," I whisper, standing to pour myself a glass.

"Strawberry wine," he corrects. "I sprung for the kind with the screw-off cap."

"Classy." I giggle and take a sip. The taste and the smell work together to snare my senses and carry me back in time. The dock behind the old warehouse on Main. The moonlight reflecting off the water. William's tongue circling my navel….

"Are you nude?"

His words pair with my anticipation and send a thrill up my spine. "I have a robe on. I believe it's the one your 'friend' Meredith was wearing the other day."

"Jealous much?"

"Maybe a little." I smile. "Maybe I should send you more dirty texts. I can't have your phone thinking she's better at that than me."

"Maybe you should."

I could. I like the idea of sending him a dirty message while he's teaching.

"What are we doing?"

I'm talking about *this,* about *us,* but he says, "I'm not sure, but let's start with that robe and see what happens." His voice has gone deep, gravelly. "Untie it for me, Cally."

My hands shake slightly as I obey. I let the ties fall to the side and slide my hand down the flat of my belly. "What about you? What do you have on?"

"Boxers."

I lick my lips. I'd tell him to take them off, but I like the image of him in nothing but boxers. "Since I started staying here, I've been wondering how you sleep," I confess.

"Honestly, I haven't done much sleeping at all. I think about you sliding between those sheets, your body laid out on the same bed I used to touch you on."

My breath hitches. "How am I supposed to resist you when you talk to me like this?"

"You're not."

"There are so many reasons we shouldn't do this." But I already know we will. I surrendered the moment I locked the door. "I'm afraid I'll hurt you again."

He hesitates a beat. "That's a chance I'm willing to take, Cal. Let me make that choice, okay?" Then, before I can reply: "Are you nude under the robe?"

"Yes."

He groans. "You've got the upper hand here."

"How so?"

"You saw me naked in the shower. It's been too damn long since I've seen your bare body. I want to see those curves I felt at the restaurant."

I shift back on the bed and fan my fingers over my belly.

"Touch your breasts for me. Touch them like I would. Let me hear you as you play with your nipples."

Desire ripples through me as I lift one hand to my breasts, cupping them, teasing my nipples with my fingers.

"God," he groans. "I love hearing you breathe when you're aroused. You're so damn responsive. It is such a turn-on."

"It's not…." I hesitate, embarrassed to say it but needing him to know, to understand. "I'm not always like this. It's you. No one else does this to me. No one else could ever turn me on this fast."

"How aroused are you? Slide your hand between your legs and tell me."

My breath comes faster as I trace my hand down my body to the needy spot between my thighs. My body is humming with arousal. Greedy with desire. When my fingers find the slickness between my legs, I whimper because my hand is a sorry substitute for his, the quiet of this empty room a poor consolation prize when I crave the weight of his body on me, his breath in my ear. "I can't," I whisper. "I want *you*."

He moans softly. "It's good to hear you say it."

I shake my head and remove my hand. This is too much. And I've reached my breaking point. "Will, I have to go."

Then I hang up the phone.

William

What the hell just happened?

I blink at my phone, try to make sense of the words telling me the call ended. *Fuck.*

I squeeze my eyes shut and throw my head back on my pillow.

Not that I'll be sleeping much tonight. Not with Cally in my head. Not with the image of her just upstairs, parting her legs at my command. Not while I'm remembering the soft, barely audible almost-purr that she makes when she's close to coming. I keep thinking of how soft her lips look before I kiss them. How swollen they are after.

At the first knock on my bedroom door, I think I'm imagining things. But it sounds again, and then someone whispers my name quietly. "William?"

After I pull open the door, I have to blink a few times to be sure my eyes aren't playing tricks on me. Cally's standing there in nothing but a white terry cloth robe.

"Cally."

She just looks at me with those big brown doe eyes. Then her hands are in my hair and her mouth is on mine. And holy hell, her lips are so damn soft, her taste so damn sweet that I'm lost.

Cupping her face in my hands, I kiss her back without hesitation. I pull her bottom lip between my teeth, and she lets out this little kitten mewl that makes me crazy. My thumb skips down her jaw until she opens under my mouth, because I have to get inside. I need to taste her, to explore her.

Mine.

"Are you sure?" I ask.

"I promise to be quiet." She rubs a thumb over my lips, and I have to resist the instinct to pull it between my teeth and suck, to watch those expressive eyes of hers flare with desire. "Please," she says softly. "Please, William. I need this. I need someone good to touch me. Please."

I drop my hands to her waist and tug her close. The slide of my hand in her robe and I'm skating my thumb across her navel. "I'm not good, Cally. I've screwed up so many times."

"You are," she breathes. "So good you can't even see it."

I yank her robe open and crush my mouth down on hers. I mean it to be a warning—because I'm not letting her go without a fight this time. But she doesn't withdraw. She moans and rocks her hips. She meets my brutal desire with her own, tugging at my hair, biting my lip.

I kick the door closed and back her against it, as if a solid surface might contain this wild and dangerous hunger pumping through me. When I move to her neck and suck that tender skin, she gasps and presses harder into me.

Another wave of lust slams through me, and suddenly I need to see her eyes, to see the pleasure on her face as I touch her.

When I pull back, she's watching me. Her lips are red and swollen, her lids heavy with desire.

I move my hand up her torso. As I brush the underside of her breasts, her eyes float closed and she arches into my hand.

"God, you're beautiful." My words are thick with arousal, gritty with the desperation I've felt since she watched me stroke myself in the shower. Fuck. I'm lost.

I dip my head to her breast, wetting it with my tongue. Cupping her in my hand, I draw her nipple into my mouth. She cries out against my neck and digs her nails into my shoulder blades as I suck and bite, rough and soft by turns. Maybe too rough, but I can't help it because she's moaning and I am desperate to claim her, to brand her.

She rocks into my thigh. I run my hands down her legs and draw her knees up, lifting her between me and the door until my cock is nestled right between her legs, only the thin fabric of my boxers between us. She wraps her legs around me and squeezes me tight.

"Goddammit, Cally." My eyes close, and I have to grit my teeth. "You're so wet I can feel it, and I haven't even taken off my shorts yet."

"What are you waiting for?" She slides her fingers into my hair and tugs my mouth down to hers.

I growl against her and curl my fingers into her hips. "Do you have any idea how much I've thought about this sweet body of yours? Do you have any idea how crazy it made me to have you sleeping upstairs, so fucking close but off limits?"

I peel the robe from her shoulders and let it drop to the floor. "You are so insanely beautiful." I drop my head to open my mouth against her breasts. One at a time, I draw the taut peaks into my mouth, between my teeth, until she cries out and arches closer.

"William," she whimpers. "Please."

I lift my head, my fingers picking up where my mouth left off and rolling a perfect pink nipple between my fingers. "What, baby? Please what?"

She shudders and presses her breast further into my hand. "Please, can you?"

I need to hear her say it, to hear the words from her lips, but I can't resist another taste and have to lower my head to her breasts again and roll a nipple against my tongue.

"God, you taste good."

Her hands thread through my hair and tug, and when I close my mouth over her and suck, the cry that rips through her is almost enough to make me go off in my shorts.

"William," she whimpers, and I love the way she says my full name. "Inside me. Please."

My breath leaves me in a rush. There they are. The words I've been waiting for. But I'm not ready.

Sliding my hands under her ass to support her, I swing around and take four long strides to the bed. I slowly slide her down my body until she's sitting on the bed. Grabbing her hips, I tug her forward until she's leaning back on her elbows and her hips are at the edge of the bed. Then I kiss my way down her body—across her collarbone, between her breasts, down her belly.

I scrape my teeth over one hip then trail my mouth across her stomach. Stopping at her navel, I circle the little jeweled piercing with my tongue before opening my mouth against the soft flesh and sucking.

She bucks her hips, and I cup her, hot and wet, between her legs.

"God, you're amazing," I murmur. She gasps at the touch of my hand.

I position her feet back on the bed so her knees are bent and she's open to me. Then I sink to my haunches and look at her.

She reaches for me. "What are you doing?"

A smile curls my lips, and I press lightly against her inner thighs until her legs fall open and she's completely exposed to my gaze.

"William," she whimpers as I trace my finger down her swollen, sensitive sex.

Her legs come together, and I press them open again and lower my head and taste her. She arches against me, crying out again until the sound of her moans, the feel of her fingers tangling in my hair, and the taste of her against my tongue has my cock aching impatiently in my shorts.

But I won't be rushed. I circle her clit with my tongue, and she trembles under me.

Lifting my head, I lock my eyes with hers. "Don't hold back, Cally. Let me make you come."

I sink two fingers inside her. She pulses around me. So damn close. Taking her clit between my lips, I suck the same moment I cover her mouth with my free hand. She trembles under my mouth, until she's pulsing around my fingers and her cry is muffled against my hand.

chapter seventeen

Cally

"GOD, YOU'RE beautiful when you come." His eyes are hot on mine as he works his way back up my body, one hand still cupping me between my legs. My limbs are limp, my body relaxed, but just the heat in his eyes reignites something in me.

Just like that, I need more.

William climbs on top of me, and I wrap my legs around his hips. I'm greeted with the long, thick shaft of his cock pressing against my clit through his cotton shorts. Just that contact and I'm whimpering—with that dangerous cocktail of pleasure, need, and nostalgia.

"I made so many damn mistakes when you were out of my life. When I you left, I lost more than my girlfriend. I lost myself." He traces my lips with his thumb, and the tenderness in his eyes nearly undoes me. "Be with me, Cally. You're my compass. My north star."

My throat is thick, and his words have tears pushing at the back of my eyes.

"I love you," he murmurs. He kisses the corner of my mouth, my ear, then my cheeks, where his lips press the wet heat of my tears into my skin. "I've always loved you."

I shake my head, needing him to understand. "You don't love me. You love the girl I used to be."

"Do you have any idea how amazing you are *now*?" His eyes lock with mine as he whispers the words. "Everything you've done for the girls and your father…the way you just picked up and left your old life? Not many people your age would do that. You work nonstop, and you're always doing for them. I don't need my memories to be head over heels in love with you, Cally. All I have to do is know you."

My heart is full and broken all at once, and I can't allow myself to return his words. I've said *I love you* so many times since leaving William, and every time it was a lie. I won't let the words be tainted by my lips. "Make love to me, William."

Something flashes over his face. My choice of words doesn't escape his notice. But that's what this is. That's what it will be between Will and me. Some people have sex or intercourse. Some people fuck. But with Will, no matter how fast or slow, tender or rough, after all these years of waiting, I know it will be making love. And that's what I need now. More than anything.

In seconds, he's off me, standing beside the bed and shucking his shorts. He slides on a condom from his end table, and I swallow hard at the sight of him—long and thick, and a little intimidating.

He lies back on the bed, his head propped against a pillow, and crooks his finger at me.

Placing a knee on either side of his hips, I straddle him. He guides me until he's pressing against my entrance.

My eyes close in anticipation of the pain-laced pleasure I know his size will bring.

"Look at me," he commands, fingers digging into my hips.

I open my eyes and lock them on his as he slowly slides inside me. My body has to stretch to accommodate his size, but he's patient and lets me adjust to him. Just having him inside me brings me close again. He stretches me and presses deep, and his eyes don't leave my face until I start moving over him, creating a rhythm for our bodies as he slides deep again and again. Pressure building, my body tightening.

He pulls me forward and cradles my ass in his hands. When his mouth latches onto one of my nipples and draws it tight, I come apart again, and he tightens his hold on my hips and rocks into me with three hard strokes before coming with me.

"Why did you keep resisting this?" We're lying in bed nude, our sweaty skin drying under the soft breeze of the ceiling fan. He took care of the condom in the bathroom and then came back to bed and drew my body against his.

"Maybe I wanted you to beg," I tease.

He grunts. "If I thought that would do it, I would have."

The humor leaves me suddenly. He deserves a real answer. "Because I'm not staying. Leaving you once almost killed me. I don't know if I can survive leaving you a second time."

He hooks his foot behind my knee and rolls us over so he's above me, his hands framing my face. "So don't leave. You have a job here. A place to live. What are you so anxious to get back to?"

My heart squeezes in my chest. Because I want what he's offering. I want to be the girl who believes in happily-ever-after again. I want to trust that everything happens for a reason.

But I'm not that girl I used to be, and Will deserves more than for me to pretend I am.

"It's not that simple."

"It can be." He presses a kiss to my collarbone. "Are you really so desperate to get back to something there, or are you running away from something here?"

My throat grows thick. I can hardly speak because I can't swallow my own lies when he's looking at me with so much love.

"Stay." He presses a kiss to the corner of my mouth. "There's nothing you need to run from. I've got you. No matter what." He kisses me again, this time right between my breasts. Right over my heart.

He settles next to me and pulls my body against his to sleep. "Hello, Cally," he whispers, and seconds later, I feel his breathing change against my neck as he relaxes in his sleep.

I lie there, wide awake, wishing it were all as simple as he believes it to be.

William

Sleeping Beauty is in my bed.

The morning sun slants in my bedroom window and across Cally's face, and I can't bring myself to leave her, though I have to open the gallery in fifteen minutes. There's something about being with this woman that washes away all the ugliness of the past two years. My mistake of an engagement to Maggie, my bigger mistake of an engagement to Krystal. I hate to think of myself as some easily analyzed psyche. A cliché case of a guy who lost his family when he was young and has spent his life since trying to build a new one.

But with Maggie and Krystal, I was always caught up in what *would* be. Securing that future—the family, the children—it was all this elusive high I couldn't stop chasing.

It was never like that with Cally. Not when I was eighteen. And not now. Cally grounds me in the moment, roots me in the here and now. She makes simply *existing* so damn perfect I forget all my anxieties about tomorrow.

Her dark lashes flutter against her cheek and she moans softly, rolling to her side and curling into me. After I made love to her the second time last night, she fell asleep in my arms. I watched her for awhile, reminding myself she was real, and here, that it wasn't a dream. I was almost back to sleep myself when she started talking in her sleep. *"I'm sorry."* That was all I could make out her long stream of murmurs. *"I'm sorry. I'm so sorry."*

She was dreaming, but I felt like the words were for me, and it shook me to think she's carrying around so much guilt. But sorry for what? For standing me up that weekend? For dropping me with a text message and just as quickly making herself unreachable? For falling into another guy's arms before a month was out? Or maybe she's sorry for all that and more. Maybe she's sorry for something I don't even know about. Something I wouldn't want to know.

Whatever it is, it doesn't change how I feel. Here, in my bed, the morning sun warming our skin, I'm surer than ever that only Cally matters.

"Mmm," she murmurs against my chest. "I need to get out of bed and get the girls to school."

I stroke her hair back from her face, tucking it behind her ear. "Already taken care of."

She jerks upright and looks at the clock. "Shit. I'm so sorry."

"Don't be. They wanted to let you sleep." I tug her hips until she slips down in bed next to me again. "And I wanted to keep you in bed as long as possible."

She rolls over and curls into my chest. "I haven't slept that well in ages."

"Sounds like you should sleep in my bed more often."

"So you're going to use my insomnia as an excuse to have your way with me?"

"When it comes to getting your naked body next to me as often as possible, I have no shame."

"You smell good." She presses her lips against my chest and licks up my sternum. "Taste good too."

I grab her hands and roll us so she's under me, her hands over her head, trapped at the wrists by mine. Her eyes flash hot as they meet mine.

I nuzzle her neck, relishing the knowledge that I'm branding her with my unshaven face.

"When are you moving back to Vegas?" I have to ask. I need to remind myself that she isn't going to be in my life forever. That she doesn't want to be.

"I don't know." She lifts her eyes to mine, her insecurities written all over her face. "I'm not a fan of long-distance relationships."

"Me either. But I think they can be done. If it's really necessary."

She sinks her teeth into her bottom lip. "Maybe it's not necessary."

"What do you mean by that?" I'm afraid to hope.

"I mean I was going back to Vegas because it was the default, the obvious next move, and—" She watches me. Hesitant. Careful. "—I'm saying I'm going to consider other options."

Something floods my chest, threating to overwhelm me. I bury my face in her neck and squeeze her tight.

Kissing a path up her neck, I draw her earlobe between my teeth, sucking until she cries out. She's like a dream in my arms. There's no way I can go into the gallery today. I need the whole day with Cally in my bed.

"I have to make a phone call," I whisper. Releasing one of her hands, I snatch my phone from the bedside table and lift my head enough to dial Maggie.

It rings four times before she picks up. "Hello?" She sounds like I woke her up. Too fucking bad.

"I need you to open the gallery for me today."

Cally's moved her free hand to my back, and she's smiling at me as she traces her fingers down my spine.

"I have plans with Asher," Maggie says.

Cally slips her hand between our bodies and skims the head of my dick with her fingertips. I growl. "Cancel them." I hang up the phone and toss it across the room.

Cally giggles beneath me. "Bossy."

I recapture her straying hand and replace it above her head. "I *am* the boss."

"You're good at it," she murmurs.

"You like being told what to do?"

"Not particularly, but when you do it, it's pretty hot." Her lips quirk and she rubs her bare, slick heat against my cock. She doesn't even need use of her hands to make me lose my fucking mind.

"Dammit, Cally. You're going to kill me."

She repeats the motion, tucking her hips. I'm all but inside her. "Don't make me wait."

"I need to get a condom." I grit my teeth as I shift so my cock isn't so irresistibly close to her wet heat. I've never wanted to be inside a woman without a condom as much as I want to be inside her. I'm already thinking about what it would be like to slide inside of her, skin to skin.

"I have a clean bill of health," she whispers. "Before you, I hadn't had sex for four years. And as for the rest, that's what birth control pills are for."

I still and study her. I'm not worried about pregnancy. Unfortunately, that's not something I ever need to worry about. "Are you sure?"

She sinks her teeth into her lip and nods.

Just as I move to slide into her, she stops me with her hands on my shoulders.

"What is it?" I ask. The idea of being inside her without that barrier is so damn appealing, but I'll stop if she's changed her mind.

"I wanted you to be my first. I wish you had been."

Aw, hell. "That doesn't matter anymore."

She runs her fingertips down my cheek and nods. "What's done is done. I know. But this? I've never had sex with a man without a condom before. I've been diligent. So, this is…a first."

I cup her face in my hands and crush my mouth to hers, hoping she feels every painful and beautiful ounce of my love for her in this moment. "That's amazing," I whisper. Then I slowly sink into her, our eyes locked as our bodies join so intimately. Skin to skin.

Cally

"Stay. There's nothing you need to run from. I've got you. No matter what." William's words haven't left my head since he whispered them in my ear yesterday morning. I'm considering. Maybe I could stay. Maybe this could be my life. My days working across the hall from this man who makes my heart race, my nights in his bed, his hands on my body. Could I really be that lucky? Will he want all that with me once he finds out the truth?

Sickness eats at my stomach at the thought. I should have told him the truth before sleeping with him. I owed him that. But I'm terrified that he won't look at me the same once he knows, and I'm not ready for the end.

"Lots of water," I tell my client. I force myself out of my reverie and offer her a bottle of water. "And no more workouts today. Let your muscles rest."

The woman takes the bottle and slips me a twenty—that tip in addition to the seventy she paid for her massage makes this a great start to the day.

"I'll be back," she promises. "Don't you leave town yet, or I'll have to come to Vegas for my massages."

"I'm considering staying in New Hope permanently," I admit. "I just need to work out some details."

"That would be amazing. You totally should. I'll send a ton of business your way."

"That would be wonderful."

I see her out the back doors and decide to head down to the gallery for a little break between clients.

Maggie is chatting with a young woman in the back, and William isn't around anywhere. I try to squelch my disappointment but I can't help it. I'm becoming accustomed to his face, his laughter, his eyes on me as I walk through the room. But I make myself resist. I'll see him tonight. Surely I can make it a few hours before setting eyes on him again.

"Cally?"

I turn to find the familiar voice. The smile falls from my face.

"I found you." Hazel eyes, broad shoulders, enough silver peeking through his dark mop to make him look distinguished. Brandon McHugh is as handsome as the day he set out to make me his.

My stomach flips and my heart pounds so fast and hard I need to sit down. "Hello, Brandon."

He runs his eyes over me, my ponytail, my mint green medical scrubs, my tennis shoes. "You're working." He's smiling but the disapproval is in his eyes.

"I am." Brandon doesn't care to have his women work. If they work, how can they do his bidding? If they work, they may not rely on him. Not that I ever dared speak these thoughts to him. Four years out from under his control, and I'm only now daring to *think* them.

"God, I've missed you."

"I—" I try to force the lie he wants to hear from my lips. *I missed you too.* That's what he wants to hear—that I love him, that he broke my heart when he started screwing around with Quinn, that I miss him desperately and I need him. But love and heartbreak have nothing to do with the mess happening inside me. It's fear.

I'm not ready for this. I wasn't prepared for my worlds to collide—my world in Vegas creeping in to infect my New Hope world. I don't want it here.

He frowns as he takes my hand. "Why are you shaking?"

To my horror, I realize I'm trembling. *How did you find me?* Not that

I covered my tracks. I didn't think I needed to. He'd only been back in Vegas a month or so before Mom died. I thought he'd get used to the idea that I've moved on. I thought *he* had already moved on. Had I really been so foolish? "What are you doing here?"

His eyes crinkle in the corner as he gives his bashful smile. "I came for you."

wish i may

chapter eighteen

William

CALLY IS on the showroom floor talking to a man who reeks of money. I watch from the loft, jealousy tearing through me, which is absurd because she's not doing anything inappropriate. Hell, she's still dressed in her massage scrubs. He could be a client for all I know. But there's something almost proprietary about the way he positions his body by hers, the way he's touching her hand.

After what happened this morning, I told myself I was going to give her some space today. I'm too damn tempted to touch her when we're together, too damn tempted to beg her to stay in my house after the girls leave, to stay in New Hope indefinitely. To stay with me. She needs time to come to those decisions on her own. She doesn't need me pressuring her.

Even before I realize what I'm doing, I'm headed down the stairs toward Cally, determined to put some space between her and this stranger.

"Good afternoon." I offer my hand. "I'm William Bailey, the gallery owner and manager. Can I help you?"

The moment the man turns to face me fully, the force of recognition slams into me so hard, I stumble back a step. He carefully releases Cally's hand and takes mine, his grip confident and strong. "Brandon McHugh."

"It's nice to meet you, Brandon," I manage, but I can feel my jaw hardening. I know that face, those eyes. Could it really be? It may have been seven years ago, but I'll never forget seeing those hands on my girl. It's him. And now he's here. "Is there anything I can help you with today? I'm sure Cally needs to get back to get clients upstairs."

"Is it going well?" Brandon asks, that proprietary hand returning to her shoulder.

"Yes," Cally says quickly. "Very well." Then, to me, "Brandon is visiting from Las Vegas. He was just—"

"Just looking for some new artwork for my New York apartment," he finishes for her.

They exchange a look, and I wonder what their relationship was. I never let Cally know I came to Vegas that summer. When I saw her with Brandon, his hand on her thigh under the table, I assumed they were together, despite how inappropriate—not to mention illegal—such an age match would have been. Was I right? Were they a couple? Her sixteen to his thirty-something? And what are they to each other now?

"Let me show you some of my favorite pieces," I offer.

"I do need to go," Cally tells Brandon. Her voice is softer, almost hesitant. She doesn't sound like herself. "We'll talk later."

"I'd like that." He runs his eyes over her until my fists are almost ready to fly at his face of their own volition. "I'd like that a lot."

Cally scurries upstairs, and I do my best to hide my jealousy and a long-held resentment he wouldn't understand. I won't give in to my caveman need to drive my fist through his face. Not until I have a reason. Instead, I usher the man toward the most expensive pieces in the gallery.

Because I'm a spiteful dick, I suggest that he probably can't afford the gorgeous glass mosaic bowl that Maggie priced at fourteen hundred dollars as a joke. And because this is obviously some sort of pissing contest to him, he buys it *and* an overpriced watercolor of the moonlight reflecting off the New Hope River. I ring him up with a smile and don't bat a lash when he pays with cash.

Only when he's gone do I feel like I can breathe again. But I'm plagued by questions about his visit and his relationship with Cally. This morning Cally suggested she may stay in town. Will his appearance here change that?

Cally

"You came." He opens the door to his hotel room and runs his eyes over me as I step in.

The black dress and tall heels I purchased for this meeting cost me everything I made this week and more, but I didn't dare show up in an outfit that would displease him. Brandon believes my appearance is for his pleasure alone, and he expects me to dress accordingly. When he finishes his visual tour and returns his eyes to mine, I know he approves. First hurdle, crossed.

I don't bother asking how he can afford the swanky downtown Indy hotel. I'm sure he had cash reserves hidden somewhere. Besides, the question would insult him. Brandon will tolerate only the best; therefore, he's in the top floor Presidential suite. He used to take me to hotels like this all over the country when he was traveling on business. He claimed to be an international jeweler. Though his business was certainly international in scope, it wasn't the jewels the Feds were worried about when they caught up with him four years ago.

"Champagne?" he asks, but his servant hands me a glass before I can answer.

I haven't stopped shaking all day. I never imagined he'd bother to come after me. I'm twenty-three now, after all, which might as well be fifty for all Brandon's concerned. Even before he was caught and thrown in prison, he was starting to get bored with me, starting to find younger girls to fulfill his desires.

I used his incarceration as an opportunity to get away from him. The feds froze all his assets, so it wasn't like I could have kept living the high life if I'd wanted to. So I found the apartment with my stoner roommates and hawked most of the jewelry and designer clothes Brandon had given me over the years. When I found out another girl had been visiting him at the prison, I had the perfect excuse to pull away. Not that I was jealous, but being a little too clingy and pretending I was hurt worked. Brandon likes the chase too much to tolerate a clingy woman. I had to work him like that. One doesn't just *leave* Brandon McHugh.

When he was released from prison and I told him I'd moved on, he took it so well. I thought he'd let me go. But he never would have showed up in New Hope if he had any intention of letting me live my life without him.

I should have known better.

I settle into the couch across from him, trying to calm my shaking hands. I need to convince him to go back to Vegas and let me finish my business in New Hope, but I have to be careful I don't piss him off.

Thinking to take a sip for courage, I put my lips to the glass then think better of it. Brandon isn't above slipping drugs in my drink to get his way. I settle my champagne on the glass-topped coffee table that sits between us.

"You're working too hard," he says, narrowing his eyes as he looks at my face. "You need more sleep. Those bags under your eyes don't do you justice."

"Maybe I'm just not as young as I used to be." I stick out my lip in a pout, as if I'm desperate for his reassurance.

"You're still beautiful, but you're tired. You can't hide that from me, sweetheart."

I shrug. *Hard work* was always a dirty word to him—especially when it came to me. He wouldn't even let me finish high school. I change the subject. "What made you decide to come?"

"You know I don't like to wait for what's mine."

A chill steals through me at that old, determined tone of a man who gets what he wants. "You took me by surprise." I force a smile and lean forward. "A nice surprise."

"Our flight leaves tomorrow," he says. "That should give you enough time to pack your things."

I'm not going with you. It's not lack of courage but presence of mind that keeps me from speaking the words. Instead, I say, "You're really going to tease me with that when I already promised the girls I'd stay until after Christmas?"

"So break your promise. I'll fly you back here with so many presents for the little rugrats that they'll be glad to send you back to me and wait for more." He comes to sit next to me and takes my face in his hands. "I need you more than they do."

When his lips touch mine, I don't try to move away. I put my hand on his sculpted shoulder and let him kiss me. When his tongue brushes my lips, I open to him, knowing the invasion will cost me far less than the consequences of denying him.

When he pulls away his eyes are smoky and he's breathing heavily. "I'd missed those lips. Four years is too long."

"It didn't seem to bother you when you were with Quinn," I pout. I hate playing this game, but I don't have a choice.

He cups my face in his big hand. "Forget her. I'm here for you now."

"Give me more time," I whisper, stroking my thumb down the side of his face. "Please, Brandon?" Before he was arrested and sentenced, I'd gotten so good at manipulating him. His obsession with me was his weakness. But I got cocky. I never should have believed he would let me be.

"Stay with me tonight," he growls. "It's been too long since I fucked that hot little body."

I lean forward and touch my lips to his, then, carefully, I reposition myself so I'm straddling him, and he's leaning back. My body wants to recoil from his kiss, but I push forward. Only when he's pulled the skirt of my dress to my waist and his hands are reaching for his belt do I pull away.

"Could I ask you for something?" I whisper.

"Of course."

"Would you book a room at that hotel where we were together for the first time? You remember? With the view of the mountains? I want our first time being together again to be special."

His hands still. "It will be."

Sinking my teeth into my bottom lip, I cut my eyes away from his. "Yes, but I'm on my...my monthly," I lie.

He growls and pushes me off his lap. "Why'd you go and get me all worked up then?"

Righting myself on the cushion next to him, I bow my head and look at him through my lashes. "I guess I was too anxious to touch you again. Not so long ago, I thought we were over."

His fingers grab my wrist and wrap tight. "We will never be *over*. You can't get rid of me."

"You left me for four years," I say, trying for a pout. "And then there was Quinn. I thought you wanted *her* now."

He yanks me forward and the skin under his fingers burns. "How can I prove myself to you? She was a passing fancy. You are the only one I ever wanted as a permanent fixture in my life."

Fixture. What an appropriate word choice. "Give me two months with the girls. Then I'll be home and everything can go back to the way it was before." I place my hand over the one he has wrapped painfully around my wrist. "You can stay with me." The offer is a gamble, but one that I must take.

"I can't stay," he growls, and there's something like anger in his eyes. "Damn parole officer doesn't want me leaving Nevada at all. I have to get back before he realizes I've gone."

"We'll make up for lost time when I get home," I promise.

"Stay my good girl. I'd hate to have to replace you."

I couldn't be so lucky.

He insists I let his driver take me back to New Hope, and I have him drop me off at Dad's because I can't risk Brandon finding out I'm staying with William.

I have two months of borrowed time. But I won't be heading back to Vegas when it's over. I *won't* go back to Brandon. But I can't be here when he comes back for me either. If I don't want to be forced back into a life with him, I'll have to hide.

chapter nineteen

William

IT'S NEARLY midnight when Cally walks in my door. The girls knew she'd be late and had dinner with their dad. Drew took care of all the necessary bedtime rituals with Gabby. But I didn't get the memo, and I sat in my dark living room, watching the front door, willing her to come through it. I'm foolishly hoping she spent the evening with Lizzy and Hanna, but I know better.

She's in a high heels and short black dress that shows off her long legs. Oblivious to my presence, she goes straight to the kitchen.

I catch her at the sink, splashing water on her face, and I spin her around and slide my hands into her hair, pressing my mouth to hers. She lets out a little squeak and lifts her hands to my chest as she opens her mouth under mine.

Her kiss is so sweet, so full of something that feels like love.

My hands go to her ass, and I pull her hard and fast against my body, needing to feel her close to me. When that's not good enough for this raging need inside me, I draw her skirt up around her waist and lift her onto the counter. She spreads her legs and tugs me forward by my shirt. I break the kiss to trail my mouth to her neck. A sexy moan of protest slips from her lips as her hands slide into my hair.

Closer, something primal demands. I nearly forget everything but our bodies. Everything except this roaring need to own. To claim. To *keep.* Because that's what's there at the root of this desire—my fear that she's going to leave me again.

I try to catch my breath and slow this down. Tracing her lips with my thumb, I skim my hand down the side of her neck before tangling it in her hair.

She tilts her head to the side to give me better access to her neck. I kiss and nip there as I find her zipper and peel the dress from her shoulders. I go to work on her bra, releasing it at the back and throwing it across the kitchen.

Her breasts are full, her nipples already hard. I take one into my hand and tease her nipple. With my other hand, I trace down the column of her spine and dip into the waistband of her panties.

She's panting in my ear and tugging on my hair to pull me closer. Moaning, she wraps her legs around me. The stiletto points of her heels dig into my back.

"Be mine, Cally. You belong to me."

She cools in my arms and presses me away. "What did you say?"

"I need to know you're mine. The asshole in the gallery. He's here for you. I can tell."

Her whole body stiffens. "How did you know?"

"Aside from the fact that he was two seconds away from whipping it out and pissing on you to mark his territory?" I take her thumb between my teeth and bite gently before releasing it. Then I place my mouth to her earlobe and treat it to a similar torture until she's pressing into me again. "You were with him tonight, weren't you?"

"Let's not do this, William," she whispers. "Not now."

She doesn't deny it and that tears me apart, but I need her too much. "Forget about the past. Forget about the future. You're here now, and what's happening between us is inevitable. You're *mine.*" I roll her nipple between my fingers and pinch until she cries softly, rocking her hips into me. "Say you're mine."

"No," she says in a harsh whisper. She shoves away my hands. "I'm not."

I stagger back. "I'm supposed to believe you belong to him? After last night?"

The sadness in her eyes makes a vice around my heart. "I'm not anyone's. I'm a human being, not a possession." She tugs off her heels and hops off the counter. Pulling her dress back up, she grabs her bra off the floor and is headed to the stairs when I stop her.

"Cally?"

She hangs her head but keeps her back to me. "I'm sorry I can't tell you what you want to hear."

William
Seven Years Ago

The Indianapolis Airport is buzzing with late Saturday morning traffic, and I wait for Cally at baggage claim, pacing, too nervous to sit.

Her plane from Las Vegas arrived twenty minutes ago, and I haven't seen her yet, but I refuse to assume the worst.

I rented a little cabin for after prom, and I already have it set up with rose petals, candles, and strawberry wine. We're going to be together tonight. For the first time.

But it's not the sex I'm looking forward to the most. It's having her in my arms again, smelling her hair, reassuring myself that I haven't lost her.

The people around me reunite with their loved ones and I try to shake this sense of impending disappointment. A mom drops her bag as she sinks to her knees and gathers a little girl in her arms. A young woman with bright eyes wraps her arms around her pierced and tatted boyfriend. I scoot back to get out of the way, scanning the crowd for her face.

The traffic around the baggage carousel clears, person by person. My heart turns stony in my chest and sinks to my gut as I watch the shiny conveyor belt turn.

All the bags are gone. Cally is nowhere to be seen.

My hands are unsteady as I pull my cell phone from my pocket and punch in her number. It rings once and goes to voicemail.

I try again. This time it goes straight to voicemail.

I'm ready to dial again when her text comes through: *Something came up. I'm sorry I can't come.*

I sink onto a bench and cradle my head in my hands. It's over. I ignored the signs because I didn't want to believe it, but I can't deny it anymore. I've lost her.

How am I supposed to let her go when she still has ahold of my heart?

Cally
Present Day

"Just imagine we're on one of those renovation shows Mom used to like watching so much."

"Does that mean the sexy hosts are going to show up?" Drew asks, stumbling forward on the riverside trail. She still hasn't completely opened her eyes, but I woke up early after a night of anxiety and little sleep, and I didn't have the patience to let her sleep in this morning. "I'm going to need some decent scenery if I'm going to be working this early on a Saturday."

"No sexy hosts, but the exterminator also promised no rats, so it's a trade-off."

It's a gorgeous morning, and I'm determined not to let last night's falling out with William ruin my day. It had to happen eventually. Better sooner than later.

As I tossed and turned last night, I realized how much I need to do before I leave New Hope. First, I need to prepare the girls for life without me. I've been taking everything on myself for too long. They're old enough to scrub walls and push a vacuum, and it's time I made them pull their weight. After all, the cabin is going to be their house, and I won't be here to take care of it. I probably won't even be able to risk coming back to check in.

I can't think about that too much.

"I better get to pick the paint color for our bedroom," Drew grumbles.

"I want to knock down a wall," Gabby says.

"No knocking down walls. I'm afraid the house would fall down."

We turn off the trail and into the woods toward Dad's.

"Who's here?" Drew asks.

I follow the direction of her gaze and my steps stutter. Dad's driveway is filled with cars, and from here I can see William and two guys I only vaguely recognize. As we get closer, I see Hanna and Lizzy leaning against Lizzy's Charger, and behind them—

Drew squeezes my arm and stops cold. "Oh. My. God."

I see him the same moment she does. Asher Logan is climbing into the back of a big black pickup, handing supplies to the guys.

Drew looks like she might vomit.

I bite my lip to keep from laughing at her. "What were you saying about needing decent scenery?"

"He's beautiful," Gabby whispers.

I roll my eyes. "Seriously? You too?" But then I realize she's not looking at Asher. She's looking at one of Will's friends, the tall, dark-haired guy with broad shoulders and wicked smile. The one Hanna likes. Max. "Come on, girls," I say, heading into the fray. "First rule is to never let them see you drool."

"Surprise!" Lizzy calls when she sees us approaching.

I prop my hands on my hips. "Are we having a party here that no one told me about?"

"A renovation party!" Lizzy says, hopping up and down so her curls bounce.

Drew grimaces next to me. "No one should be that perky before nine a.m."

My eyes connect with William's. I know without asking that he's responsible for this. He just winks at me as if last night in the kitchen never happened. *Too. Damn. Good.*

"You didn't have to come."

The guys shrug, and Max says, "We owe Will. Anyway, we're happy to help."

"Okay, everyone," Will announces. "The Dumpster will be here any minute. Let's start with the carpet and the linoleum in the kitchen. Once we get all that out, we'll tackle the walls and be ready for the new flooring by this afternoon."

"New flooring?" I whisper. Everyone's already headed toward the house and I'm standing here, blinking at Will like an idiot.

"New flooring," he says carefully, his eyes on me. "A couple of appliances."

I don't even have words. I know I should feel…something. Anything other than this crazy out-of-body confusion, like I've been dropped into someone else's life. "But…how?"

"Hey, Bailey!" Max calls from the front porch. "Where do you want the furniture?"

"Coming!" He winks at me and then disappears into the house.

A couple of hours later, the old carpet and linoleum are gone, Sam and Asher are patching the bad spots on the roof, and Max and William have started working on the rotted planks on the deck, pulling off the bad ones and replacing them with new. The sun is high in the sky and cutting through the trees, turning the autumn day hot. William peels off his shirt and tosses it aside, giving me a hell of a view as I try to tape the windows for painting.

Next to me, Drew clears her throat and nudges me in the side with her elbow. "The first rule is to never let them see you drool."

By lunch, I don't know whether to tell William off or kiss his feet. First, the truck arrived with the flooring, then another truck brought a new stove and refrigerator, and a third brought new living room furniture and loft beds for the girls and desks that go under each.

It's too much, and if it were all for me, I wouldn't accept it. If it were all for me, I'd be angry. But Gabby and Drew are practically bouncing with excitement, and instead of being angry I'm just…grateful. I'm grateful William could do this for them. I'm grateful that, for once, it's not all on my shoulders. But even so, there's something unsettling about the grand gesture. Something that doesn't sit right.

"How much do you hate me right now?" William asks behind me.

I turn slowly. He's a sweaty mess from tearing up the carpet, and he looks a little unsure as he studies me, but I've never been so attracted to someone in my life.

I grab his hand and pull him around the side of the house, where we can talk without curious eyes watching us. "Thank you for arranging this."

He shifts his hand under mine and entwines our fingers. "You're welcome."

I force myself to ask the question that's been needling me more and more with every gift he's given. "You know this doesn't change things between us, right?"

The smile falls from his face. "What do you mean?"

"You can't buy me, William. I appreciate everything you've done for us, but I'm not for sale."

"I didn't think you were." His hard jaw starts to tick. He runs a hand through his curls and looks up at the trees as it trying for patience, but his eyes burn with anger when they turn back to me. "Is that why you think I did this? Is that why you think I'm giving you a deal for your studio, why you think I let you and your sisters stay with me? You think I'm trying to *buy* you? What the fuck kind of asshole do you think I am?"

"No! Of course I—" But I can't deny it when that's exactly what I just accused him of. That's exactly what I'm afraid of.

"Last night you accused me of treating you like possession, but I have *never* thought of you that way. A possession is something you own, something you control." He tugs me close until my body is pressed against his and his mouth is brushing my ear. "I don't want to control you. I want you to be mine. Don't you see the difference?"

My heart pounds in my chest, stumbling painfully as if it's trying to race away from this conversation. "There is no difference for a lot of guys." *There was no difference for Brandon.*

"I want your heart. I have no interest in buying it or controlling it. I want you to give it to me freely. Because you already own mine. You always have. You always will."

"And my body?" I can't help myself. I have to ask. "For some men, being *his* means wearing the clothes he picks out, expressing the opinions he wants me to hold, and letting him fuck me the way he wants to fuck me."

One hand drops to my waist, lower, and he draws my body close to his, fingers squeezing my hip. "I don't want to dress you. If you're in a sexy skirt or in those scrubs your wear for work, all I want is to *un*dress you. And I don't want to own your mind, I want to explore it." His mouth brushes my ear as he speaks. Arousal shoots like an electric pulse down my spine. "But I *do* want you to let me fuck you the way I want to fuck you. But only because I'm yours as much as you are mine, and every time I touch you, I feel like I've been put on this Earth to make you come."

His mouth opens over mine. I'm clinging to him, my nails biting into his shoulders, my legs unsteady beneath me. He backs me up until has me against the side of the house, and I suddenly wish everyone else was gone, so I could take him up on the promise in his eyes.

"You're mine, Cally," he whispers. "I don't give two fucks if that sounds too caveman or possessive for you, because when it comes to you, I am."

chapter twenty

William

TODAY HAS been shit. Because I want Cally so much it hurts. Because despite our little conversation outside her dad's house yesterday, she avoided me after the girls were in bed last night. Because even angry with her, I'm happier than I've been in years.

But mostly my day has been shit because I know Cally and her sisters are moving back home tonight, and even though I'm going to see her at the gallery most days, letting Cally go in any form goes against every instinct I have.

When I get home from work and walk in my door, my nose is assaulted by garlic and basil. I don't make it more than a few steps before Drew appears in a white dress shirt and black pants, a linen napkin draped over her arm. "Your table is this way, sir," she says, motioning toward the dining room.

"What's going on, Drew?" I walk into the dining room, and Gabby, dressed just like her sister, pulls out a chair for me to sit.

The table is set for two with taper candles burning in the center and flickering shadows on the walls. Bowls of spaghetti, salad, and garlic bread wait, and a wine bottle sits on ice in a stainless steel bucket. I pick it up to see they've chosen strawberry wine.

"Did Cally do this?"

Drew grins and shakes her head. "Nope. She's not home yet." She slides her phone from her pocket and looks at the time. "She'll be here any minute."

"Does she know?"

"It's a surprise." Gabby grins. "To thank you for letting us stay."

Tenderness toward both of these girls tugs in my chest. "The strawberry wine?" Out of all the wines in the rack, I'm curious how they knew to choose this one for me and Cally.

"It's Cally's favorite," Drew says with a shrug. "She doesn't drink often, but when she does, this is what she likes."

Damn. I swallow. "Thanks."

The front door opens. "Drew?" Cally calls. "Gabby?"

Drew scurries to greet her, and Gabby just grins at me.

"This way," Drew says, ushering Cally into the dining room. "Your dinner awaits."

Cally's jaw drops and her eyes go wide as she looks at the table and then me. "Did you do this?"

I shake my head. "Your sisters were the masterminds behind this evening."

Gabby pulls out the chair opposite mine. "Please, have a seat."

Cally obeys and watches in mute fascination as the girls fill our plates with food and our glasses with wine.

"Enjoy," Drew says, placing a silver bell on the table. "And please ring this if you need anything. We'll be in the family room with our movie."

"Unless you call us, you'll have *plenty* of privacy," Gabby says with a nod.

With that, both girls leave the room.

Cally runs her finger over the condensation on her wine glass. "Strawberry wine," she says with a baffled shake of her head.

"Drew said it's your favorite."

She smiles at me and takes a sip. "She's right."

"Not much changes."

She stiffens. "Everything changes."

I don't want to argue. Not tonight. So I change the subject. "Are the girls looking forward to sleeping in their new beds?"

"They are, and Dad's ready to have them back. He misses them. I think they miss him too. He's planned this big trip to the Indianapolis Children's Museum, and Drew isn't even complaining about it." She smiles. "Did I tell you Dad got another job?"

"Really? That's great."

"Apparently his obsession with everything spiritual is finally paying off. He got a guest-lecturing gig up at The Center. It doesn't pay a ton, but it will help a lot until he can get adjunct work at the college next semester. That plus the part-time research gig and I'm finally feeling semi-confident in his ability to support the girls."

Her phone rings and she slips it from her pocket and looks at the screen. Something flashes across her face. Worry? Anxiety? "Do you mind if I take this?"

"Go ahead."

She steps into the hall to take the call, but I can still hear her side of the conversation.

"Hello?… I'm glad.… I miss you too.… I know.… No, I can't talk about this right now. I'm in a meeting.… I promise.… You too."

She avoids my eyes when she slips back into her seat.

"Brandon?" I ask.

She stops her fork halfway to her mouth and lowers it before speaking. "Yes."

I won't bother pretending I wasn't eavesdropping. "You miss him."

"It's…complicated." She shakes her head. "How do you know about us anyway? What did he tell you when he was at the gallery?"

I take a long drink of my wine before answering. She has no idea I came to Vegas looking for her after she dumped me. "He's the one you left me for," I say carefully.

Her brow furrows. "I didn't leave you for another man. I— Wait. Why would you even think that? What did he tell you?"

"I came to Vegas seven years ago. That summer? I came and I tracked you down and your neighbor told me you were at some fancy restaurant, so I took a cab and sure enough…there you were. You were in this fancy dress drinking wine and sitting with this rich older guy. It was Brandon."

"You came to Vegas?"

"My girlfriend fell off the face of the earth," I say softly. "I wasn't okay at letting that text message be the last words between us."

"I had no idea you came."

"Brandon was the one you were talking about yesterday. The one who told you how to dress, what to think—" I lower my voice. "—how to fuck."

She pushes her food around her plate and avoids my eyes.

"Everything changed after he showed up."

"Brandon's visit was just a reminder that my life isn't as simple at it was when I lived here as a teenager."

"You don't have to be with someone like that. You deserve better."

"Please. Let's not do this?"

I take a breath and make myself ask the question I've been pushing from my mind. "Do you still love him?"

She lifts her head and her eyes connect with mine. "If I did, would you still insist I be *yours*?"

"No." My chest aches and I can't understand her question in the context of the desperation that's written all over her face. "If you loved him, if he was the one you wanted…." I swallow. "I want you to be mine. I'm won't lie about that. But you can't belong to someone you don't give yourself to."

Her jaw goes slack and her eyes soften. "It says a lot that you believe that, William Bailey."

We take our meal in silence for the next few minutes, though in truth neither of us is eating much. When I can't stand it anymore, I reach across the table and take her fingers in my hand, squeezing. We finish our meal and take the dishes to the kitchen before finding the girls in the family room.

"So are you madly in love and going to have babies yet?" Drew asks from the couch, her tone bored.

Cally picks up a pillow and knocks Drew softly on the head with it. "Twerp. Get your things. We need to get going."

Someone honks out front and Drew and Gabby jump to their feet and grab their bags. "That's Dad!" Drew calls, running toward the front door. "You two behave."

Then the slam of the front door echoes through the house, and we're alone.

"I shouldn't stay," she whispers, looking at her shoes.

"Just for a drink," I promise. There's too much we've left unsaid tonight. "I hate to see a fine bottle of screw-top wine go to waste."

"I guess you know my weaknesses. Meet me on the patio?"

I grab the wine and head out to find Cally looking at the stars.

"I should have known you'd be looking at your stars."

She gives me a sad smile. "It's really beautiful. I guess I'd missed it more than I realized."

"You still wishing on stars?" I settle into the chair beside her and hand her a glass of wine.

"Thanks." She takes the glass but doesn't drink. "Not in a long time."

"Why not?"

"Kid stuff, I guess."

"That doesn't sound like the Cally I used to know."

She eyes me wearily. "I'm *not* the Cally you used to know."

My jaw tightens. "You're not the only one who's changed. You're not the only one who's had to make shit decisions."

"Says the man who just up and bought us a house of new furniture." She crosses her arms then shakes her head, looking away.

I'm instantly pissed. "Money doesn't make everything easy. I know you always thought it did, but you have no idea what it was like to grow up without my parents, no idea how much I would trade to have known what it was like to have them there."

"But it helps," she says softly. "Having money means you didn't have to make as many 'shit decisions' as I did. And my parents? They might have been alive, but—" She shoots up out of her chair. "Dammit, I don't want to do this."

I catch up to her at the French doors and press my hand against the glass before she can open them. Frustration ticks in my jaw. Fear of losing her churns my stomach. I'm sick of everything being left unsaid between us and too scared of the answers to demand the truth. "You don't want to do *what*?"

She turns to face me, leaving her body between me and the door, my hands blocking her in on either side. "I don't want to play the *who-had-the-worst-childhood* game."

"That's not what I was doing. You just shut me down every time the past comes up, like I'm incapable of understanding what your life was like after you left."

She scoffs. "Like you're an open book about yours?"

"Try me."

"You and Maggie were together." It's not a question.

"Briefly." I don't want to go there. Not with Cally. But if this is the conversation she needs to have in order to open up to me, so be it.

"She still cares about you. She's worried I'm going to hurt you. Again."

"I'm a big boy. I don't need Maggie looking out for me."

"But she does." Her hand slowly rises to touch my face, and I stay perfectly still, resisting the urge to turn a kiss into her palm. Resisting the urge to kiss her until we have both forgotten this conversation and are thinking only of each other's bodies. "And then you married her sister Krystal."

She caught up fast. But what do I expect? This is New Hope. There are no secrets here. If anything, I should be surprised she had to come all the way back to New Hope for the grapevine to deliver the news. "Krystal and I were never officially married." Not that we didn't get way too fucking close for comfort. Stupid on my part. "It seemed like the right decision at the time, but it didn't work out, and that was for the best."

"But they're all so protective of you. You're not the bad guy to them."

"I screwed up. They've forgiven me."

Her eyes dip to my mouth before lifting to connect with mine. "Which part was the screw up?"

I ball my hands into fists, resisting the urge to touch her. "All of it. Both of them."

"Yeah, you're an open book, alright."

"Jesus? Is that what you want? You want to know where I fucked up? You'll show me yours if I show you mine? Is that it? What are you so desperate to hide from me?"

"We *all* have parts of ourselves we don't want anyone to see."

I drag a hand through my hair and turn away from her. Because she's right. And I can't look her in the eyes while I confess my life's biggest failure. "After I went to college, Maggie…she needed me."

"The poor little rich girl needed you? I'm sure she did."

"It's not mine to tell, Cally, but I can tell you *I* fucked up. She came to me, she needed help, and I put her back on a bus and sent her home."

"You weren't responsible for her. A college student, you were barely more than a kid yourself."

And I was hung up on a girl who dumped me for a rich asshole at least fifteen years older than me. I hang my head. "It doesn't matter. She was terrified, and I sent her right back into the fray."

"What fray?" She shakes her head. "I don't understand what could have been so bad. The maid didn't clean her room well enough? Not enough boys falling at her feet?"

She's trying to pick a fight, but I won't take the bait. "Exactly. You don't understand. You aren't the only one who's had to make shit decisions, and neither am I. When I realized what I'd inadvertently done, I couldn't forgive myself. I was obsessed with protecting her, and when I came back home from grad school, that obsession turned into something else."

"You fell in love with her."

I shrug. "I loved her. That doesn't mean it was a healthy love."

"Then Krystal?"

"Krystal picked up the pieces when Maggie left me. She loved me and she wanted all the same things I wanted. She made me forget that I'd lost Maggie."

"And Krystal? Did you love her?"

"Of course I did. I wouldn't have put a ring on her finger if I didn't."

"But Maggie had just left you. You poor thing, so broken-hearted you only needed two-point-five seconds to fall for her sister. Was it that easy for you to get over me too?" I turn, and she's thrown her hand over her mouth. Regret pulling at her features. "I shouldn't have said that."

"Because you already know the answer."

"I'm not so different than Maggie," she whispers. "You always wanted to save me. To fix me and my broken family. Hell, look at us now. You're just coming to the rescue again."

"I can help and I want to. What's *wrong* with that?"

"I want more."

She can have more. She can have anything. Everything. "Then it's yours."

She tilts her chin, looking up at her stars again. "I don't want to be rescued. Been there. Done that. Lived with the self-loathing."

"Tell me what you want."

"I want a man who's just as saved by my love as I am by his." She lifts her shoulders. "Someday. But I don't *need* it. All I need now is to help my sisters and get by."

"I'm sick of you dancing around your past."

I don't really expect her to reveal anything, so I'm surprised when she speaks. "Mom's love affair with Vicodin became an obsession. She was too stoned to even give twenty-dollar hand jobs anymore."

I flinch. "Cally…."

"We got food stamps, but she'd sell them for drugs. A hundred dollars that was supposed to buy my sisters and me dinner became a handful of precious pills for her." Her eyes fill and she looks away from me. "Within a month of moving to Vegas, I got a job, two jobs, but it was never enough. And then I'd talk to you, and you were planning for college and picking out the car your grandmother was going to buy you for a graduation gift. You lived in a completely different universe than me, and I couldn't handle it."

I take her shoulders and turn her to look at me. "I wish you would have told me. I could have helped. I could have—"

"What?" She laughs. A cold, hollow sound that doesn't hold an ounce of humor. She pushes at my chest, and I back up and drop my arms. "What would you have been able to do? Send money? And then keep sending money? An eighteen-year-old boy responsible for supporting a family of four? Mom would have had your trust fund cleaned out before you even finished college."

"I don't care about the fucking money. I would have given it all up for you."

"I loved you," she whispers. "I loved you enough to let you go. That's the truth. Someday soon I'll have to do it again, and it will still be the truth, even if you can't accept it."

I wrap my arms around her and crush her against me, holding on too tight because I'm terrified of what will happen if I let go. "Don't. I need you to believe again. I need you to be brave. You hold on to me, and I'll hold on to you."

She clings to me, her hands wrapped around my biceps as she lifts to her toes and presses her mouth to mine. I hold her tight, pouring everything I feel into the kiss until all the tension has drained out of her body. "I can't stay," she murmurs. "This is only for now. It can't be forever. Please don't ask me for something I can't give."

I don't answer, don't let myself think about what she's leaving me for—or whom. I scoop her off her feet and carry her to my bed. I undress her slowly, exploring her body with hands and mouth. When I slide into her, she clings to me, cries her pleasure into my neck. I make her come again and again, taking everything she offers from her body since she won't give me her heart.

chapter twenty-one

Cally

IN THE last month, the leaves have turned, days have cooled, and I feel like we're racing toward the end of my time in New Hope. Every day I stay is another day I'm risking Brandon returning. He promised me two months, but the promise of a selfish man means nothing, and I would be smart to leave now.

Life has been deceptively good since the girls and I moved back into Dad's. William and I go to football games and cheer on his alma mater, and then he takes me back to his house and makes love to me. I insist our affair is temporary, but I can tell he thinks he can change my mind.

Dad has settled into his role as primary care provider for the girls, and though money hasn't been easy, there's been enough that I've been able to put some back for my new life. Thanksgiving is just around the corner, and this morning William told me he wants us to host a dinner for our friends and families at his house. I need to disappear before Thanksgiving, so his plans only fill me with despair. He misunderstood my reaction and teased me about my lack of cooking skills until we were both laughing away my fears. Then he spent the rest of the morning making love to me.

Each day, I find myself counting down the minutes of my workday, anxious to get home to William, to savor these last days together. Today is no different.

But first I have to finish with this client. This is the third time in as many weeks that Carl York has been in for a massage. Normally that wouldn't bother me. The fact that he's mentioned his wife leaving him and how lonely he is *at least ten times* leaves me a little uneasy. But I shrug off the feeling.

"That's our hour." I reposition the sheets to cover his chest. "Take your time, and I'll meet you in the waiting area."

He moans. "When's your next client? I'd like to add thirty minutes."

"Okay." This is something I usually don't allow unless the client makes arrangements before we start, but I'm available, and as much as I need the money, it's foolish to say no. "I could do another thirty. Is there an area you want me to focus on?"

Before I realize he's grabbed my hand, he's pressing it onto his hard-on over the sheet. "Right there, baby."

I slam my fist down on his dick, then twist around to bend his to the back of his hand. "*Bitch!*" he cries.

I release him and step back, queasiness churning my belly. "We're done, Mr. York. But if you ever try anything like that again, I'll be doing some deep tissue work on your balls. Understood?"

He rolls to his side and draws his knees up to his stomach, moaning. Fucking asshole deserves it. I'll go back to living on peanut butter sandwiches and invite rats to be my roomies before I work with a guy who treats me like that.

I turn to leave but when I reach the door, his words stop me. "Don't act so fucking righteous. I know who you are. I checked up on you. You want to act like you're better than your mama, but I know the truth."

When I leave the room, I'm shaking. I don't want to be here when Carl leaves, so I exit the apartment and go out into the gallery's loft reception area. Maggie shoots me a worried look from the couch where she's tapping away at her laptop. "Are you okay?"

I force a smile. "Yeah. Everything is fine. I just—"

I run to the sink and vomit, heaving and heaving until my stomach is wrung dry and my mouth tastes like bile.

"Yeah, you're downright peachy," Maggie mutters. I hear her getting up, but I don't look. I need to compose myself. I've been practicing massage professionally for almost four years, and I've never had anyone try anything like that. But none of my clients knew about my past. None of them knew I once sold myself to keep my sisters off the street.

I rinse out my mouth and clean out the sink, but even then I leave the water running. The sound gives me the illusion of privacy I need right now.

When I finally turn it off and turn around, Maggie's leaning against the wall, her arms crossed. "Carl York? Seriously, you let that piece of shit on your massage table?"

I plaster on a smile. "Made a good impression on you too, did he? Is he still here?"

"He's gone and not very happy with you. What happened?"

"He wanted me to jack him off. Pushed my fucking hand onto his hard-on."

Maggie's breath leaves her in a rush. "That's assault, Cally. You need to call the cops, file charges."

I shake my head. "That's the last thing my business needs. I can't take that sort of hit." Not now. Not when I'm stockpiling as much cash as I can so I can start a new life.

"It's exactly what your business needs. File charges when some asshole pulls that shit. That sends a message loud and clear about what kind of business you run. You have to make sure people know that's not what you're about."

"And why is that?" I lift my chin and feel all the anger that's been simmering inside me for the last fifteen minutes rise up. "Does the spa by campus have to make sure their clients know they aren't there to give 'happy endings'? Why am I any different?"

"Don't be like that."

"I want to know. Why is it different for me? Because I'm poor, so my massage practice is really just a front for my real specialty of giving hand jobs? Is that what people think? Or maybe they think that because my mom felt like it was what *she* had to do, I'll feel the same way?"

Her eyes go sad. "Just because what people think about you isn't fair doesn't mean they won't think it. Trust me. I know."

"What do you know?" I laugh, and it sounds so empty, so miserable. "You're a *Thompson*. You have money and influence. Everyone in this town loves you guys."

Her face changes and the sympathy in her eyes is replaced with something else. Something harder. "Nobody cared that I was a Thompson when they found out the sheriff was fucking me. I was fifteen, and he was cheating on his wife. With me. The fact that I said *no* was just a technicality to people around here. He left town, and some people saw what he did for what it was—a man with power over me, a much older man, using that power to fulfill his own sick desires. Some people got that. They got that I was a victim. They got that even when you have a crush on your dad's best friend and wear tight shirts around him, *no* still means *no*." She shrugs. "But others? Others *never* got that. You weren't here to see a good portion of this town turn against me because of the sins of a grown man, but it happened, and don't you dare tell me that I don't *get it* just because my family has money."

My throat is thick with shame and embarrassment. Not only am I being as judgmental as everyone else, I should have known better. This was what William was talking about when he said he failed Maggie. This is the part he wasn't telling me. "Jesus, Maggie. I had no idea."

Her shoulders rise on a long inhale and her expression softens. "It's better now, but I had to stop allowing them define who I am. You're going to have to do the same thing. Don't let what they think about your mother influence the way you see yourself. Your mom did stuff for money, but you're better than that."

I blink at her, stepping back until my shoulder hits the wall. "My mom did what she had to do." I just didn't understand that until I was pushed into the same corner. At least she called the shots when she sold out.

"I don't know one way or the other," Maggie says. "But it doesn't matter what she did or didn't do. The truth is irrelevant to some people. They believe what they want. Especially assholes like Carl who are just looking for an excuse."

"Don't tell William about what happened today."

She chews on her lower lip for a moment, studying me. "I think that would be a mistake."

"I won't take another appointment from Carl. It'll be fine. Please?"

She crosses her arms, disapproval clear in her eyes. "It's not mine to tell, but think about what I said, okay?"

I don't know what Will would do if he found out about what happened tonight, but I'm sure that, like Maggie, he'd want me to file charges. But I can't tell anyone what Carl did because I'm too terrified he'll share what he knows about me.

"Maggie, what does Carl do for a living?"

"He's some sort of PI, I think. Pics of husbands cheating on their wives, that kind of thing."

I swallow and make myself ask, "Do you have any idea who might have hired him to find something out about me?"

Maggie frowns. "Who would do that?"

But I already know the answer.

"You want to act like you're better than your mama, but I know the truth."

If someone hired a private investigator to look into my past, it won't be long before William finds out what I haven't had to courage to tell him. I got caught and sent to juvie when I met with the second man Anthony sent me to. I have no doubt that's how Carl York found out the truth. I assumed my juvenile record would be sealed, but I wasn't so lucky. When I was arrested for breaking and entering at nineteen, the court decided not to seal it. I had a box of jewelry in one of Brandon's homes that I was trying to get to after he was sentenced. Only it wasn't his house anymore, and I got caught.

Was I ever going to tell William the truth about my first years in Vegas? Or was I hoping my past would just disappear if I wished hard enough?

I know what I need to do, and when I leave my massage studio I go straight to my car. There's no question in my mind who hired Carl, and I need to make sure she lets me tell William the truth before she can.

Venus Salon is a swanky place by campus where all the sorority girls get their hair foiled and nails painted. The place is bustling on this Friday night, with every chair in the salon occupied and several people in the waiting area.

I'm two steps inside the doors when I spot Meredith.

She crosses her arms around her middle at the sight of me, hugging herself as she approaches. "Can I help you?"

All eyes are on us. "Can we go somewhere private to talk?"

Her jaw is hard, her disgust with me all over her face, as if my presence repulses her. "Fine. Follow me."

We cut through the salon. The stylists stop working and stare as us as I follow her back to the office. I could swear I hear one of them mutter *"Home wrecker"* as I step into the office.

Meredith closes the door behind me. "What can I do for you?"

I frown as she lowers herself into a chair. Her face is pale. "Are you okay?"

She waves a hand. "I'm fine."

"I...." I should have thought this through. What am I going to say? How am I going to convince her to stay quiet? And if she agrees to wait, do I really have the courage to tell William myself?

Before I can figure out what to say, she motions to the chair across from her. "Will you sit? I wanted to talk to you anyway, so I'm actually glad you're here."

I swallow. Shit. Am I too late?

"I have a proposition for you."

"A what?"

"Twenty thousand."

I cross my arms. "Twenty thousand what?"

"Dollars."

I blink at her, then my breath rushes from my chest. "You're blackmailing me?" My heart pounds.

"What? How could I blackmail you?"

"I don't have that kind of money."

"Exactly. That's why I'm offering it to you. Twenty thousand dollars. A little gift from me to you. I know about your dad's house."

I feel like I've been dropped into the wrong conversation. Nothing she's saying makes sense. No matter what she tells William, she hates me. Why would she want to give me money? "What about Dad's house?"

She raises a brow. "The foreclosure? The auction? What, are you so busy screwing my man that you aren't even reading the mail that comes to your house? I have friends at the bank. Your dad is eighteen months behind on his mortgage. They've given him every opportunity, but time's up. The bank is auctioning it off? I suppose you don't mind. You'll just move your crew in with Will, continue to suck him dry, huh? Real classy."

My stomach flips, turns sour, and tightens on itself all in one painful moment. "Dad's house is being foreclosed on?"

She leans forward and narrows her eyes at me. "Are you seriously that clueless?"

"I had no idea." And she's not far off the mark. I've been too caught up in my own temporary fairytale.

Is she telling the truth about the house? Does Dad know? Has he been keeping this from me? Then the rest of her words sink in. "You're offering me twenty thousand dollars to save my house?"

She laughs. "There you go. Finally catching on. Good girl."

"What's the catch?"

She drops her gaze to the desk where she drums her perfectly manicured nails. Her voice isn't as cocky when she speaks again. "I think you know."

"William," I say softly.

"You came back into town like you'd never left. Swept in and stepped right back into his life, with no mind to the fact that you were pushing me out. I'll give you twenty thousand. You can save your little sisters' home and then leave town." She crosses her arms and leans back in her chair. "Or maybe you'll just take the money and run, screwing over your family like you screwed over Will by coming back. I don't care. I just want you gone."

My world spins wildly as she explains what she's already arranged—an account in my name that she'll wire the money to as soon as she's satisfied I've made a clean break with William and left town.

When she's done explaining, I ask, "And if I don't take it?"

Sighing, she shakes her head. "Don't be stupid, Cally. Eventually William is going to come to his senses and see that you're not the girl he wants to spend his life with."

"Is this why you hired Carl York? So I wouldn't have a choice? So I'd have to take your money?"

"Carl York? The PI? Why would I hire him? The foreclosure is public record."

I feel like I've been sucker punched in the solar plexus. If she didn't hire Carl, who did?

"Think about it," she says. "It's a lot of money."

"Bribing me to leave isn't going to buy you William. He's not for sale." I put the words out there. Intentionally baiting her to see if she knows more than she's saying, to see if she'll say, *"But you are."*

"That's a chance I'm willing to take. Will and I were good together. He'll come around. But do you want to know that truth?"

No. I don't want to know the truth. I want to hide from it in fantastical beliefs about wishes and destiny. The truth has done me no favors.

"Even if he doesn't want me back—which, let's face it, he will—it would be worth every penny just so I didn't have to see him with you."

Electric bill, gas bill, water bill. My hands shake as I tear through the stack of mail on Dad's kitchen counter.

I freeze when I see it. The New Hope Bank logo on the front left corner. The letter is addressed to my father and explains how the auction will work and the amount he must pay by next Friday if he wants to keep his house.

My stomach goes into a free fall, my heart following shortly behind.

I don't realize he's watching me until I hear him clear his throat. "I've been sending them as much as I can." Worry wrinkles my father's brow and draws his features downward. Suddenly, he looks much older than he is.

"If you've been sending money, why are you going into foreclosure?"

He takes the letter from my hands and taps it nervously on the counter. "I was already so far behind, and I wasn't able to catch up fast enough."

I close my eyes. "If you would have told me, we could have cut our losses on this place and moved you and the girls somewhere else. Instead, you've been throwing good money after bad, and now you're going to lose it all."

"I thought it would work out." His eyes are so sad, and my heart breaks for him. One of the smartest men I've ever met caught up in a delusion.

"*This* is how things 'work out' when you don't take care of them, Dad. *This* is what happens. Everything falls apart and all the work you've done, all the sacrifices you've made amount to nothing."

"Then maybe *nothing* is exactly what the Universe knows we need," he says softly.

"No!" I point my finger in his face and my body trembles with sudden rage. "The *Universe* wants you to take care of your shit. This isn't something that's going to get better by wishing on stars. *Destiny* can't swoop in and save the day."

"Everything happens for a reason, Cally. You have to believe that."

"Believe it? I believe it's an excuse for people who don't want to take responsibility for their own decisions. It's a dream world for men who can't deal with the fact that they've let their families down." I want to rail at him, to tell him the rest. I want to scream that while he was in India telling himself that 'everything happens for a reason,' I was in Vegas, spreading my legs for the highest bidder.

But I bite my tongue. I keep the truth locked inside because I may have sold my body but I didn't sell my heart. And my heart won't let me destroy my father with what I've done.

"You *set me up* for disappointment. You taught me all that magic bullshit and we lost everything." I might spare him from the whole truth but he needs to understand the consequences of his beliefs. "When we first moved to Vegas, I thought the shit life we were living was *my fault*. I hadn't wanted to leave and I had a terrible attitude about it. When Gabby cried at bedtime because her piece of bread wasn't enough to fill her belly, I thought I wasn't *believing* hard enough. Don't assign all your spiritual nonsense to us losing this house. Because that's on *you*."

Dad's eyes fill with tears, and I regret even that much of my confession. Then, out of the corner of my eye, I see Drew as she runs from the room.

"Shit," I mutter.

"I had no idea," Dad says, and the horror on his face is so terrible I wish more than anything I could take it all back. I wish I could package up the terrifying reality of those early days in Vegas and lock it away where it can't hurt anyone else.

"Of course you didn't," I whisper. My anger leaves as quickly as it came, and now I just feel empty.

"I wish you would have…If I'd known…Your mother said…"

"Yeah. I wish you would have known too." I shrug awkwardly. "What's done is done. And we made it out alive."

"You're mother never told me how bad it was."

She was too stoned. But I don't say it. "I need to talk to Drew."

I leave my dad to deal with his shock and find her alone in her room, sitting in a corner, her knees drawn to her chest.

"You made me love this piece-of-shit house," she mutters. "You made me love it, and now I'm losing it too."

"I'm sorry, Drew," I whisper. "I'm going to find a way to fix it. I promise."

"Call Brandon," she says. "Call him and tell him we need money for the house. He'll give it to you."

I squeeze my eyes shut. I've limited Drew's understanding of my relationship with Brandon on purpose. I wouldn't want her to know the truth about her big sister. But as a result, she sees him the way he sees himself, as a knight in shining armor who swept in and saved my family from a life on the streets. "We can't ask Brandon," I say carefully. "I'm not with him anymore."

"Well, it was stupid. Really fucking stupid moving us here. Gabby's finally acting like a normal kid and now she's going to be homeless."

I swallow, but I can't choke down the guilt and regret clogging my throat.

She shrugs, picks at the carpet with her big toe. "Does this mean we have to leave New Hope?"

"No, of course not," I say in a rush. "You're staying. I have to figure out what to do about the house, but you're absolutely staying."

She flicks her eyes up to meet mine. "What about you?"

"I can't," I whisper. And the words tear my heart in two.

chapter twenty-two

Cally

I AM head over heels in love with William Bailey, and it hurts like a bitch.

When I was a little girl, I believed I would grow up and fall in love. I believed that loving would be as natural as breathing. I believed love was inevitable and that it would feel like being wrapped in a warm fleece blanket on an autumn day.

I was right about everything but the last. I had no idea how much love could hurt, and it feels like it's done nothing but hurt me for seven years.

For the last four hours, I covered the floor for Will at the gallery while he set up the new exhibition for opening night this weekend. His muscles bunched and stretched under his T-shirt, and when he caught me watching, I pretended not to be hot and bothered.

Every stolen glance, every time he passes me and stops for just a second to kiss my lips, every squeeze of my hand or pinch of my ass, fills me with hope and breaks my heart all at once.

I haven't told him the sordid truth about my past. Though if someone hired Carl to find out, Will's going to find out soon, whether I tell him or not. I haven't told him about Dad's house either, and time's running short on that too.

William positions another painting and turns to me with a grin, his baby blues sending my girly bits into a whining fit of, *Please!* and *I want that.* "You okay?"

"I'm fine. Good. Great." *I'm a babbling idiot incapable of constructing an intelligent sentence in your presence.* I've been like this since I found out about the foreclosure yesterday. Because the only choice I have is to take Meredith's money. It's pretty ironic that she's offering, since I was planning to leave anyway, but it still kills me to take it. Because if Will doesn't hate me when he finds out what I did seven years ago, he'll hate me for taking her bribe.

He steps closer and takes my face in his hand, tilting my chin up as he studies me. My heart slams in my chest, and my whole core is filled with the push-pull, pain-comfort that comes with loving someone you have to let go. "I think you're working too much."

"I'm fine," I promise.

The bell over the front door jingles, and Hanna and Lizzy Thompson stroll into the gallery.

"We're here to kidnap Cally," Lizzy announces.

Hanna nods. "She works too much, and we're dragging her along for martini night with the girls."

"You guys—"

"We won't take no for an answer," Lizzy says, cutting me off.

"I have to close up for Will so he can finish putting up the fall exhibition."

"Stop being such a workaholic and *live* a little," Lizzy says.

"Back us up, Will," Hanna says. "She works constantly. It's not healthy."

Will's studying me, and I duck my head under his assessing gaze. "They're right," he says. "You need a break. And it's slow today. I've got this. No problem."

"I told you I'd stay and—"

He waves away my objection. "It's not a big deal. The twins are right. It's not healthy to work all the time. You'll burn out." He tugs me against him and lowers his mouth to my ear. "Or you could take me up on my offer to run away with me for a weekend. Cancel your appointments? Spend next weekend in bed in our hotel suite?"

My stomach flips—because, if I take Meredith's money, by next weekend, I'll be gone. I turn to the twins. "Fine. I'll go for one drink."

Lizzy grabs my arm and pulls me toward the door. "Let's get her out of here before she changes her mind."

"Bye," I call lamely over my shoulder as I leave.

"Hello," William calls back.

"Hello," I whisper.

Lizzy pushes me through the doors and rolls her eyes. "I think I just threw up in my mouth a little."

Her Charger is parked out front and she doesn't release me until she's opened the passenger door and shoved me half inside.

I rub my wrist. "Man, you weren't kidding when you said *kidnap*."

"Are you okay?" Hanna asks from the back. "Lizzy doesn't know how strong she is sometimes."

"She's fine!" Lizzy slams my door and comes around to climb in her side. "Brady's for margaritas, or The Wire for martinis?" she asks as she slides her key into the ignition.

"Martinis," Hanna says.

Lizzy turns the car in the direction of The Wire, and I'm almost relieved that they came for me. This might be the only chance I have to say goodbye.

"Would you stop thinking so much?" Lizzy asks. "All you're doing is sitting there, but those wheels in your brain are so busy cranking away, it's making my brain feel like a slacker."

Hanna taps my shoulder. "Thank you for coming with us. We've missed you."

Something squeezes in my chest. "I've missed you guys too."

Lizzy flashes me a sad smile before returning her gaze to the road, and I know there's something they're not saying.

At the Wire, it appears every table is taken, but I follow the girls back to a booth and am surprised to see Maggie waiting there.

"I didn't know you were joining us!" I slide in next to her and grab the martini menu.

Maggie exchanges a meaningful look with her sisters, who have taken their positions in the booth across from us.

I set down the menu. "What is it?"

Again with the secret sisterhood of exchanged glances, then, Lizzy: "We need to talk."

"Drinks first!" Hanna protests.

Maggie nods. "Hanna's right. This calls for vodka."

So I sit there with anxiety tearing up my stomach as we wait for our drinks to arrive—Grey Goose with olives for Maggie, chocolate for the twins, and a vodka tonic for me.

"Enough with the suspense," I say after we get rid of the waitress. "What's up?"

"There are some rumors," Hanna hedges.

"And we think you should know about them," Lizzy finishes.

I smile but I don't need a mirror to know it's shaky and doesn't reach my eyes. The PI. Whoever he was working for has told everyone the truth about me. I was hoping it wouldn't get around until after I left. I wince, thinking of my sisters. No. I was hoping it would *never* get around. "What is it?"

Again, the girls exchange looks. Lizzy clears her throat. "Meredith is pregnant."

"Everyone is saying it's Will's," Hanna continues, "and…the timing is right."

I take a swig of my drink. "Pregnant," I murmur. *Holy shit.* No wonder she wants me to leave town.

"She's not coming out and *saying* that it's his." Lizzy puts her hand on mine.

"But she's not denying it either," Hanna adds.

"People are starting to whisper about you," Lizzy admits. "They're calling you a home wrecker."

"Because apparently men in this town aren't responsible for their own dicks," Maggie mutters.

"We're telling them what's what," Hanna assures me. "Despite how she likes to spin it, Will and Meredith were *not* an item when you got to town."

"We don't think Will knows," Lizzy says softly. "But we think you should tell him before she does."

Maggie clears her throat. "Ladies, would you let me and Cally speak privately for a minute?"

The twins scoot out of the booth, leaving me and Maggie alone.

"Listen," Maggie begins, "I like you, and I like how happy Will is when he's with you, so I'll tell you something I wouldn't tell anyone else. There's no way that baby is Will's."

My mouth is dry, and I down half of what's left in one gulp. "I'm pretty sure they slept together," I say. "Even assuming they used protection, nothing is one-hundred-percent effective." What was it Maggie said after I first moved back? That all Will wanted was to get married and have a family? If I hadn't shown up, would he and Meredith be happily pursuing that dream by now?

She gives me a sad smile and drops her eyes to her drink. "Would you just trust me on this one? Meredith may be pregnant, but it is *not* his baby."

Slowly, I nod. I'm sure she's trying to reassure me because she sees the panic on my face. But she doesn't understand that I can't give William what Meredith can. And I love him enough to let him have with her what he can't have with me.

"Would you excuse me for a minute?" I push out of the booth before she can answer. Suddenly it's too hot in here and I need some fresh air. I don't make it to the door before someone grabs my arm.

When I look up, Meredith's eyes are boring into mine. "Look who's here."

I step back. Shit. I don't want to face her tonight. "Hey, Meredith."

I try to side step her, but she holds on tight. "I had an interesting chat with Carl York today." She actually smiles, as if what Carl told her about me is the best possible news. "I wonder how much William knows about your escapades as a *call girl* back in Vegas."

I stumble backward and my feet tangle under me as my back hits a tray. The next thing I know, glass is shattering and I'm soaked with beer. The smell is more that my stomach can handle but I force myself to take slow, steady breaths.

"I'm so sorry," I say to the waitress, who is also soaked, eyes wide in horror.

"It's okay," she mumbles, dropping to her haunches to pick up shards of glass.

Meredith shakes her head slowly. "Some people cause you nothing but trouble."

I'm stuck in place and before I can unfreeze myself, Lizzy rushes over and grabs towels off the bar. "Let me help you with that." She flashes me a worried look before dropping to her haunches.

"My offer still stands," Meredith says, and then she turns and leaves.

As I busy myself with helping the girls clean up the mess, my stomach surges into my throat at the thought of that bitch living the life I want. A life with William. His babies in her belly. I'll get out of the way and let Will make his choice, but now I know I can't take her money. Because I'm not for sale anymore.

I make excuses to leave early, but Maggie follows me outside. She takes me by the shoulders, determination gleaming in her eyes. "It's not whether or not you make the mistake. It's how you handle it."

"I—"

She squeezes my shoulders. "Do you understand?"

I blink at her and realize she heard Meredith. Maggie knows. "I can't *fix* that," I whisper, and to my horror, tears are spilling down my cheeks. "I can't change what I did."

"You explain what happened. You tell him the truth. You'd be amazed what William Bailey can forgive."

chapter twenty-three

William

"Hey there, Bailey, Carl York here. You're one difficult man to get ahold of!"

I frown into my cell phone. I've been sending his calls to voicemail, trying to forget I hired him. Carl doesn't seem to want me to forget. "What's up, Carl?"

"I got that information you wanted. About that Brandon McHugh guy." He whistles, long and low. "It's a good 'un too."

"I don't need it anymore." Anything I need to know about Cally's ex, she can tell me.

"Oh boy, you want to know this. Trust me."

I close my eyes and rub my temple. The gallery is closed for the night, and I'm alone in my office preparing the last minute details for this weekend's exhibition opening. I don't want to deal with Carl. I want to go find Cally and take her home to my bed.

"Listen," Carl says, "it's up to you, but you already paid me. Might as well get what you paid for, right? You don't have to decide now. I'll put it in the mail so you'll have it all. I gave you an extra piece in there too— did a little digging on Cally Fisher. I was curious, so it's on the house. In the meantime? I wouldn't touch her with a ten foot pole...." He chuckles.

"If you know what I'm saying. I know I won't be getting any 'massages' from her again, that's for sure."

I can practically hear his air quotes around the word *massages*. Fucker. I hang up before he can say more.

Cally

My dad is going to have to face losing the house. My little run-in with Meredith tonight made that clear to me. The reality of the situation sucks, but I don't see an alternative. The truth is, I won't be around to bail Dad out, and he needs to learn to make better decisions.

When I pull up to the cabin, my heart drops like a thousand shards of glass into my already aching stomach.

Brandon McHugh is leaning against a black SUV. His long legs are crossed at the ankle as he flashes that charming smile in Drew's direction.

The way he's looking at her makes me want to cut off his balls with a rusty razorblade.

I hurry out of my car. "Drew, go inside and set the table for dinner."

Drew scowls. "I'm not hurting anything."

"Go!" I order.

He watches her run into the house. My fifteen-year-old sister. And all at once, I both wish I had a gun and am glad I don't. He turns his attention back to me and shakes his head slowly at my jeans and T-shirt. "Cally baby, I hate seeing you dressed like that."

"You're early," I say softly. "We said two months."

"I have business in Indianapolis and Chicago, so it appears your time's up. Your sisters are settled, and I'm done waiting."

There's no use arguing. I knew this could happen. "Okay." I look over my shoulder to make sure the girls aren't around to hear. "When do we go?"

His jaw tightens. "I have business to attend to. I'll come for you tomorrow night. But buy some new fucking clothes before then." He sneers. "I can't look at you in that shit. You look *old*."

I force a smile. "Of course."

"You should bring your sisters with you. They're cute. I'll take good care of them."

My stomach pitches. "Not an option," I say steadily. "Dad has legal custody."

He grins. "Drew likes me."

"I have to get their dinner ready." And buy a gun. I really have to buy a gun.

Cally
Seven Years Ago

The moonlight calls my name through the bedroom window, and the stars wink at me from the dark midnight sky. Stardust kisses my fingertips. My wishes float in the air like dandelion fluff, waiting for me to catch them. I try to concentrate, to focus so I can stretch to take one into the palm of my hand.

He stops me before I can grab the wish. His hand on my arm, his erection at my back.

His mouth is hot on my ear, and I think of William in a tuxedo. Good, beautiful William, waiting for me to get off the plane so he can take me to prom.

I lost my virginity tonight, just like William and I planned. I wore a beautiful dress that clung to my curves. Sipped wine through the dinner at a fancy restaurant. Danced. An evening orchestrated for perfection. So much just as we planned, and nothing as we planned.

Goosebumps race across my bare skin as his fingers skate up the back of my spine.

"I wanted you from the first moment I saw you. I would have paid anything to have you." Fantasy mingles with reality. His words are hot

against my neck, and I close my eyes and imagine William is holding me, speaking to me. The way it was supposed to be. The drugs make that easier than it should be, but I hide inside the fantasy of me and William as this man slides his hand between my legs. I imagine William is holding me after prom, seducing me with his fingers until neither of us can resist, imagine it's William preparing to slide into me again.

"*William*," I murmur.

The man flips me to my back—suddenly, painfully, violently. He pins my hands on either side of my head, squeezing. "What did you call me?"

I blink up at him, and my fantasy skitters away into the night.

"What's my name, sweetheart?" The man over me demands. "Tell me my name."

I try to catch my breath, reorient myself. I lock my gaze to the piercing hazel eyes of the man who bought and paid for the right to my body. The man who owns me now.

"Say it."

"Brandon," I whisper. "Brandon."

William
Present Day

Brandon McHugh is outside Arlen Fisher's cabin, leaning against a gleaming black Cadillac Escalade, smoking a cigarette. He gives me a disinterested once-over as I swing my leg off my bike.

I went to The Wire to track down Cally after Carl York's call, but the girls told me she went home. Idiot that I am, I assumed that meant my house, but she wasn't there.

"Can I help you?" Brandon asks.

"I'm here for Cally."

"She's not available right now. Want me to tell her you stopped by?"

Her car is parked right in front of me, but I'm not going to argue. I shove my hands into my pockets and glare at him. "What are you doing here?"

"I could ask you the same question."

"Me? I'm her boyfriend."

He inclines his chin. "Hmm. That's funny, because when Cally and I made plans for her to move back to Vegas with me, she didn't say anything about a *boyfriend*."

His words are a punch in the gut, and I have to hold strong against my instinct to stagger back. "I'm sure there's a lot she hasn't told you."

"Oh, hell." He chuckles. "I'm such a fan of irony."

I want to knock that grin right off his face. "Where is she?"

He grunts, then cocks his head. "You're not fucking my girl, are you?"

"If you have to ask, is she really your girl? Why don't you get out of here? If she wanted to be with you, she'd be living in Vegas."

He laughs again. "My *wife* and I were just figuring out the details of her return."

Wife. The word slams into me, and I spin on him, nails biting into the flesh of my palms. "Excuse me?"

"Cally's little sisters showed me everything you fixed up for their daddy inside, not to mention the outside. Well done. Can't say I blame you. But she's good. You have to give her that. Not even a couple of weeks away from having me to take care of her, she found you. I guess she knows what men will do for a taste of that pussy."

I don't even make the decision before my arm is swinging. And soon I'm nothing but my anger and my fists and the sharp pain radiating from where his fist connects with my jaw. His fists land twice—a wrecking ball into my cheek and nose—before I manage a solid swing at his jaw. Then I lose track of where I've been hit and the number of punches we've thrown. All I care about is bringing this asshole down, and we're wrapped up in each other, still going hard, when someone pulls me off him.

I'm breathing hard and my vision's blurry. My face feels wet, and I wipe my nose and find my hand covered with blood.

I can faintly make out Cally's dad standing over me, and she's standing a few feet beyond him, hands on her hips. Between us is the asshole. Her *husband*. He hops to his feet and grins like it's nothing.

"There will be no violence on my property," Arlen Fisher growls. He's a quiet man, and that's probably the most I've heard him speak at one time. I wonder if he'll say more or threaten to call the cops, but he just nods, as if he has complete faith that his order will make it so, and then he turns and walks into his house.

"What do you think you're doing?" Cally asks, and I don't know if she's talking to me or him or both of us. I don't fucking care. I just want away from this. From her.

I push myself off the ground, and pain starts settling in places I don't remember getting hit. My side, my left bicep. My knuckles are screaming and the whole right side of my face is on fire.

He slaps her ass, and even though I just promised myself I was getting out of here, I'm ready to go again.

"Will, please," she whispers before I can swing. "Don't." For a quietly whispered word, it's wrapped in enough sadness that I know I've already lost her. He's here for her, and she's going with him. He's the reason she told me she can't stay. Can't or won't?

Her father reappears and hands me a wet towel. I nod gratefully and press it against my bloody nose while Cally takes Brandon's arm and walks him to his car.

"I can't believe she'd be with someone like that."

Her father is staring at me, and I realize I said the words out loud.

"Don't make the mistake of thinking that people don't continue living their lives just because you're not around," he says softly. "Cally isn't the same girl you were with seven years ago, and if you keep trying to pretend she is, you're both going to get hurt."

I draw in a breath. Cally's been trying to give me the same warning and I've ignored her, but suddenly it's painfully obvious that she was right.

I walk back to my bike and every step sends pain radiating through my ribs. Cally is standing at the SUV, using a washcloth to wipe blood from Brandon's face. When she sees me watching, she steps back and drops her hands to her sides. Her eyes go sad as she looks me over.

"Are you okay?" she asks.

I swing my leg over my bike and pain ricochets through my core. "Fucking fabulous." Then I start the engine and pull away. Because I can't handle the idea of her seeing me like this. And because, for the first time, I finally understand what she was telling me. She's not the same woman she once was, and we can't have the relationship we once had.

Cally

"Baby," I whisper. "You're hurting me." William's gone, Brandon's pissed, and my world is shattered.

Fury burns in Brandon's eyes. "You little slut. You've been fucking that asshole."

I shake my head. "No," I whisper. "It's not what you think." My purity, the idea that I had only ever been with *him,* was everything to Brandon. I don't want him going after Will. I can't have him hurting Will more than he already has.

"You fucked him and now you expect me to take you back, to take care of you?" His hands slide from my shoulders to around my neck, resting there, waiting for an excuse. My dad is just inside the house and I say a silent prayer that he's watching, that he'll be able to protect me if Brandon snaps.

"I didn't sleep with him," I say, slowly lifting my hands to his face. "I don't want to be with anyone but you." I have to calm him down before his hands tighten any more at my neck.

"Don't lie to me, Cally. Not about this."

"I wouldn't." The lie is a dangerous one. All he would have to do is ask around town and he'll learn the truth. I've been careless, too determined to soak up every ounce of a life I knew I'd have to leave behind.

"I *saved* you," he whispers, his face going sad and his hands dropping from my neck to take mine. "You were days from being on the street and I saved you."

That's his favorite story to tell. He'd hold me at night and repaint our ugly beginnings in the broad strokes of his twisted perception. As if he didn't pay Anthony tens of thousands of dollars for the privilege of taking my virginity. As if he didn't force me to marry him so he could control me even more than before. "I helped your family. How do you repay me? You don't even visit me while I'm in prison."

"I—I didn't think you wanted to see me," I lie. "You were with her."

But I can tell he sees through my excuse now. He always has.

"I told myself I would get you back as soon as I got out, but you tried to push me out of your life like I didn't *save* you." He has tears in his eyes. Actual, glistening *tears.* "You. Hurt. Me," he growls, hands returning to my neck. "I thought you would need me again after your mom's drug overdose. I was so sure that would bring you back to me."

"Brandon," I gasp when his hands tighten. "You're hurting me."

He stumbles back, his hands curling into fists. "I can't look at you right now." Then he climbs into his car and tears out of the drive, kicking up dust.

I don't know how long I'm standing there before I feel Gabby at my side. "I don't like him," she says. "He came to the apartment the morning Mom died. I never liked him."

I turn and blink at her. "Brandon was at the apartment the morning mom died?" Then Brandon's words sink in. *"I thought you would need me again after your mom's drug overdose. I was so sure that would bring you back to me."*

I never told Brandon mom died of a drug overdose. I told him she had a heart attack. Just like I told everyone else.

"I was so sure that would bring you back to me."

Suddenly, everything is too clear. After years, Mom was doing better, even holding a steady job. Then suddenly a drug overdose? And how did Brandon know?

I thought I could run away. I thought I could hide from Brandon. I thought leaving New Hope would be enough to protect the people I love. But the only way I can protect them is if I give Brandon what he wants. They won't be safe until he has me or he's in prison again.

Will's house is dark, but I'm sure he's here. Where else is he going to go with his face torn up like that?

The door's locked, but he gave me a key last month when I was staying here with the girls. When I tried to give it back, he insisted I keep it. Now I'm glad.

Evening sunlight slants through the windows and spills across the hardwood floors at the back of the house. I know I haven't seen the last of Brandon. He'll be back for me soon. He was pissed. Ugly, nasty angry, and I don't have long. Not unless I want him to come after William. Brandon bought me years ago, and in his mind he still owns me.

But my heart belongs to William.

William's kitchen and living room are empty. He's not resting on the couch in the family room like I thought he might be. I follow the dark hall to the master bedroom and find his curtains drawn, making it darker in here than the rest of the house. In the dim light trickling in from the hallway, I spot him, sprawled on top of the comforter in nothing but his boxer briefs.

I step into the room quietly. The soft and steady rise and fall of his chest gives me the courage to go closer so I can look at his face. His cheek is twice the size of the one opposite it, and the bruise there extends up to his eye, which is puffy and possibly swollen shut. His lip is cracked.

I continue my study of his injuries and drop my gaze to his bandaged knuckles and the angry red bruise at his ribs.

"What are you doing here?"

I jump at his words. He's awake but not moving. "I just came to check on you," I say softly, lowering myself on the edge of the bed by his side. "I've been worried."

He reaches to the bedside table and clicks on the light. "You seemed real damn worried about me when you were tending to your *husband's* injuries."

I swallow the hurt his words bring and don't bother defending myself. "I didn't want him to hit you again."

"I can handle myself."

Of course he can against most guys, but Brandon eats and breathes fighting. God knows what new skills he learned while he was locked up. Just remembering coming outside to see Brandon swinging at Will is enough to make me lose my breath all over again.

I have to touch him. In the near-darkness, I find his lip and trace the split with my fingertip. Then I touch his swollen cheek, his puffy eye. "I thought he was going to kill you." He doesn't reply, nor does he complain as my fingers take inventory of the rest of his face—the injured and healthy spots equally.

After my hands have finished their tour and slide to his hair, my lips follow the path of my fingers in reverse. I kiss his swollen eye, his cheek, his jaw. He doesn't move.

When I come to his mouth and finally press my lips to his injured ones, he grabs my wrists and holds me still. Suddenly, my tentative exploration of his wounds becomes his exploration of my mouth. His hands are in my hair, and he's pulling me down on the bed, rolling until I'm under him.

And today sucked so badly I let myself have this moment like a reward for enduring. Here, in the dark of his bedroom, his nearly naked body over my fully clothed one, everything between us falling to pieces, this kiss is the least we deserve. It feels like a secret gift we're both entitled to. So I open under him, kissing him back and rubbing my tongue against his, and when his hand snakes up my shirt, hot and greedy, I arch into his touch like Brandon isn't coming for me, like kissing William when I need to be telling him goodbye isn't the worst idea I've ever had.

I have to touch him. I need it more than I need air. But when I explore his body, his breath leaves him in a hiss and his lips abandon mine.

"I'm leaving tomorrow night," I whisper.

"He's making you. Before he ever showed up in town, you were thinking of staying. He's making you leave, isn't he?"

"I want to go." The words are heavy with lies and I fight to heave them off my tongue. "I'm sorry."

"You can tell me if you're scared. I'll protect you from him."

But who will protect you from Brandon? I swallow. I don't know what's going to happen tomorrow, and I need William to let me go. "Why would I be scared of my own husband?"

"You can tell me the truth, Cally."

I roll back my shoulders. "The truth is that I'm leaving, just like I planned from the beginning."

The pain in his eyes isn't just the physical kind. I've hurt this man. Just like I knew I would.

chapter twenty-four

William

"YOU CAN leave then." I roll off her and sit on the edge of the bed, cradling my head in my hands. When she doesn't move, I growl, "Go back to your husband, Cally."

She sits up and positions herself next to me. So damn close it hurts. She rests her elbows on her knees, her head in her hands, and I realize for the first time what a wreck she is. She looks like she hasn't slept for days, like she's been ravaged by grief and worry and…more.

She lets out a long, slow breath. "Meredith's pregnant. Did you know that?"

"What does Meredith have to do with anything?"

"Everyone is saying it's yours."

I have to laugh at that. Same old joke coming back to me. "I can guarantee you it's not mine."

"But you slept with her before I came back. It could be."

"Just—" I shake my head and push off the bed. Why are we even talking about this? "Believe what you want, okay? It doesn't fucking matter anymore."

"It does matter," she whispers. "It matters because she can give you the life you want. The marriage, the children. I can't."

"Right. Because you're already married."

"I'm sorry I didn't have the courage to tell you the truth about…my past. But I was up front with you about what I could and couldn't offer."

I can't stomach this conversation. I love Cally enough to need more from her. "You weren't *up front* with me about the fact that you were married." She draws in a shaky breath, and I'm so damn hurt, her pain only pisses me off. "Whatever. I'm done with this conversation."

"I was selfish and I'm sorry for that." She turns to me and puts her hand to my face. A tear rolls down her cheek. "I hope you have an amazing life. You *deserve* an amazing life."

"*Leave*," I growl. "Put your key on the front table on your way out."

She walks to the door and hesitates.

"Goodbye, Cally."

Cally

Saturday night, I'm waiting for Brandon with a packed suitcase and an illegally purchased gun.

If I tell Brandon I won't go with him, I risk him hurting me, or worse, hurting William, Dad, or one of the girls. But I can't go back to being his doll and living under his rule. Three years of that was three too many. The worst kind of prison is the kind that disguises itself as home.

My grand plan is to wait until I know Brandon has drugs in his possession and tip off the police. It shouldn't take long since I know that's the "business" he's in town for. The gun is Plan B. A pretty shitty Plan B, but better than none at all.

My phone rings. I don't recognize the number, but I accept the call because I expected Brandon to be here by now and I'm starting to get nervous. If he killed mom, what else will he do?

"Hello?"

"Cally?"

"Drew? Where are you?"

"I'm in Indianapolis." She's whispering and her voice is thick with tears. "I'm at the big hotel by the stadium. Can you come get me? Please?"

The whole world goes still around me. She told me she was staying with a friend tonight. "What are you doing there?"

"I'm scared. Please come get me." She takes in a shaky, hicuppy breath. Hell, she's crying. "Please."

"Are you with Brandon?" Even as I hope she'll say no, I already know she is.

"Don't be mad. He said that if I came with him, he'd give me the money for Dad's house, but he's scaring me. He gave me these clothes. A dress and this skimpy underwear and he made me put them on." Another shaky sob. "He said he'd kill me if I called the police. He has some people here in the other room now. He doesn't know I'm on the phone. He keeps calling me *Cally* and he won't let me leave. I'm scared. Please come get me."

"I'm on my way." Fear skates through my stomach on a razor edge, leaving shreds behind. I close my eyes and grab my purse. My gun is inside, and I say a prayer I won't have to use it. "I'll be there as fast as I can."

William

The last thing I am in the mood for tonight is the opening for the fall exhibition. The doors to the event opened an hour ago, and I've spent most of it in my office, hiding my face and my mood from unsuspecting patrons.

There's a knock on my door, and I ignore it, leaning back in my chair and closing my eyes. My solitude is destroyed at the scrape of a key in the lock. Which can mean only one thing: Maggie. No one else has the key to my office.

She sweeps through the door, wearing a long, strapless black dress, her hair in some sort of twist at the back of her head. The minute she sees me, her jaw drops and her eyes widen.

"Holy shit!"

"I know. I really make this suit, don't I?"

She grins and tilts her head to inspect the bruises on my face. "Of course you do, and once I get past the ground burger someone made of your face, maybe I can appreciate that. What happened?"

"I cut myself shaving."

She props her hands on her hips and narrows those sharp green eyes. "Does this have something to do with Cally?"

"She's not responsible for my stupidity."

"Who did this?"

"Give the credit to the asshole she's married to."

Her face falls and she lowers herself into a chair. "She's married?"

"She's not only married, she's leaving. Or she already left. Fuck if I know." I lean back. My body aches in places I didn't know I had, and my heart hurts so fucking bad I wish I could cut it out of my chest. "I knew she had secrets, but I never imagined this."

"Did she tell you the rest of her secrets?"

"The rest of what secrets? She's fucking married. If there's something worse than that, I don't want to know it."

"The truth is always more complicated than it appears," Maggie says softly. "Maybe the same is true of her marriage."

I shake my head. "She was talking about staying until the first time he showed up, then everything changed. I thought maybe she was afraid of him."

"How do you know she's not?"

I set my jaw against the pain, remembering the conversation. "I asked. I told her I'd protect her." And fuck if my pride isn't in worse shape than my face. She chose him over me. I should be used to this shit by now.

"You big idiot. How hard did he hit your head? A woman who's afraid of her husband is going to lie about it nine times out of ten. But when looking at the mess said husband made of her lover's face, she's going to lie about it one-hundred percent of the time. She's trying to protect you."

I hear a sharp gasp and I look up to see Meredith standing in the doorway.

"Who did this to you?" she demands. Her heels click against the floor as she rushes over to me and gently touches my face. "You don't have to tell me. I already know that girl has something to do with this. I wish you'd stay away from her."

"You should see the other guy," I grumble.

She turns to Maggie. "What happened to him?"

"I'm sitting right here," I growl.

"He got in a bar fight."

Meredith narrows her eyes. "A *bar* fight?"

Maggie nods sagely. "I told him he needs to stop hanging out at the titty bar, but does he listen to me? *No*, he doesn't."

I scowl at her. "Seriously?"

"I don't believe for a second this happened at a titty bar," Meredith says.

She shrugs. "Tell your sweet little girl here the truth, Will. Tell her you can't get enough of the titty bar."

"Would you both stop saying *titty bar*?" I blow out a hard breath, hoping to send some of my frustration with it. "Maggie, will you excuse us? Meredith and I need to talk."

"Fine," Maggie says, standing begrudgingly. "I'll be downstairs doing *your job* if you need me. But think about what I said."

I wait until Maggie closes the door behind her before I speak. "I hear congratulations are in order."

Meredith's cheeks flush and she drops her gaze to her hands. "Thank you."

"I also hear everyone thinks it's mine."

"I didn't say that. Not to anyone."

"But you didn't correct them."

"I thought it would be better this way. You know, in case we reconcile."

"Do you hear yourself? You're batshit crazy, woman."

She lifts her eyes to mine and they're glistening with unshed tears. "I'm not crazy. I'm in love. Your grandmother told me you can't have children. She told me about the football accident. I knew how much you wanted a family and I thought….Well, I thought if I could give it to you, maybe you'd choose me."

She's biting her lip and worry lines crease her forehead. She's really beautiful, and I know she can give me all the things I've spent the last three years craving madly—a life, a family, love. But I don't just want those things. I want them with Cally.

"I'm sorry," I say. "You and I will never work."

"Because you love Cally."

"Yeah." And it's true. I still love her. Still want her. I'd forgive her for all of it to have her in my arms just one more time.

"Well, at least you know she loves you too."

"How do you figure?"

She looks at her hands for a minute before bringing her eyes back up to meet mine. "I offered her twenty-thousand dollars to leave town and stay away from you."

"You did what?"

"I thought she was going to take it. I really did. But she didn't." She shakes her head. "I love you, and I knew she needed the money."

"Jesus, Meredith! That's not love! That's manipulation. You've got to be kidding me."

She throws her hand over her chest. "I don't *want* her dad to lose the house. I thought it was a nice compromise. But apparently she's going to let you pay for *that* too."

"Why would her dad lose the house? What are you talking about?"

"She didn't tell you? Arlen Fisher's house is in foreclosure. The bank is going to auction it off."

"Shit." I drag a hand through my hair. Of course she didn't tell me. She doesn't want my money.

"Can I ask you something without you getting angry with me?"

"You just told me that you offered the woman I love twenty-thousand dollars to leave town."

She nods. "Okay. Point taken. So, nothing to lose, right?"

"I don't want to talk to you about Cally." I push back my chair and stand.

"This isn't about her. Not exactly." She stands too and skirts around me until I'm looking at her. "You say you want family and stability, but have you ever noticed that you tie yourself to women who you know can't or won't give you that?"

I step back. "I don't know what you're talking about."

She lifts a finger. "First, Maggie, who never loved you, not the way you deserve at least." She holds up a second finger. "Then Krystal, who would have been the perfect choice—except she's Maggie's sister, so that was doomed from the start." She holds up three fingers. "And now Cally? Even if you can get over her juvenile record, she's married, and to a man who spent the last four years in prison no less. You say you want something real and I'm standing right here, but you're choosing her instead."

My jaw hardens and it aches from where Brandon's knuckles connected with it yesterday. "What do you want from me, Meredith?"

She shrugs. "I just want you to be honest with yourself. It's okay if you want to be alone. It's really all you've ever known—being alone and wishing for more. That's safe for you. But at least do me the courtesy of admitting it."

"I don't want to be alone. But that doesn't mean I want to be with you." I exhale slowly. "I never meant to hurt you." Then her words sink in. "Cally's husband spent the last four years in prison?" Jesus. How young was she when she married him?

"Didn't you read the file Carl York put together for you? It's all in there. The dirt on her husband, their marriage certificate, the juvie record from her escapades as a call girl."

Her words hit me hard and unprepared. "Her escapades as what?"

"You didn't even look at it, did you? You're rejecting me for a former *prostitute*. Don't you get that?"

I ignore her and dig through the stack of paperwork on my desk until I find the unopened manila envelope Carl York mailed to me. I tear it open and flip through the papers, past the background check on Brandon McHugh, past Cally's juvenile record, until I reach the copy of their marriage certificate. The date stares up at me in bold, black print. "She was sixteen."

"Her mom would have had to give written consent. You'd think she would have looked into him before permitting it." She leans over me and flips through more papers until she pulls the one she's been looking for. "Two years before he married Cally, he got picked up with an underage prostitute. Apparently he has a thing for the young ones. Heck, maybe prostitution is how they met. Like in *Pretty Woman*."

I'm already grabbing my keys. I need to find her. I need to stop her from leaving. Her words echo in my head. *I loved you enough to let you go. That's the truth. Someday soon I'll have to do it again, and it will still be the truth, even if you can't accept it.* She isn't leaving with Brandon because she loves him. She's leaving because she loves me.

"You really don't care about her past?" Meredith asks behind me as I rush toward the door.

"It's called unconditional love, Meredith. I recommend you try it."

Maggie bursts into the office. "I just got a call from the Marion County jail. They're holding Cally for shooting her husband."

chapter twenty-five

Cally

Last night, I did something I've wanted to do for seven years. I told my story to the police. The whole thing. From my mom's drug addiction to the loan I took from Anthony to how I came to meet and marry Brandon McHugh to why I shot him.

Okay, I did two things I've wanted to do for seven years. I told the police my story and I shot the bastard who thought I was something that could be bought.

Honestly, once I'd told my whole story, I think the detectives were surprised I didn't aim for center mass when I found Drew in his hotel room.

Brandon will be going back to prison. There was already a warrant for his arrest in Nevada, and he had all sorts of drugs in his hotel room. I don't know too many details. I don't care about anything but the fact that Drew is safe, and I managed to get away from Brandon without killing him.

When the police cruiser drops me off at Dad's, the sun is starting to rise. The first thing I do is look for Drew. She's sitting on the couch, arms wrapped around her middle, and I sink down next to her and pull her tight against me.

The silence is sweet, and I'm scared to break it. When the police came, they separated us for questioning, so I didn't get to ask any questions.

Right here, in this quiet moment, I am blissfully ignorant of what happened to her before I got to the hotel room. I almost don't want her to speak, as if me not hearing the truth could save her from it. But that only works one way, and tonight it's Drew that needs saving.

"I'm going to ask you questions, and I need you to tell me the truth."

"You're going to be so mad at me," she whispers. It's dark in the living room, the morning sun just now starting to show her head outside our windows. I can barely make out the tear streaks that glow against her perfectly smooth skin.

"What's done is done, Drew. I need to know some things."

"Okay."

I take a breath. It feels like the first I've taken in days. My chest is still tight with panic. Even with Drew next to me—safe—it's still hard to breathe. "Are you hurt?"

"He slapped me. Shoved me a little. But I'm okay."

My squeeze my eyes shut. Questions are screaming through my brain at a hundred miles an hour. *Why did you go to a hotel room with him? Why did you lie to me? What were you thinking?* I have to push them all aside. *Triage.* "Did he rape you?"

She spins to me. Her eyes are big and her red-painted mouth is slack, her cheeks smeared with mascara. She looks so young. Like a child caught playing in her mother's makeup.

"I need to know, Drew." But more, she needs to tell it. I can't have a dark secret eating my sister from the inside, not when I know the kind of damage that can do.

Her teeth sink into her bottom lip and she tugs at her too-short skirt. I recognize the outfit as the one Brandon had me wear the first night he had sex with me. God help me, he was trying to recreate that night with Drew. "No. He didn't touch me. He kissed me. Groped me over my clothes a little. But I cried and that pissed him off. He didn't have a chance to do anything else."

Thank you, dear God. Something loosens in my chest and I can breathe a little deeper. "That's good. That's so good."

"I was so scared, Cally. I know that's what he planned." Her words are muffled by her sobs. "I thought that maybe I should do it, you know.

He said he wanted to help us. To save me, to save our house. I just had to be—" She hiccups out a sob. "I just had to be his good girl. But I couldn't…."

"Never!" I force myself to relax, force my voice to quiet. I could scream at her. Scold her. Tell her how stupid that was. And maybe I'll do all of that. Another day. When my heart isn't so completely pulverized. "You don't ever sacrifice yourself like that. You are worth more than a pretty dress. More than a meal on the table. More than a house. You hear me? Never forget what you're worth." It hurts so much to have this conversation that I almost want to ask her to stop. Instead, I reach over, and grab her hand from where she's fidgeting with her skirt. I lace our fingers together, and I squeeze. "There are some parts of yourself that, once you sell, you can never get back."

"Are you in trouble? For shooting him?"

"Not much." I'll have to go before a judge, but my lawyer didn't think I'd have to do much beyond some community service hours for the illegal handgun.

"I should have listened to you. You told me to stay away from him."

"Shh." I pull her against my chest and stroke her hair. "It's over now. You're safe."

William

Cally's leaving. I keep repeating the words to myself, as if maybe that will make them finally sink in.

She's here now. I can hear her in the apartment upstairs. But she's leaving.

I turn off the gallery lights and lock the door. When I went to Indianapolis last night, they were questioning her and wouldn't let me see her. Then this morning when I went to her dad's place, the trunk of her car was open and suitcases were piled inside. I tried not to panic, but Maggie heard her on the phone canceling her appointments for next week, and I can't deny the truth anymore. *She's leaving.*

I need to see her before she goes. Feel her. Taste her. I need to make sure I never forget her.

I catch her in the massage room.

"Are you okay?" My voice is rough, as battered as my heart and body.

"I'm fine." She gives me a soft smile but it falls away when I push her against the wall. "Well, hello to you too."

Pushing close, I spread her legs with my knee until she's positioned against my thigh.

"I'm so sorry," she whispers, sliding her hands into my hair. "For everything."

I open my mouth against her neck and suck, not caring that it will leave a mark. I'm desperate to chase away the gnawing pain I've felt since Brandon called her his wife, to wash away the horror I felt at reading the file Carl put together. When I think about her selling her body to someone, when I think how bad things must have been to make her resort to that, I want to punch something. I want another shot at Brandon.

I grip the bottom of her shirt in both hands and pull it off over her head before shoving her pants from her hips.

"Yes," she whispers. "Please. I need you." But then I drop to my knees and press my open mouth against the cotton polka dots of her underwear, and she stops talking altogether.

I slide my tongue against her panties, saturating them with my tongue as my hands find their way up the back of her thighs and take an ass cheek in each hand.

"Oh my God."

Repositioning my mouth right over her clit, I suck at her through the cotton. Her hands are in my hair, pulling as her hips rock instinctively toward my mouth.

I grab her wrists and position them at her sides, holding them there as I kiss my way up her body.

Her eyes are on me, dark and smoky with need, and I draw her hands from her sides to above her head, where I shackle them with one of mine.

She's so fucking gorgeous in a lacy pink bra and polka dot panties, her chest rising and falling as she tries to catch her breath from my assault.

I can't resist those perfect lips, so I press my mouth to hers, slide our tongues together until she's rocking into my thigh again.

"I'm going to release your hands, but I want you to leave them above your head."

Her dark eyes go smoky with approval as I pop open the front release on her bra. Her breasts fill my hands and I lower my head, drawing her nipple into my mouth, toying with it with my tongue, then teeth. She cries out and her fingers tug on my hair, forcing me to stop too soon.

"Hands above your head," I order. Heat flashes in her eyes as she obeys, and I return to her neck, trailing my mouth over the sensitive bit of flesh under her ear and down to her collarbone. I flatten my palm against her stomach and fan my fingers over her hipbones, my thumb over the ring in her navel.

"Turn to face the wall," I command.

She obeys without question and leaves her hands above her head as I explore the bare skin of her back with my hands and then my mouth. She obeys me completely with her stillness as I explore her. As I trail kisses down her spine, I slide off her panties. With one hand around her hip, I slide the other between her legs.

"Slide your legs apart for me."

She leans into the wall and does as I ask, arching enough to expose her sweet sex to me.

"*Jesus*. You're so damn beautiful." I cup her with my hand, using my fingers to tease her as I scrape my teeth over one ass cheek then the other.

She whimpers, and I drive two fingers inside of her, curling them until her legs are unsteady and her muscles are flexing. When she's close, I open my mouth to that sensitive spot just at the base of her spine and suck until she's coming apart on my hand.

Cally

I'm clinging to the wall for dear life as I recover, but I've hardly caught my breath when William's mouth is back at my ear. "Face me, sweetheart."

I turn on wobbly legs and reach for the button on his jeans, desperate to get him nude, to feel his skin against mine. I unzip him and release him from his boxers. Before I can push them off his hips, he's hoisting me up between his body and the wall, sliding into me fast, hard, and hungry.

I cry out in pleasure as he pushes deep.

"That's right, baby," he murmurs. "Let me hear you."

He uses the strength in his arms to hold me up, and his muscles bunch under his shirt. He's manic, driven by something he isn't sharing with me. He presses his face into the crook of my neck, and all I can do is hold on and pray he's finding what he needs in me.

He's swelling inside me, so close to the edge, and he groans into my neck and presses my weight into the wall so he can slip his hand between our bodies. He's holding back, putting off on his own release.

"Come for me again, sweetheart. Let me feel you." His fingers are relentless against me, his whispered demands hot in my ear. It doesn't take long before I shatter. Only then does he let go, his hips jerking and his head falling back as he finally releases inside me.

After, he takes me to the shower in the apartment and washes me slowly and thoroughly, pressing gentle kisses to where his mouth was rough minutes before.

We don't bother going back to his place or getting dressed. We lock the doors to the apartment and curl up on the couch, clinging to each other.

I keep thinking the words I need to say but they refuse to find their way to my tongue. But I don't want to ruin the perfection of this moment by explaining my ugly past.

"Why'd you do it?" His question is so soft, I almost don't realize he's speaking.

"What?"

He swallows so hard I can hear it. "Is it true? You were a prostitute?"

My heart pounds, but I concentrate on the feel of his skin under my cheek, his arms wrapped tightly around my waist. "It's true."

"That's why you broke up with me, isn't it? Your mom was stoned out of her mind and you sold yourself for money for your sisters." His voice is so calm, so rational—a complete contrast to the chaos of pain and hope warring in my chest. How can he know this and not hate me?

"I messed up," I confess. "I took a loan from a man I knew I shouldn't trust, and when I couldn't pay it off, he threatened Gabby and Drew."

"You became a call girl to pay off a loan?"

I shake my head against his chest, then push myself up so I can look at his face. His eyes are full of hurt, and I wish I could take that away for him. "This is what the man does. He finds women who are in trouble and he gives them loans to keep them afloat. Then he requires them to 'work off' their debt."

"Jesus," he breathes. He squeezes me tight and pulls my head down to his chest again.

"I can hardly think about it. I hate thinking that anyone else touched you, but to think men paid for it." A shudder moves through him, and he sits me up and climbs off the couch to pace. "Dammit, Cally, you were a fucking virgin. Didn't he know?"

I close my eyes. His agitation makes me feel both better and worse. Better because I'm not alone. Worse because now he's suffering with me. "I was more valuable to him once he found out." I swallow hard, not wanting to share this ugliness with him, but knowing I need to tell him more. "I gave blow jobs to a few of his special clients, and then he played them off each other and gave the highest bidder my virginity." I want to spare him the pain I see on his face, but I make myself keep going. "Brandon won that honor."

He stops pacing and runs a hand over his face.

I make myself keep going. "Knowing I'd been a virgin only fueled Brandon's obsession with me." An obsession that began the moment I ran out of his condo, too terrified to do what I'd been sent to do.

"But what you told me was true? You've been tested? You're healthy?"

"Of course! I wouldn't have risked giving you something."

"I'm not worried about me, Cally!" He pulls me off the couch and crushes me to his chest. "You're all I care about. Don't you get that?"

"I was telling you the truth when I told you I haven't been with any-one for four years. It's true. Brandon bought my virginity, but the man who'd given me the loan expected me to keep working. He threatened my life, my sisters. Brandon said he'd pay the guy off, get him to leave me alone, if I'd marry him. He promised to take care of me and give me money for my family, so I told mom I was in love with him and made her consent."

"Did the girls know any of this?"

I shake my head. "Not about the loan or the prostitution or even the marriage. Mom and I thought it would give them the wrong idea about when they should get married and agreed not to tell them. Brandon gave me just enough to keep them off the streets but never enough that I felt like I could run away. He controlled every aspect of my life from the moment he bought me until he was put in prison four years ago."

He pulls me into his arms. "I wish you would have told me."

"I hated the idea of you knowing what I'd done."

He presses his lips to my hair. "I think I knew. I told you I would imagine the worst, and when I saw the look in your eyes when I brought up the past, I knew it was much worse than anything I'd imagined before."

"I'm sorry I couldn't tell you. I thought you'd hate me."

"How could I hate you for something like this?"

I shrug. "I made a choice."

He takes my shoulders and steps back until I'm looking him in the eyes. "A choice made out of fear is no choice at all."

I snuggle back into his heat. Through the sliding glass doors that look out over the river, I can see the stars cradled in the dark night sky. I take my time, selecting a favorite for the first time in seven years, and then I muster the courage to dare one more wish. "I love you," I confess. "I never stopped."

"I love you too. Always." He tangles his hand in my hair and holds me close. "Don't leave me, Cally. You fill my hollow places. You make me whole. Please stay."

I lean back and frown up at him. "Where do you think I'm going?"

"I saw you packing your car this morning. There were suitcases in your trunk, and you were canceling all your appointments."

"Just five days. Asher Logan's letting me use his beach house on Lake Michigan for a week with the girls. Drew needs some time before going back to school."

He squeezes me tighter. "And after that? You're staying?"

"There's nowhere else I'd want to be."

chapter twenty-six

William

SEEING CALLY for the first time in a week is like a punch in the gut and an instant high all at once. Midweek, I caved and asked Maggie to tell me the address, but she refused, promising me the best thing I could give Cally right now is time.

So I made it five days and now she's standing in front of me in long sleeve T-shirt, her hands tucked into the pockets of her jeans. The wind whips her dark hair around her face, and she looks so damn beautiful I can't resist reaching out to tuck some of those wild wisps behind her ear.

"What are you doing here?" she asks softly.

"The bank is auctioning the house today," I explain, as if she wasn't already painfully aware of this fact.

Her shoulders tense. "I know you mean well, but sometimes people need to face the consequences of their decisions. For my dad, that will be losing this house."

"You won't let me buy it for you then?"

"I won't," she whispers.

"What about us?" Lizzy asks from behind me. She and Hanna were in the back of my car and apparently decided now was as good a time as any to make their presence known.

"What?" Cally asks. "You guys don't have enough money to buy this house."

"Not alone," Lizzy says, "but maybe if we went in with some friends."

"They say when you're young is the best time to invest," Hanna says sagely.

I nod, just as an oversized black pickup pulls in the drive.

"What's Asher Logan doing here?"

"I guess maybe he's looking at investment properties too," I say. "And this is a prime piece of real estate, right by the river, not to mention the sentimental value it holds. He and I bonded over that roof, you know. Can't put a price tag on male bonding."

Max and Sam appear next, cutting through the grass up the trail from the paved path along the river. "Count us in, too," Max calls. "That dock back there has the best fishing all along the river."

Cally's eyes brim with tears. "You guys."

"I'm in, too," Gabby says behind her. Cally turns and Gabby places a bright pink Minnie Mouse bank in her hands. "You got this for me when you took us to Disney Land. You told me to save for something magical. I think this place will do just fine."

Drew steps forward next, her jaw hard and her eyes moist. "I'm in, too," she says, handing Cally a wad of cash. "That's what I was saving for a new iPhone, but I don't need it. My best friends are all here in New Hope."

Cally looks at the Minnie Mouse bank and cash in her hands. "So you're all going to go in together and buy my dad's house?"

I lift my hands. "Not me."

Her brow wrinkles. "Not you?"

I shake my head. "I can't have you accusing me of trying to buy you when I ask you to be my girl. But the rest of them, yes."

"As long as you're in this town," Hanna says, "you don't have to face anything alone."

"I—I don't even know what to say."

"You can tell them that won't be necessary," Arlen calls, the porch screen squeaking behind him as he comes down into the lawn to join everyone else. "I visited the bank this morning and got it taken care of."

Cally's jaw goes slack, but I'm sure mine does too.

Arlen shifts uncomfortably as everyone stares. "While you girls were gone last week, I auctioned off my books."

"The autographed ones?" Cally's eyes are wide. "You've been collecting those my whole life."

He lifts a shoulder in an awkward shrug. "My daughters are more important than some autographed papers."

"Daddy," Cally whispers. Then in three long strides she's wrapping her arms around him and leaning her head into his chest.

"Does this mean Asher Logan isn't going to be part owner of a house with me?" Drew asks. "Because that is a total bummer."

Asher grabs something out of his truck and walks it over to Drew. "Here you go, kiddo. How's that for a consolation prize?"

Her eyes go wide as she takes the CD from his hands. "Oh. My. God. Is this the new album? It doesn't even release for months!"

He grins. "Thanks for being such an awesome fan."

"Huh," Lizzy says. "My mom said she wanted to see me do something responsible with my money. I guess I'm going to have to find something else now."

"We could go shoe shopping?" Hanna suggests.

"That's a plan," Lizzy says. "Maggie, can you and your stud give us a ride back to Mom's?"

Everyone clears out and the girls head back into the house with their dad, and finally I'm alone with Cally.

I clear my throat. "I have a bone to pick with you."

Cally

I spin around at the sound of Will's voice.

His eyes blaze, nearly predatory, as he takes three slow steps and closes the space between us. "You tried to get rid of me by pushing me off on some other woman."

I hang my head and study my shoes. "I just want you to have the best life possible."

"Yeah, but I would have thought you'd do better. Meredith? She's scheming and manipulative and kind of a bitch."

I snap my head up and bite back my smile.

"I mean, sure, she's beautiful, and you're right about me wanting kids. It's true, I do. And I guess it's nice that Grandma likes her, though—between you and me—I think me falling in love with troubled girls keeps Grandma's mind young. You wouldn't want my grandmother to get senile, would you?"

"No," I say, keeping my face somber. "I wouldn't want that."

"And, anyway, Meredith is a blond, and I know that's a thing for a lot of guys, but I really prefer brunettes."

"It's important to know what you want."

He's so close I can feel his heat and have to fight the urge to wrap myself up in his warmth. "If you wanted to choose the woman for me to spend my life with, you totally missed the boat. I thought you knew me better than that."

"My apologies. Maybe I could try again if you gave me a bulleted list."

"Hmm…well, I'm not really into girls who will let me own their mind. I'd like a girl who can think for herself."

"That's important."

He settles his hands on my hips and lowers his mouth next to my ear. "And I don't mean to be picky, but she needs to be amazing. You know the type, loves with all of her heart and thinks I'm a sex god."

A wicked tendril of electricity zips up my spine. "Hmm, and how would you confirm that?"

He nips at my earlobe. "Maybe by the way she screams my name when I make her come."

I swallow. Hard. "I'm not sure I want to know how other women sound when you make them come."

He pulls back and his eyes drop to my mouth. He's a breath away. I could push up on my toes and taste those lips. "But you asked what I want."

"The baby's really not yours?"

"I can't have kids, Cally. The baby's not mine." He cups my face in his hand. "So I guess you need to add to that list a woman who could handle life with a man who can't have children. She'd need to be okay with fertility interventions or adoption."

My eyes fill. "I could handle that."

"I could also use a decent massage." He grins and rolls his shoulders back.

"We might be able to arrange that."

"I want you, Cally." Then his mouth is on mine and his hands are in my hair. This isn't the gentle, loving kiss of my high school sweetheart. And I don't kiss him back like an innocent girl with her first love. This is the hard, punishing, demanding kiss of a man who's finally taking what he wants and the woman who's giving it to him.

I open under him and moan into his mouth, clinging to his shirt as I surrender to the kiss—the brush of our tongues, the wicked nipping of his teeth.

When we finally break the kiss, he leans his forehead against mine and we both struggle to catch our breath. "Now it's time for you to head back in the house and break the news to your father."

"What news?"

"That his girls won't all be living with him. That you're moving in with me. I'm also going to need you to divorce that asshole you're married to. Call me a caveman if you must, but I don't share."

epilogue

Cally
Six Months Later

WHEN I get home from the massage studio, the house is dark and empty.

My phone buzzes in my hand, and I open the text message: *Go to the bedroom.*

Biting back a smile, I follow my boyfriend's command and make my way down the hall. But when I get there, I don't see William like I expect to. Instead, there's a formal black gown draped across the bed, a floor-length number with ribbons tied in little bows at the shoulders. It looks vaguely familiar, but I can't place it.

I'm not surprised when my phone buzzes again.

Get dressed. I'll pick you up in thirty minutes.

What's he up to?

I'm pulling off my clothes when another text message comes through.

Wear the black silk panties, the ones with the ties at the sides.

I text back, *Care to tell me where you're taking me?*

And ruin the surprise?

I shower quickly with the floral body wash that makes him crazy, then I dress carefully. I take special care as I tie the panties at each hip, imaging him untying them later. For my bra, I choose black lace that makes his blue eyes go smoky when he looks at me.

The dress is a soft flowing material that glides against my skin and makes me feel beautiful.

I don't put on much makeup, just a little lip-gloss and some eyeliner and mascara, and I leave my hair down so he can tangle his hands in it when he kisses me.

I'm just stepping into my shoes when he texts me again. *I'm out front when you're ready.*

A ridiculous case of the nerves has my stomach somersaulting as I walk out the front door.

William is leaning against a black stretch limo dressed in a tuxedo, legs crossed at the ankle as he waits for me. He holds a single red rose.

"I thought you said you didn't want to dress me?"

His lips turn up in a grin. "I didn't. Drew pulled that dress out of storage for me."

I blink down at the familiar gown and have to shake my head. How had I forgotten my own prom dress? "Where are we going?" I ask again.

He winks at me and opens the door, taking my hand to help me into the limo. "You'll know soon enough."

When he's seated next to me, he pours me a glass of champagne, and I have to shake my head in awe. "Am I forgetting some sort of special occasion?"

He dips his head and presses his lips to mine. "Every day you're in my life is a special occasion."

I take a single sip from my glass before he takes it from my hand and the limo comes to a stop. "Short ride," I mutter, only a little disappointed that I didn't have enough time to enjoy it.

"Don't pout. The limo's ours all night." He winks at me as he helps me out onto the sidewalk. "Later, we'll let him drive us around while we make out."

I frown at the building before me. I'm missing something. "You brought me to New Hope High School?"

He offers me his arm, and I slide my hand through it and allow him to escort me inside the heavy gymnasium doors. The doors swing closed behind me and I can hardly believe what I'm seeing. The room is dark save for the twinkling white lights draped across the ceiling and a dim light illuminating the dance floor. My best friends are already dancing—

Lizzy, Hanna, and Maggie wearing prom dresses, arms draped around their dates.

I spin around and William pulls me close. "Happy prom night," he whispers in my ear.

Wrapping our arms around each other, we start to dance from where we stand. "I thought about taking you to the actual prom," he says, his hands cupping my butt. "But then I couldn't touch you like this. I didn't want to finally get prom night with my girl and be expected to behave."

I grin. "We couldn't have that."

His fingers tie something cool around my wrist.

"Diamonds?" I shift my hand back and forth, watching them twinkle in the light.

"Stardust," he corrects. "I want you to always believe you deserve whatever you can wish for, Cally. As long as you'll let me, I'll make your wishes come true."

"They already have," I whisper. "I love you so much, William Bailey. You're my dream come true, and I'm so grateful I found you again."

"Hmm…then do you mind if I borrow them to make a wish of my own?"

I grin. "What's that?"

"I know you've already given me more than I should ask for, but I'm one of those spoiled rich kids who thinks he should have everything he wants."

"You're not spoiled. What is it? What do you want?"

He releases me and draws a box from his pocket. "I wish you would marry me, Cally Fisher."

My throat is thick with tears and happiness, but I nod and press my lips to his. "You don't have to wish for me, William. I'm already yours."

The End

author's note

There is a common argument that prostitution is a victimless crime—a transaction between two consenting adults that harms no one. However, in the United States, we're beginning to take another look at what is truly happening in these so-called "consensual" transactions and, in some cases, reclassify them as human sex trafficking. Authorities have found that very often the prostitutes are coerced into a life they don't want to be living, manipulated through addiction, poverty, and fear. It is all too easy to dismiss a prostitute's troubles, to tell ourselves "she made the choice," but as William tells Cally, a choice made out of fear is no choice at all.

other titles by
Lexi Ryan

New Hope Series
Unbreak Me
Wish I May

Hot Contemporary Romance
Text Appeal
Accidental Sex Goddess

Stiletto Girls Novels
Stilettos, Inc.
Flirting with Fate

Decadence Creek Stories and Novellas
Just One Night
Just the Way You Are

contact

I love hearing from readers, so find my on facebook page at facebook.com/lexiryanauthor, follow me on Twitter @writerlexiryan, shoot me an email at writerlexiryan@gmail.com, or find me on my website: www.lexiryan.com.

acknowledgements

I must thank my husband first. Without him, my books just wouldn't be possible. Brian, thank you for the time, encouragement, and patience you gave me through this book and all the others. For sending me to the "satellite office" to work when the kids won't leave me alone, for listening to my endless out-of-context plot concerns, and for proving day after day that happily-ever-after exists outside of my head. I love you and those rotten kids something fierce.

My friends and family, who celebrate my successes as their own, cheer me on every step of the way, and pimp my books out to every literate adult they meet. I am humbled by your enthusiasm and grateful to have built a life surrounded by such amazing people.

To everyone who provided me feedback on and cheers for William and Cally's story along the way—especially Adrienne Hogan, Marilyn Brant, Violet Duke, Megan Mulry, Annie Swanberg, and Lauren Blakely—you're all awesome and I'm lucky to call you my friends.

Thank you to the team that helped me package this book and promote it. Sarah Hansen at Okay Creations designed my beautiful cover, and if I have my way she will do many, many more for me. Rhonda Helms, thank you for the insightful line edits, and Sara Biren at Stubby Pencil Editing for proof reading. A massive shout-out to Jessica Estep of Ink Slinger PR for your amazing and tireless work to promote me and my books, and to all of the bloggers and reviewers who help her do it. Amazing. Every one of you.

To my agent, Dan Mandel for getting my books into the hands of readers all over the world—you're making my dreams come true.

To all my writer friends on Twitter, Facebook, and my various writer loops, thank you for your support and inspiration. I must say, ours is the coolest water cooler in all of the workforce.

And last but certainly not least, thank you to my fans. To those who read *Unbreak Me* and sent me notes begging for William to get his happily-ever-after, knowing you wanted to read his story as much as I wanted to write it was a thrill. I appreciate each and every one of my readers. I couldn't do this without you and wouldn't want to. Thank you for buying my books and telling your friends about them. Thank you for asking me to write more. You're the best!

~Lexi

play list

Wish I May Playlist

Gotye, Kimbra—*Somebody That I Used to Know*
Kings of Leon—*Sex on Fire*
Passenger—*Let Her Go*
Ani DiFranco—*Sorry I Am*
Miley Cyrus—*Wrecking Ball*
Sara Bareilles—*Gravity*
The National—*Slipped*
Ani DiFranco—*Letter to a John*
Kodaline—*All I Want*
William Fitzsimmons featuring Rosi Golan—*You Still Hurt Me*
Katy Perry—*Roar*
One Republic—*Counting Stars*

Excerpts from
Marilyn Brant and Jen McLaughlin

Dear Readers: One of the few activities I love as much as writing is reading. On the following pages, you will find the description of and excerpts from two books I loved: Marilyn Brant's *The Road to You* and Jen McLaughlin's *Out of Line*, both available now. Enjoy!

About the *The Road to You*

Sometimes the only road to the truth...is one you've never taken.

Until I found Gideon's journal in the tool shed—locked in the cedar box where I'd once hidden my old diary—I'd been led to believe my brother was dead. But the contents of his journal changed all that.

The Road to Discovery...
Two years ago, Aurora Gray's world turned upside down when her big brother Gideon and his best friend Jeremy disappeared. Now, during the summer of her 18th birthday, she unexpectedly finds her brother's journal and sees that it's been written in again. Recently. By him.

The Road to Danger...
There are secret messages coded within the journal's pages. Aurora, who's unusually perceptive and a natural puzzle solver, is hell bent on following where they lead, no matter what the cost. She confides in the only person she feels can help her interpret the clues: Donovan Mc-Cafferty, Jeremy's older brother and a guy she's always been drawn to—even against her better judgment.

The Road to You...
Reluctantly, Donovan agrees to go with her and, together, they set out on a road trip of discovery and danger, hoping to find their lost brothers and the answers to questions they've never dared to ask aloud.

In that expectant space between silence and melody, our trip began...

Excerpt of *The Road to You* © Marilyn Brant

I could count on one hand the things I knew were true about Donovan McCafferty:

He was twenty-three—just over five years older than I was.

He'd escaped into the Army at age eighteen and, except for a few quick but memorable visits, hadn't returned to Minnesota until this past winter.

He had an excellent mechanical mind.

And he made me very nervous.

Underneath my skin, every nerve fiber was fast twitching. Just thinking about Donovan always did that to me...

It was 7:05 p.m. by the time I got to the auto-body shop where he worked. They closed at seven, but the light in the back was on and I knew he was in there. Not because I'd caught even one glimpse of Mr. Tall, Dark and Intense yet, but because the only other car in the lot was a crimson Trans Am with the giant Firebird decal in black and gold across the hood. His, of course.

I pushed open my car door, grabbed my tote bag with Gideon's journal tucked safely inside and inhaled several lungfuls of the cloying summer air.

I didn't make it more than five steps before Donovan came out. A solid, broad-shouldered, six-foot-two mass of frequently impenetrable emotions. Not impenetrable enough this time, though.

Even at a distance of half a parking lot, I detected two powerful sensations that crashed, one after the other, into my awareness:

One, he was hugely curious about why I was here.

And, two, he very much wished I hadn't been.

He walked up to me and cleared his throat. "Car trouble, Aurora?" He glanced at my hand-me-down Buick, which had done nothing but purr contentedly during my drives around town. Donovan was the type to have noticed this, so I could tell he knew it wasn't the car.

I shook my head. "I need to show you something," I told him. "Privately."

A small flash of amusement quirked one corner of his mouth upward. I was surprised he allowed me to read this, especially since he knew I could. Surprised he was letting me see that one of his possible explanations for my presence was flirtatious in origin—even as he immediately dismissed the idea.

I rolled my eyes. "It's not like that."

He pressed his lips together, but the amusement still simmered just beneath the surface. "Too bad. 'We're both *young* and *inconspicuous*,'" he said, parroting the hideously embarrassing words I'd said to him two years ago at our brothers' secret high-school graduation party..

I fought a blush. "We're not *that* young," I told him, trying to stand straighter and look older. "And we're not inconspicuous *here.*"

"Ain't that the truth." He turned and motioned for me to follow him inside. Led me into the back office and ushered me in. "You want me to close this door, too? Snap the blinds shut?"

He was mocking me, but there was a layer of concern beneath it. He knew something serious was up. In a town of 2,485 people, where you'd run into the majority of the residents a handful of times each week, I'd spoken with Donovan McCafferty in private exactly six times in the past five years.

Here's to lucky number seven.

Coming October 2013!*

About *Out of Line*

Desperate to break free…

I've spent my entire life under my father's thumb, but now I'm finally free to make my own choices. When my roommate dragged me to my first college party, I met Finn Coram and my life turned inside out. He knows how to break the rules and is everything I never knew I wanted. A Marine by day and surfer by night, he pushes me away even as our attraction brings us closer. Now I am finally free to do whatever I want. I know what I want. I choose Finn.

Trying to play by the rules...

I always follow orders. My job, my life, depends on it. I thought this job would be easy, all the rules were made crystal clear, but when I met Carrie Wallington, everything got muddy. She's a rule I know I shouldn't break, but damn if I don't inch closer to the breaking point each time I see her. I'm ready to step out of line. And even worse? I'm living a lie. They say the truth will set you free, but in my case…

The truth will cost me everything.

Excerpt of Out of Line © Jenn McLaughlin

Though my urge to run was strong, I forced myself to act casual. I'd been running away enough. It was time to stand still. "You do realize I can handle a grabby-hands boy by myself, right? I dealt with you, after all."

He stepped closer, towering over me. "Ginger, you have no idea how to deal with me."

I stiffened. "I know that if I kissed you now, you wouldn't push me away."

"Of course I wouldn't. Look at you." His gaze dipped over my body, and when he met my eyes again his own were blazing and hot. "Any man would kiss you back."

"You'd push me away after." He lifted a shoulder but said nothing. He was so darn condescending and cocky. "Why are you at another frat party that I just *happen* to be at? Who are you? Why are you following me?"

Finn leaned against a palm tree and looked far too casual, but he reminded me of one of those lions on the Discovery Channel. He looked perfectly calm on the surface, but in a second he could be all deadly and lethal. "I'm here because I was taking a walk down the beach, and I saw you and that loser kissing. Then I saw you push him away. I wanted to make sure you were okay, but now I'm wishing I had bashed his head into the fucking wall before I let him go."

My heart rose to my throat. "Why?"

"Because you should be kissing *me*," he practically whispered. "Not some college boy who doesn't know what he's doing."

He closed the distance between us. And as soon as his hands were on my hips, his mouth was on mine. The familiar sensations he'd awoken in me came to life, and I clung to him. His tongue entwined with mine, and he grabbed my waist, yanking me against him.

I lifted up on tiptoe, trying to get closer, and moaned softly. He needed to do that again. And more. This is how a kiss was supposed to feel. This is what it was supposed to do to me. I might be inexperienced, but even I knew what a good kiss felt like.

And. This. Was. It.

*** *Available now!* ***

This paperback interior was designed and formatted by

Made in the USA
Columbia, SC
21 May 2021